Charles M. Schulz

PEANUTS™

Special thanks to the Schulz family, everyone at Charles M. Schulz Creative Associates, and to Charles M. Schulz for his singular achievement in shaping these beloved characters.

Cover
Pencils by **Bob Scott**
Inks and Colors by **Justin Thompson**

Trade Designer: **Jillian Crab**
Assistant Editor: **Alex Galer**
Editors: **Matt Gagnon & Shannon Watters**

For Charles M. Schulz Creative Associates
Creative Director: **Paige Braddock**
Managing Editor: **Alexis E. Fajardo**

ROSS RICHIE CEO & Founder • MARK SMYLIE Founder of Archaia • MATT GAGNON Editor-in-Chief • FILIP SABLIK VP of Publishing & Marketing • STEPHEN CHRISTY VP of Development
LANCE KREITER VP of Licensing & Merchandising • PHIL BARBARO VP of Finance • BRYCE CARLSON Managing Editor • MEL CAYLO Marketing Manager • SCOTT NEWMAN Production Design Manager
IRENE BRADISH Operations Manager • CHRISTINE DINH Brand Communications Manager • DAFNA PLEBAN Editor • SHANNON WATTERS Editor • ERIC HARBURN Editor • REBECCA TAYLOR Editor
IAN BRILL Editor • CHRIS ROSA Assistant Editor • ALEX GALER Assistant Editor • WHITNEY LEOPARD Assistant Editor • JASMINE AMIRI Assistant Editor • CAMERON CHITTOCK Assistant Editor
KELSEY DIETERICH Production Designer • EMI YONEMURA BROWN Production Designer • DEVIN FUNCHES E-Commerce & Inventory Coordinator • ANDY LIEGL Event Coordinator • BRIANNA HART Executive Assistant
AARON FERRARA Operations Assistant • JOSÉ MEZA Sales Assistant • MICHELLE ANKLEY Sales Assistant • ELIZABETH LOUGHRIDGE Accounting Assistant • STEPHANIE HOCUTT PR Assistant

kaboom!™

PEANUTS Volume Four, October 2014. Published by KaBOOM!, a division of Boom Entertainment, Inc. Peanuts is ™ & © 2014 Peanuts Worldwide, LLC. Originally published in single magazine form as PEANUTS: Volume Two No. 9-12. ™ & © 2013 Peanuts Worldwide, LLC. All rights reserved. KaBOOM!™ and the KaBOOM! logo are trademarks of Boom Entertainment, Inc., registered in various countries and categories. All characters, events, and institutions depicted herein are fictional. Any similarity between any of the names, characters, persons, events, and/or institutions in this publication to actual names, characters, and persons, whether living or dead, events, and/or institutions is unintended and purely coincidental. KaBOOM! does not read or accept unsolicited submissions of ideas, stories, or artwork.

A catalog record of this book is available from OCLC and from the KaBOOM! website, www.kaboom-studios.com, on the Librarians Page.

BOOM! Studios, 5670 Wilshire Boulevard, Suite 450, Los Angeles, CA 90036-5679. Printed in China. First Printing.
ISBN: 978-1-60886-427-0, eISBN: 978-1-61398-281-5

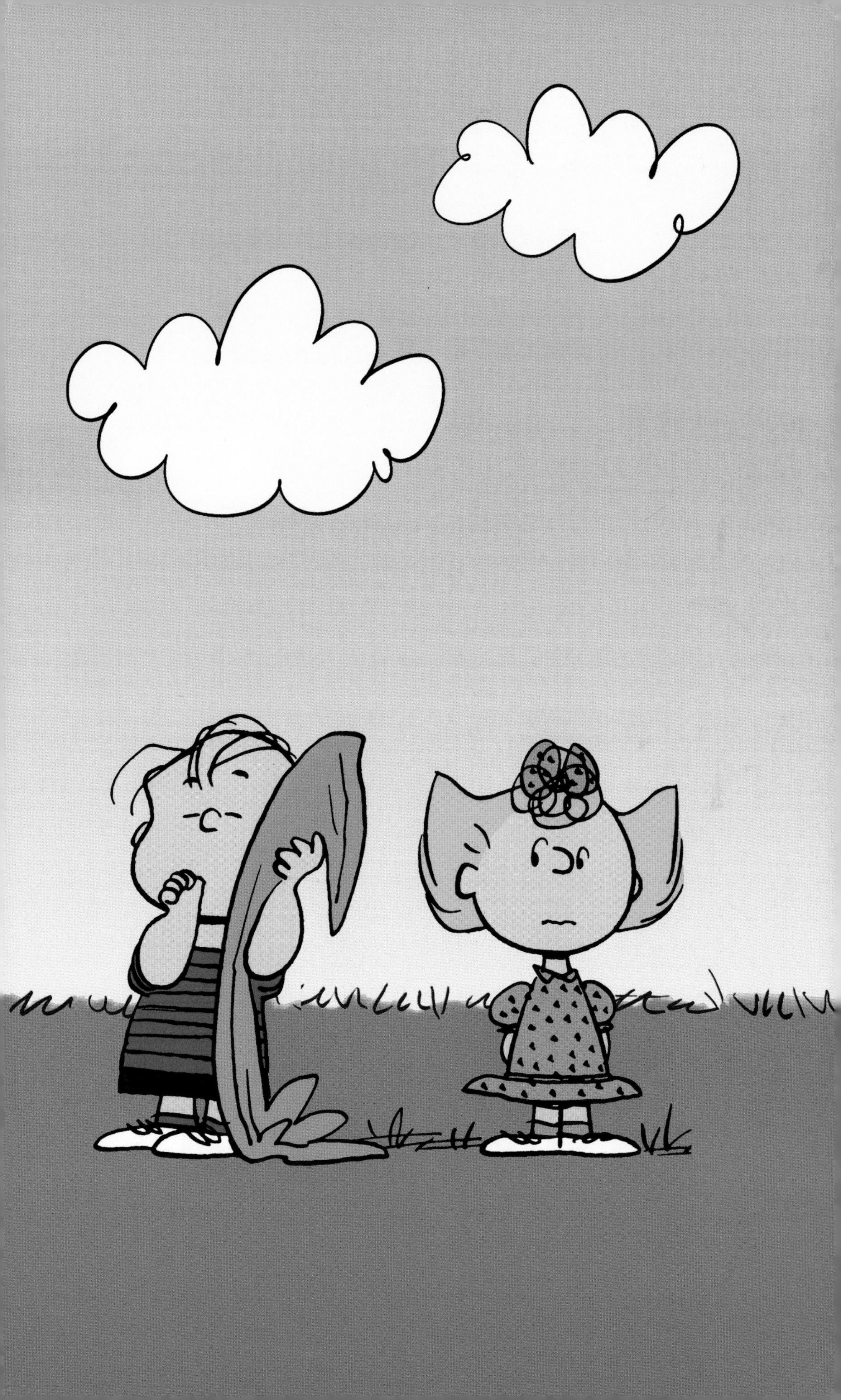

Table of Contents

Classic Peanuts Strips by

Charles M. Schulz

Colors by **Justin Thompson, Donna Almendrala & Art Roche**

From the Drawing Board
Composed by **Justin Thompson**
Designed by **Iain R. Morris**

Write & Wrong p 7
Story by **Alexis E. Fajardo & Nat Gertler**
Pencils by **Stephanie Gladden**
Inks by **Justin Thompson**
Colors by **Lisa Moore**
Letters by **Alexis E. Fajardo**

LOL Lucy p 13
Story & Pencils by **Vicki Scott**
Inks by **Paige Braddock**
Colors by **Donna Almendrala**
Letters by **Alexis E. Fajardo**

Dogtor Is In p 20
Story by **Jeff Dyer**
Pencils & Inks by **Mike DeCarlo**
Colors by **Lisa Moore**
Letters by **Steve Wands**

Have Dish Will Travel p 25
Story by **Caleb Monroe**
Pencils by **Mona Koth**
Inks by **Mark & Stephanie Heike**
Colors by **Lisa Moore**
Letters by **Steve Wands**

Lucy's Loophole p 30
Story by Caleb Monroe
Art by Robert Pope
Colors by Lisa Moore
Letters by Steve Wands

Be It Ever So Humble p 33
Story by Caleb Monroe
Art by Jeff Shultz
Colors by Lisa Moore
Letters by Deron Bennett

Twinkle Thinkle p 47
Story by Nat Gertler
Art by Jeff Shultz
Colors by Lisa Moore
Letters by Steve Wands

Brush Up Your Beethoven p 51
Story & Layouts by Vicki Scott
Art by Andy Hirsch
Colors by Lisa Moore
Letters by Alexis E. Fajardo

Tuxedo Junction p 58
Story & Art by Charles M. Schulz &
Paige Braddock

Number Crunch p 63
Story & Colors by Art Roche
Pencils by Scott Jeralds
Inks by Justin Thompson
Letters by Donna Almendrala

Movie Time p 73
Story by Nat Gertler
Art by Andy Hirsch
Colors by Lisa Moore
Letters by Steve Wands

Tutor Trouble p 82
Story by Jeff Dyer
Pencils by Stephanie Gladden
Inks by Justin Thompson
Colors by Nina Kester
Letters by Alexis E. Fajardo

When You Wish Upon A Pumpkin p 89
Story by Jeff Dyer
Art by Robert Pope
Colors by Lisa Moore
Letters by Steve Wands

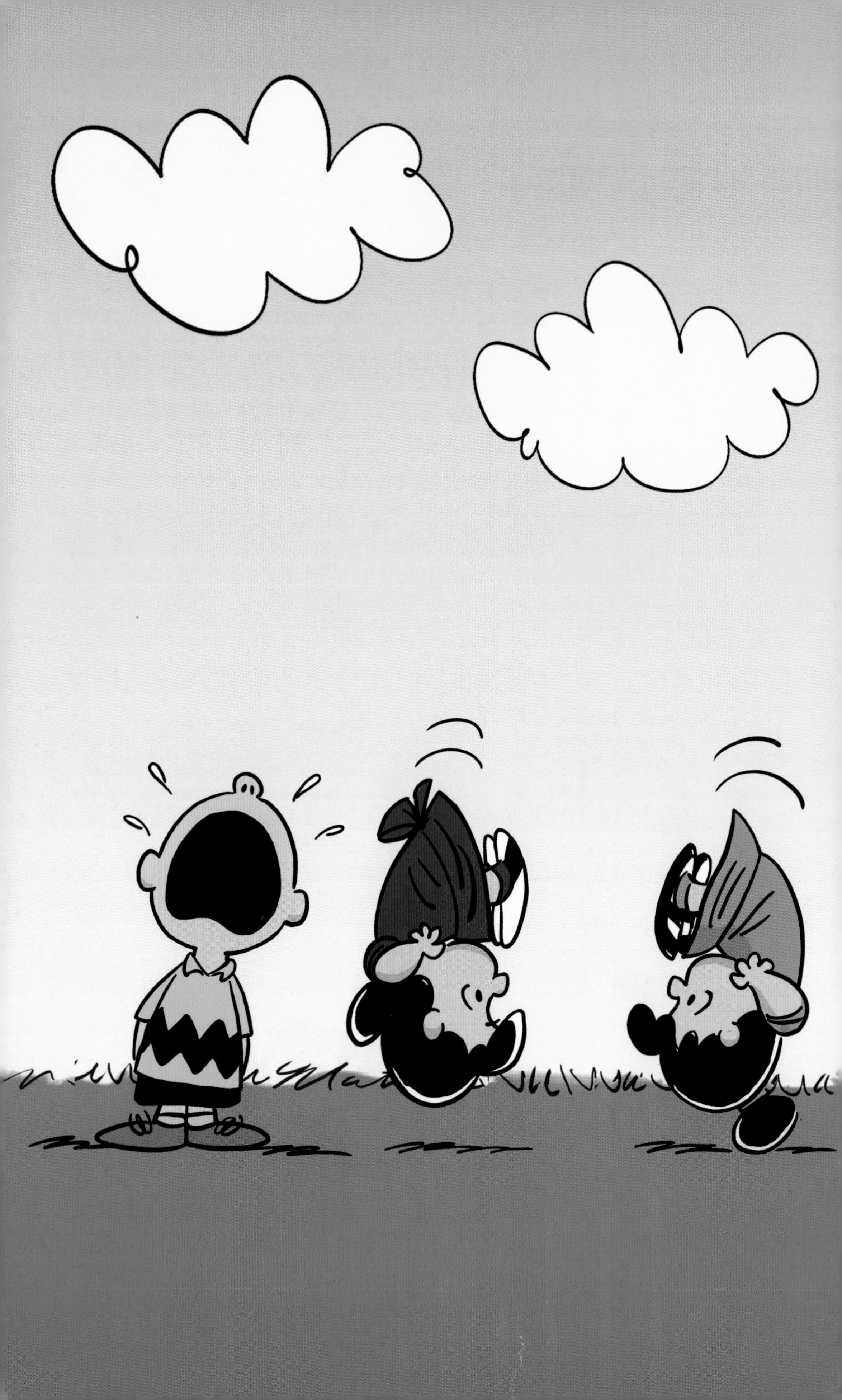

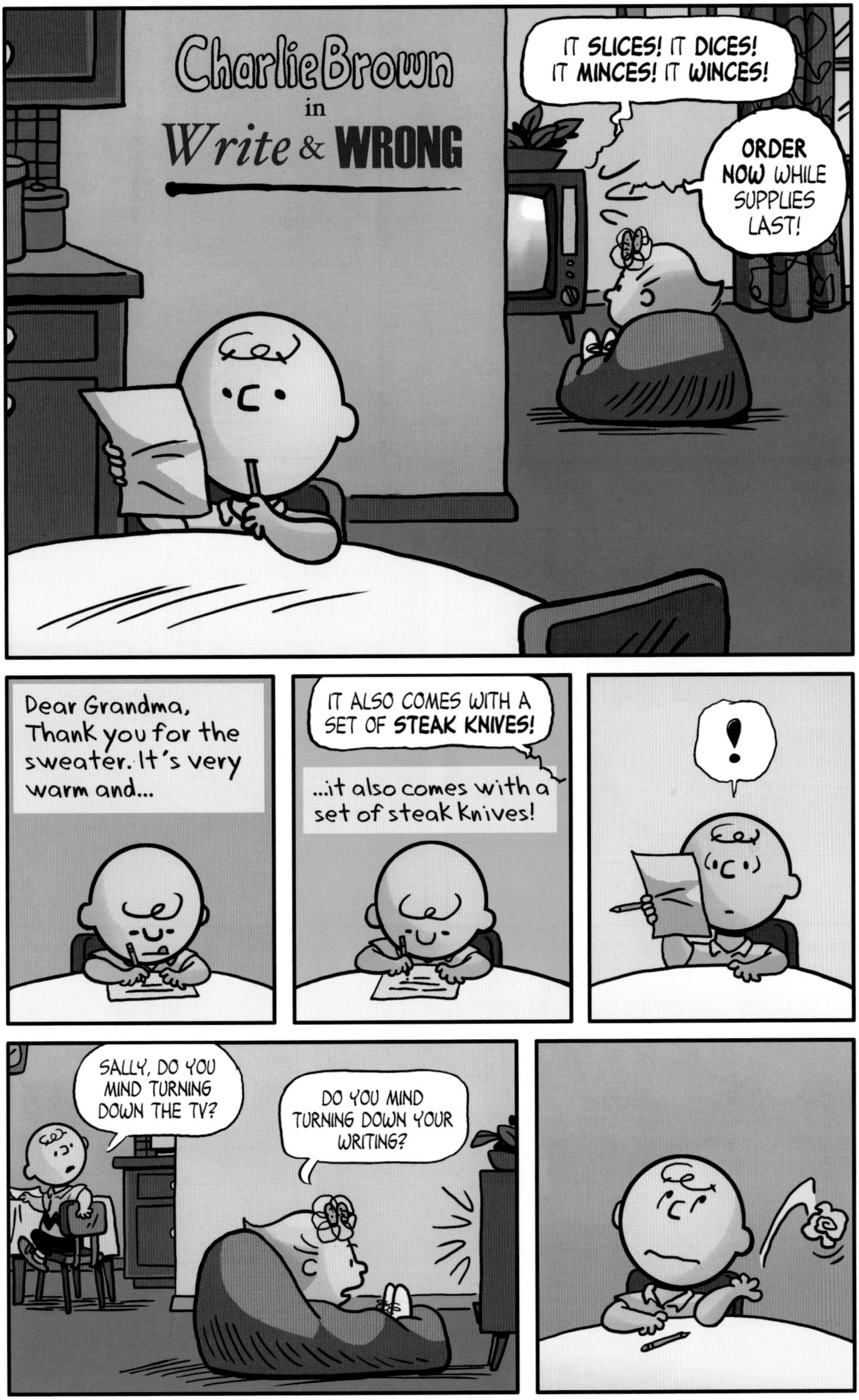

Charlie Brown
in
Write & WRONG
IT SLICES! IT DICES! IT MINCES! IT WINCES!
ORDER NOW WHILE SUPPLIES LAST!
Dear Grandma, Thank you for the sweater. It's very warm and...
IT ALSO COMES WITH A SET OF STEAK KNIVES!
...it also comes with a set of steak knives!
!
SALLY, DO YOU MIND TURNING DOWN THE TV?
DO YOU MIND TURNING DOWN YOUR WRITING?

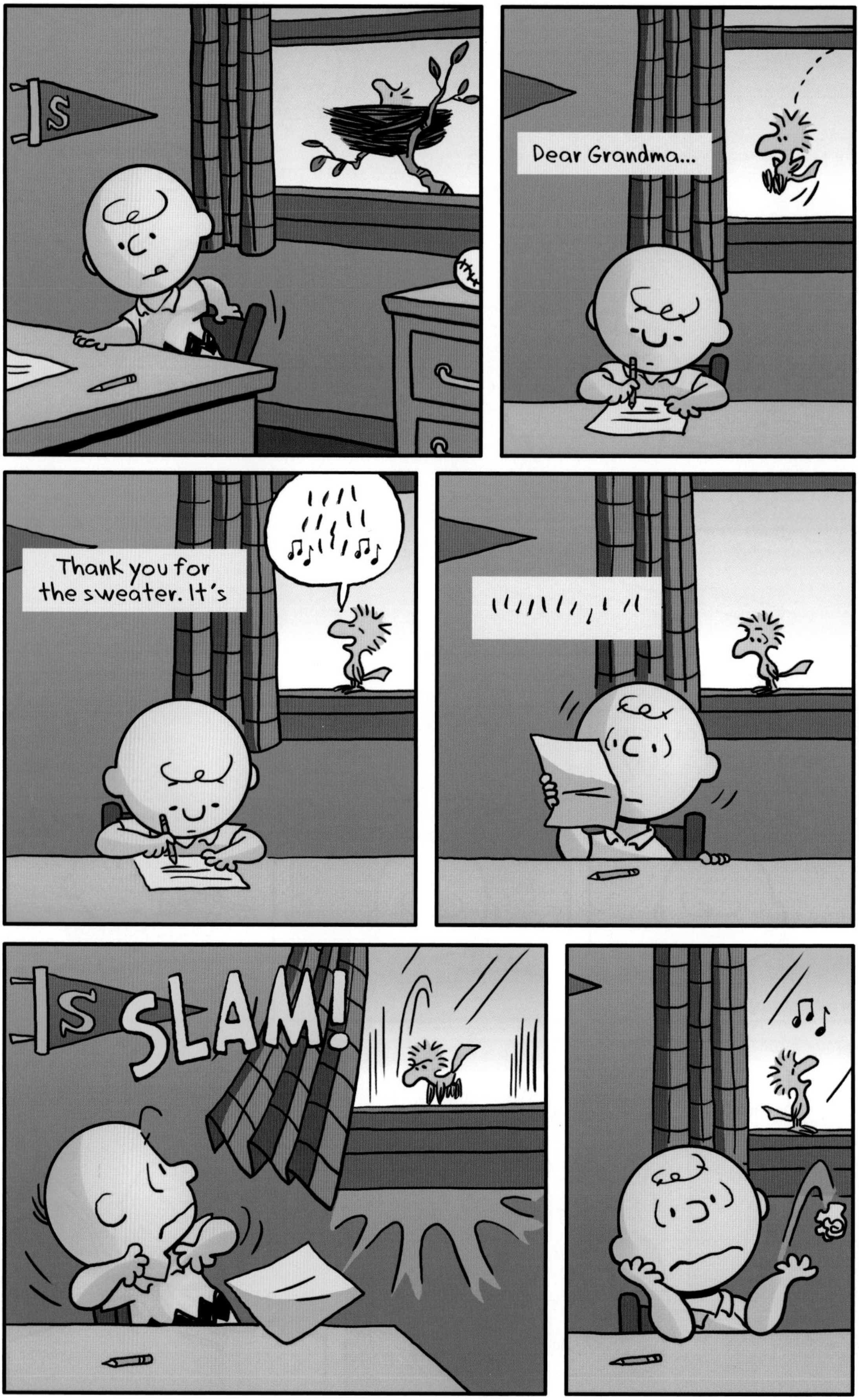
Dear Grandma...
Thank you for the sweater. It's
SLAM!

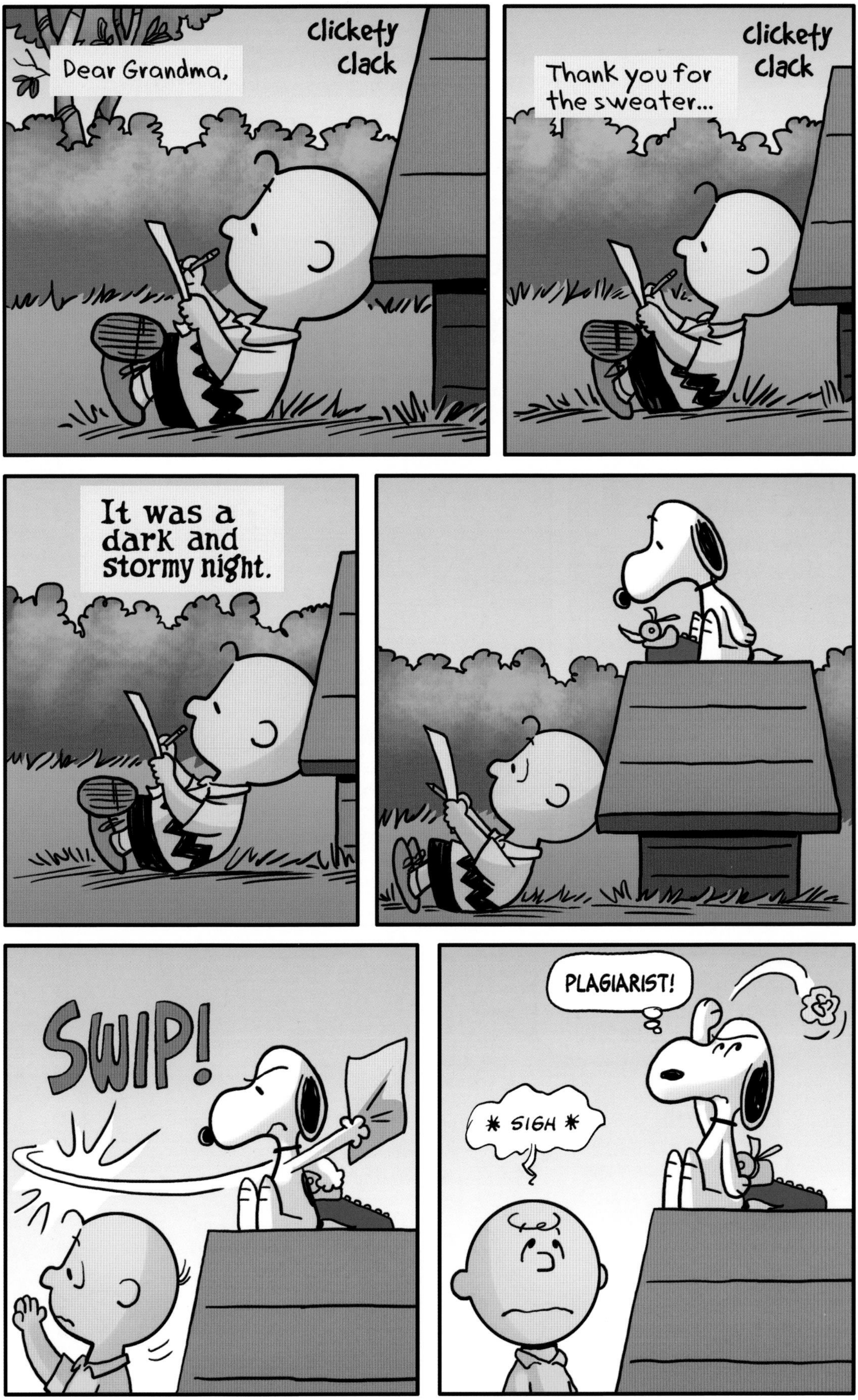
Dear Grandma,
Clickety clack
Thank you for the sweater...
Clickety clack
It was a dark and stormy night.
SWIP!
* SIGH *
PLAGIARIST!

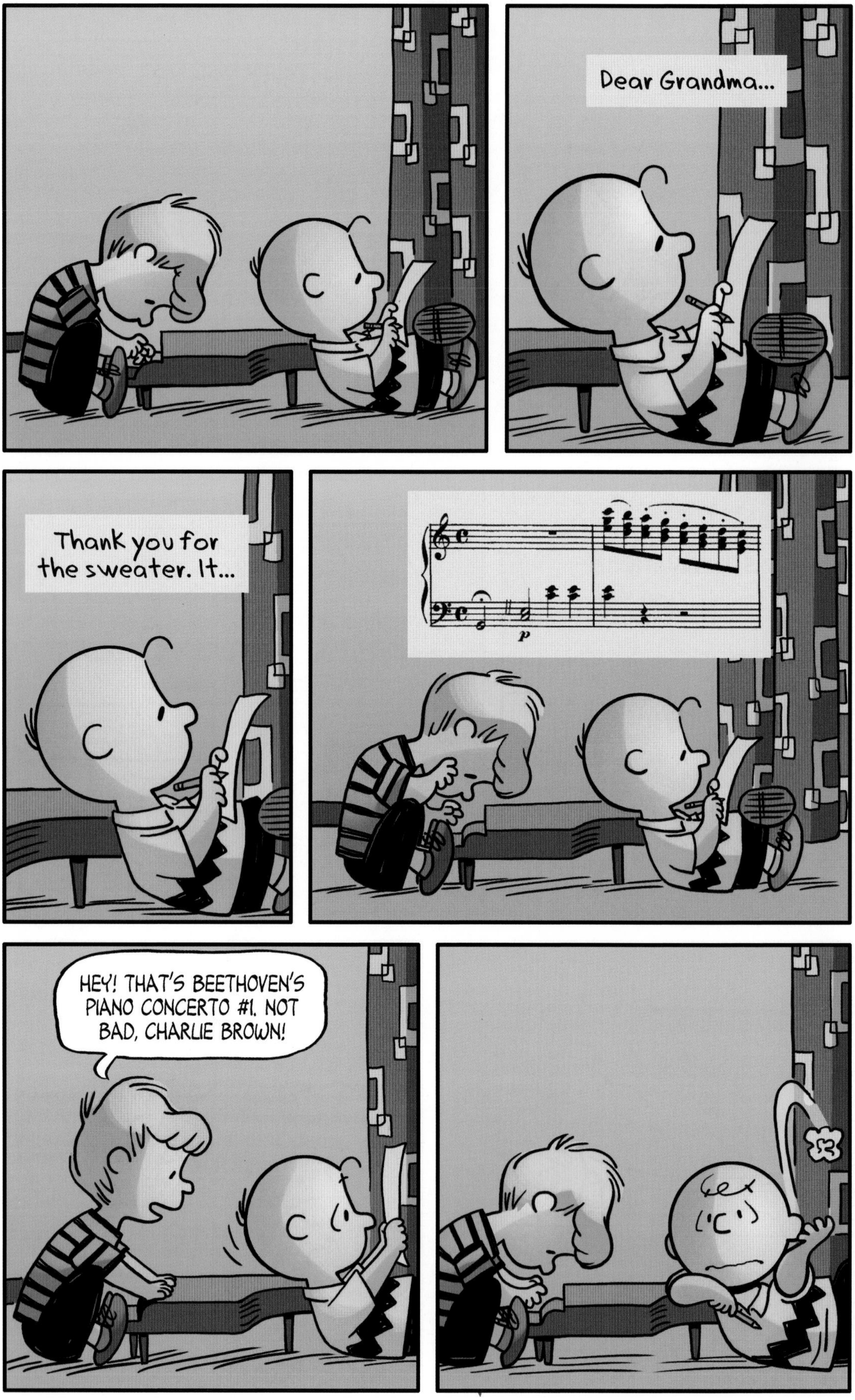
Dear Grandma...
Thank you for the sweater. It...
HEY! THAT'S BEETHOVEN'S PIANO CONCERTO #1. NOT BAD, CHARLIE BROWN!

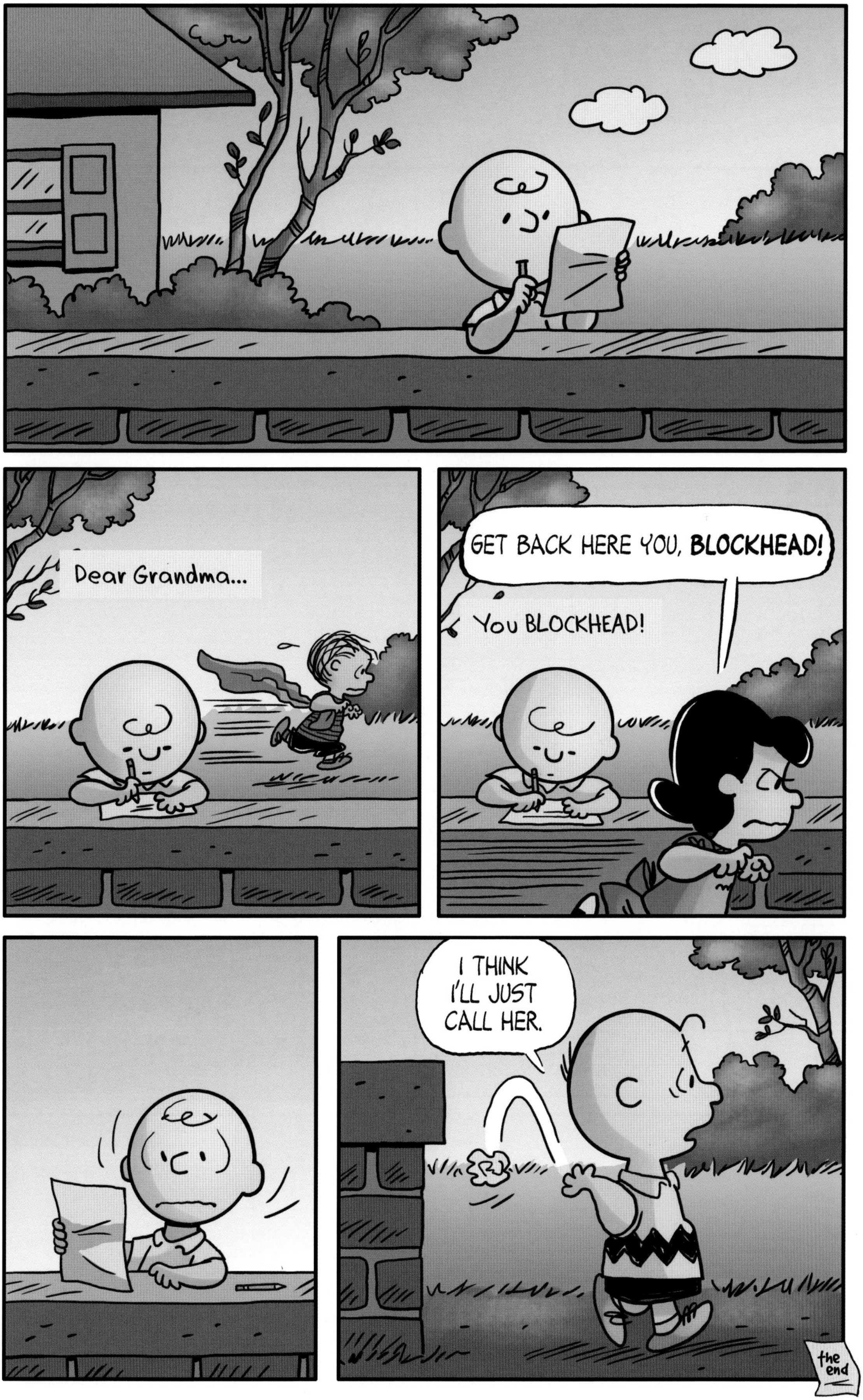
Dear Grandma...
GET BACK HERE YOU, BLOCKHEAD!
You BLOCKHEAD!
I THINK I'LL JUST CALL HER.
the end

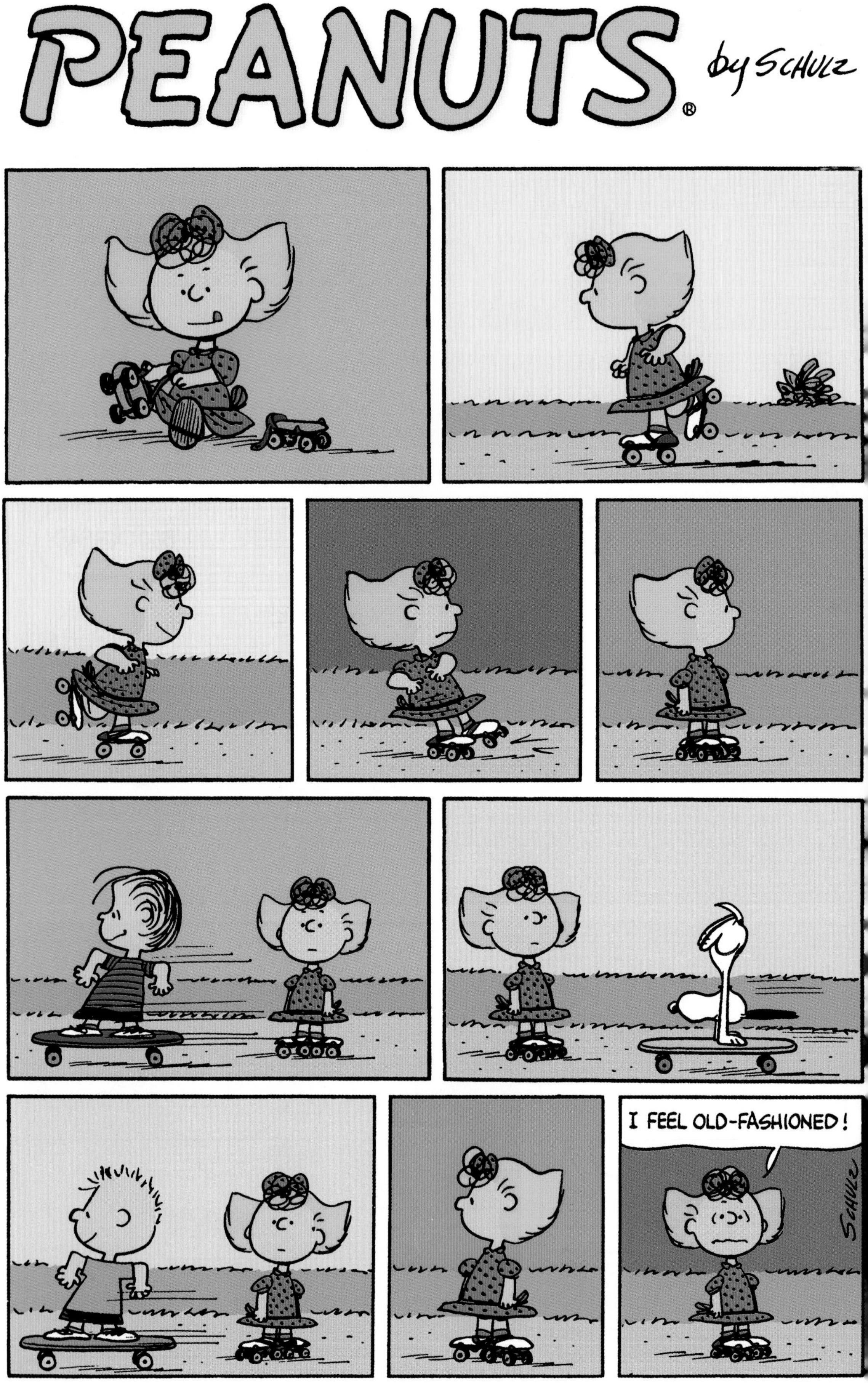
PEANUTS®
by SCHULZ
I FEEL OLD-FASHIONED!
SCHULZ

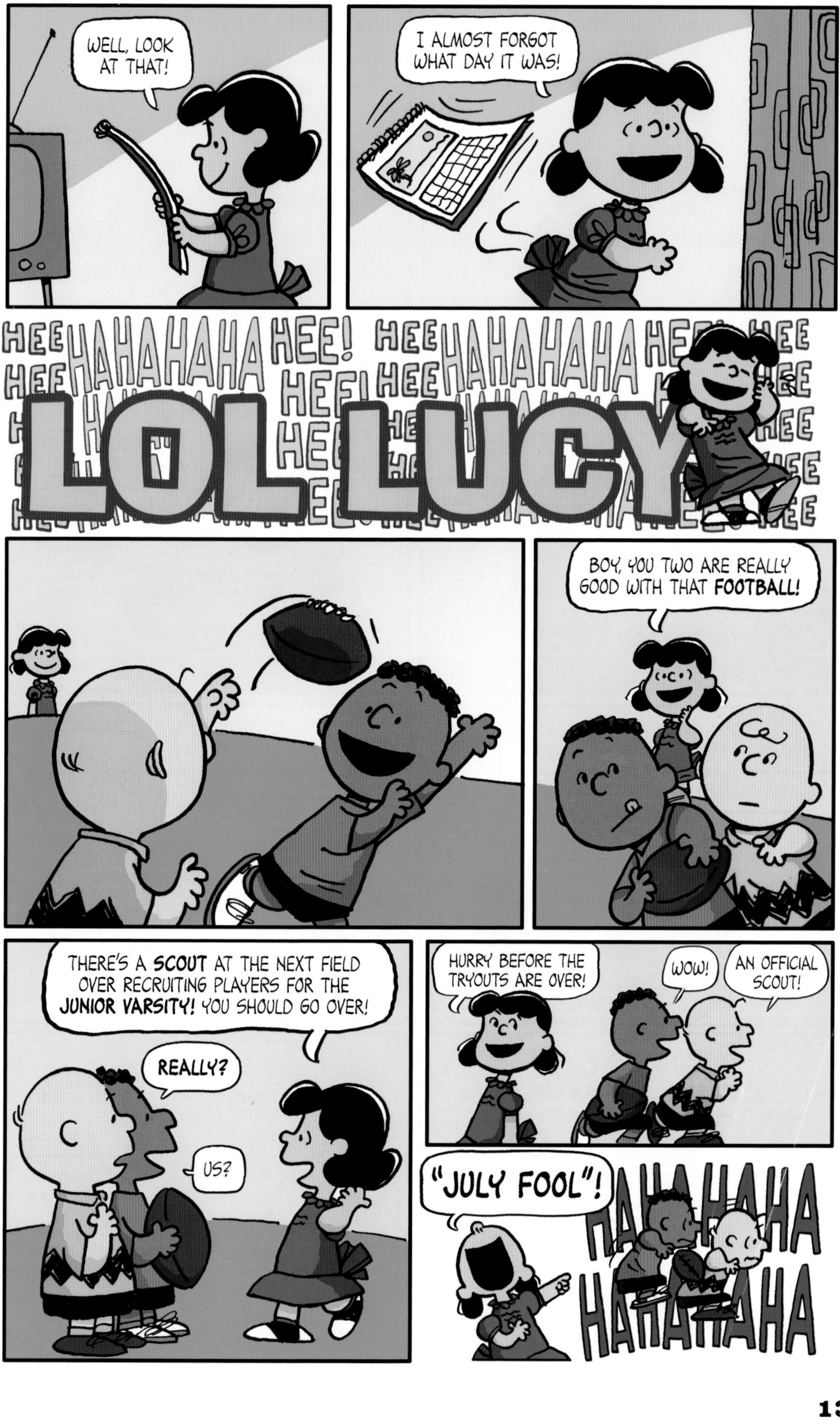
WELL, LOOK AT THAT!
I ALMOST FORGOT WHAT DAY IT WAS!
HEE HAHAHAHA HEE! HEE HAHAHAHA HEE
LOL LUCY
BOY, YOU TWO ARE REALLY GOOD WITH THAT FOOTBALL!
THERE'S A SCOUT AT THE NEXT FIELD OVER RECRUITING PLAYERS FOR THE JUNIOR VARSITY! YOU SHOULD GO OVER!
REALLY?
US?
HURRY BEFORE THE TRYOUTS ARE OVER!
WOW!
AN OFFICIAL SCOUT!
"JULY FOOL"!
HAHAHAHA
HAHAHAHA

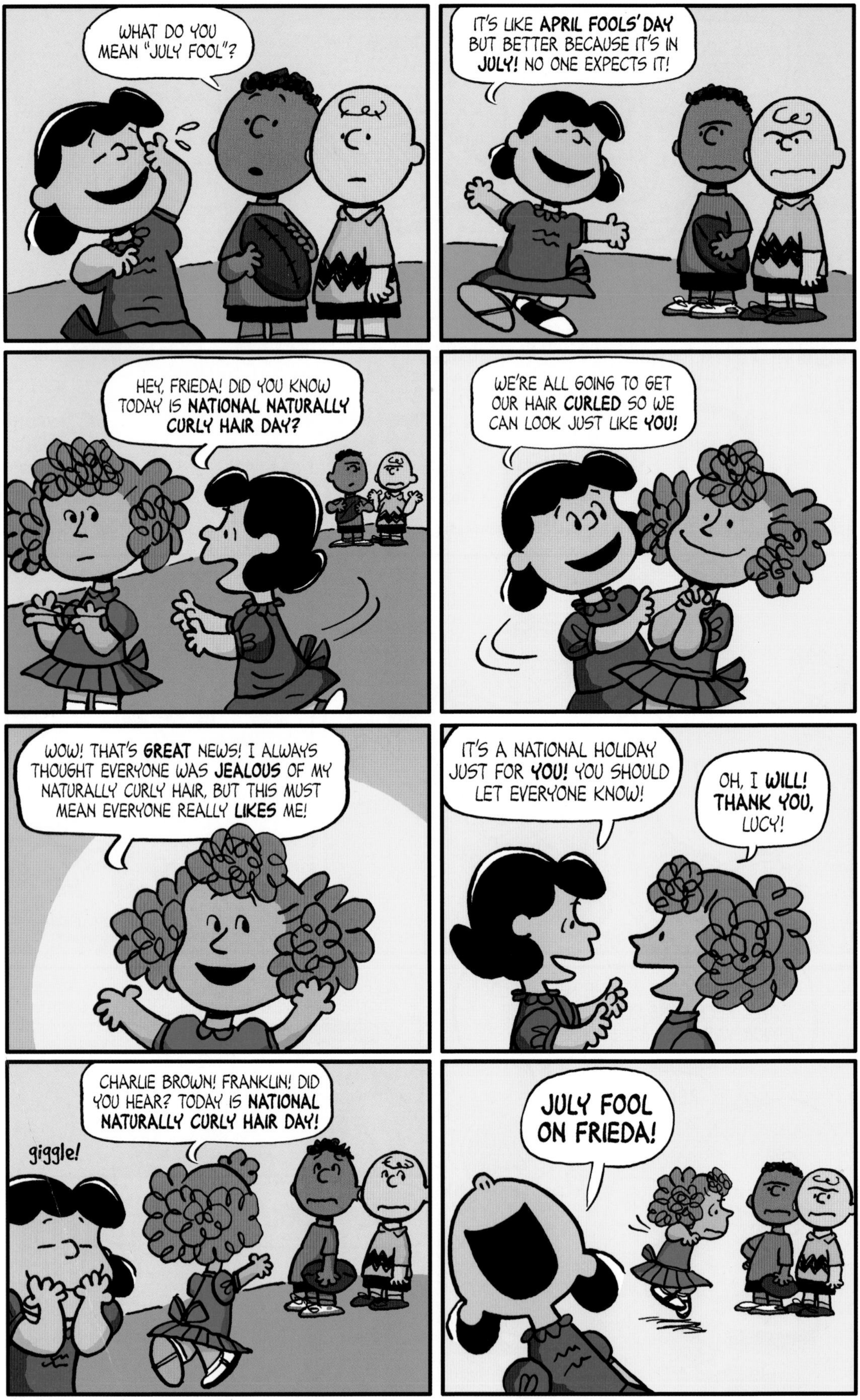
WHAT DO YOU MEAN "JULY FOOL"?
IT'S LIKE **APRIL FOOLS' DAY** BUT BETTER BECAUSE IT'S IN **JULY!** NO ONE EXPECTS IT!
HEY, FRIEDA! DID YOU KNOW TODAY IS **NATIONAL NATURALLY CURLY HAIR DAY?**
WE'RE ALL GOING TO GET OUR HAIR **CURLED** SO WE CAN LOOK JUST LIKE **YOU!**
WOW! THAT'S **GREAT** NEWS! I ALWAYS THOUGHT EVERYONE WAS **JEALOUS** OF MY NATURALLY CURLY HAIR, BUT THIS MUST MEAN EVERYONE REALLY **LIKES** ME!
IT'S A NATIONAL HOLIDAY JUST FOR **YOU!** YOU SHOULD LET EVERYONE KNOW!
OH, I **WILL! THANK YOU,** LUCY!
giggle!
CHARLIE BROWN! FRANKLIN! DID YOU HEAR? TODAY IS **NATIONAL NATURALLY CURLY HAIR DAY!**
JULY FOOL ON FRIEDA!

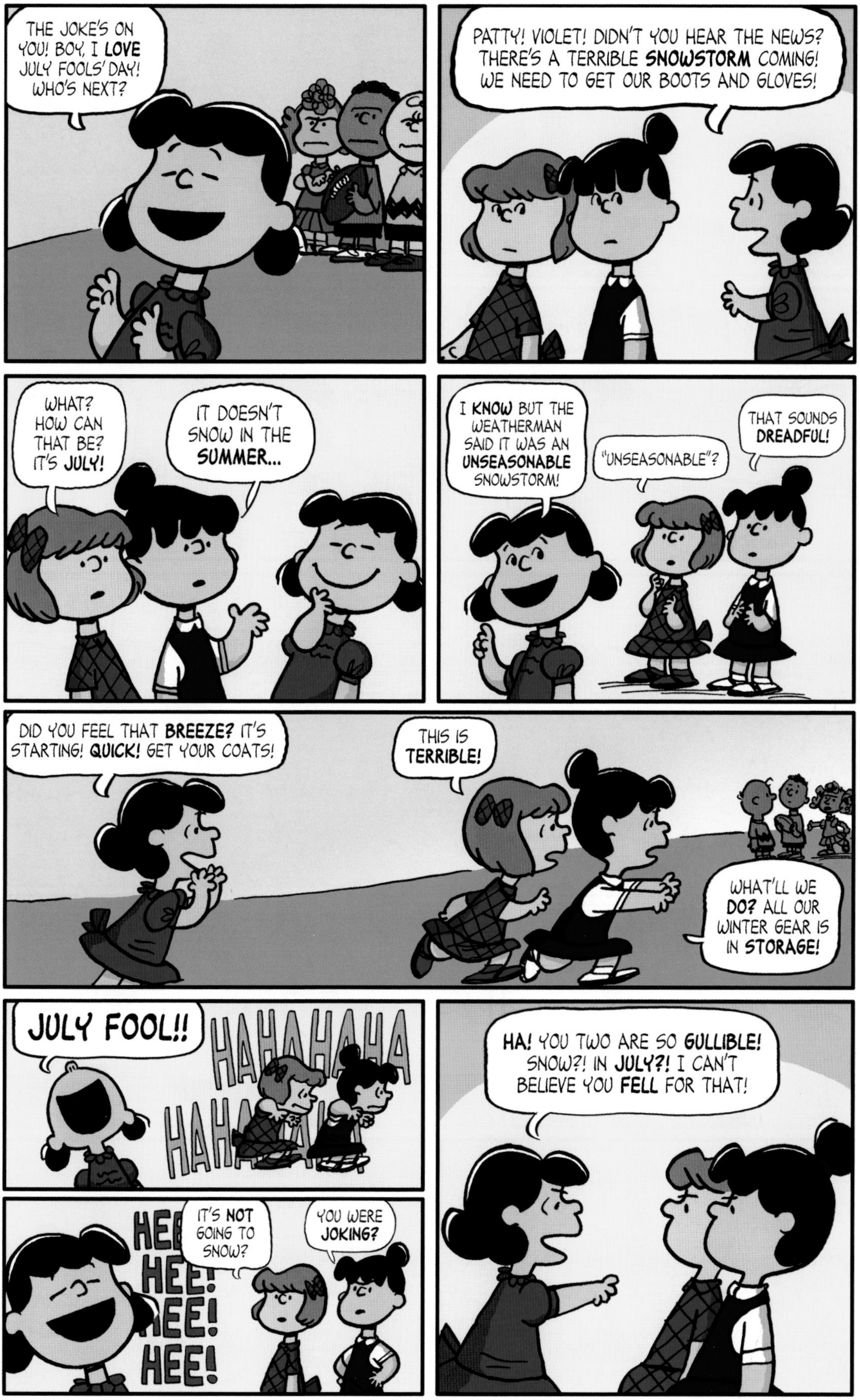
THE JOKE'S ON YOU! BOY, I LOVE JULY FOOLS' DAY! WHO'S NEXT?
PATTY! VIOLET! DIDN'T YOU HEAR THE NEWS? THERE'S A TERRIBLE SNOWSTORM COMING! WE NEED TO GET OUR BOOTS AND GLOVES!
WHAT? HOW CAN THAT BE? IT'S JULY!
IT DOESN'T SNOW IN THE SUMMER...
I KNOW BUT THE WEATHERMAN SAID IT WAS AN UNSEASONABLE SNOWSTORM!
"UNSEASONABLE"?
THAT SOUNDS DREADFUL!
DID YOU FEEL THAT BREEZE? IT'S STARTING! QUICK! GET YOUR COATS!
THIS IS TERRIBLE!
WHAT'LL WE DO? ALL OUR WINTER GEAR IS IN STORAGE!
JULY FOOL!!
HAHAHAHA
HAHA
HEE
HEE!
HEE!
HEE!
IT'S NOT GOING TO SNOW?
YOU WERE JOKING?
HA! YOU TWO ARE SO GULLIBLE! SNOW?! IN JULY?! I CAN'T BELIEVE YOU FELL FOR THAT!

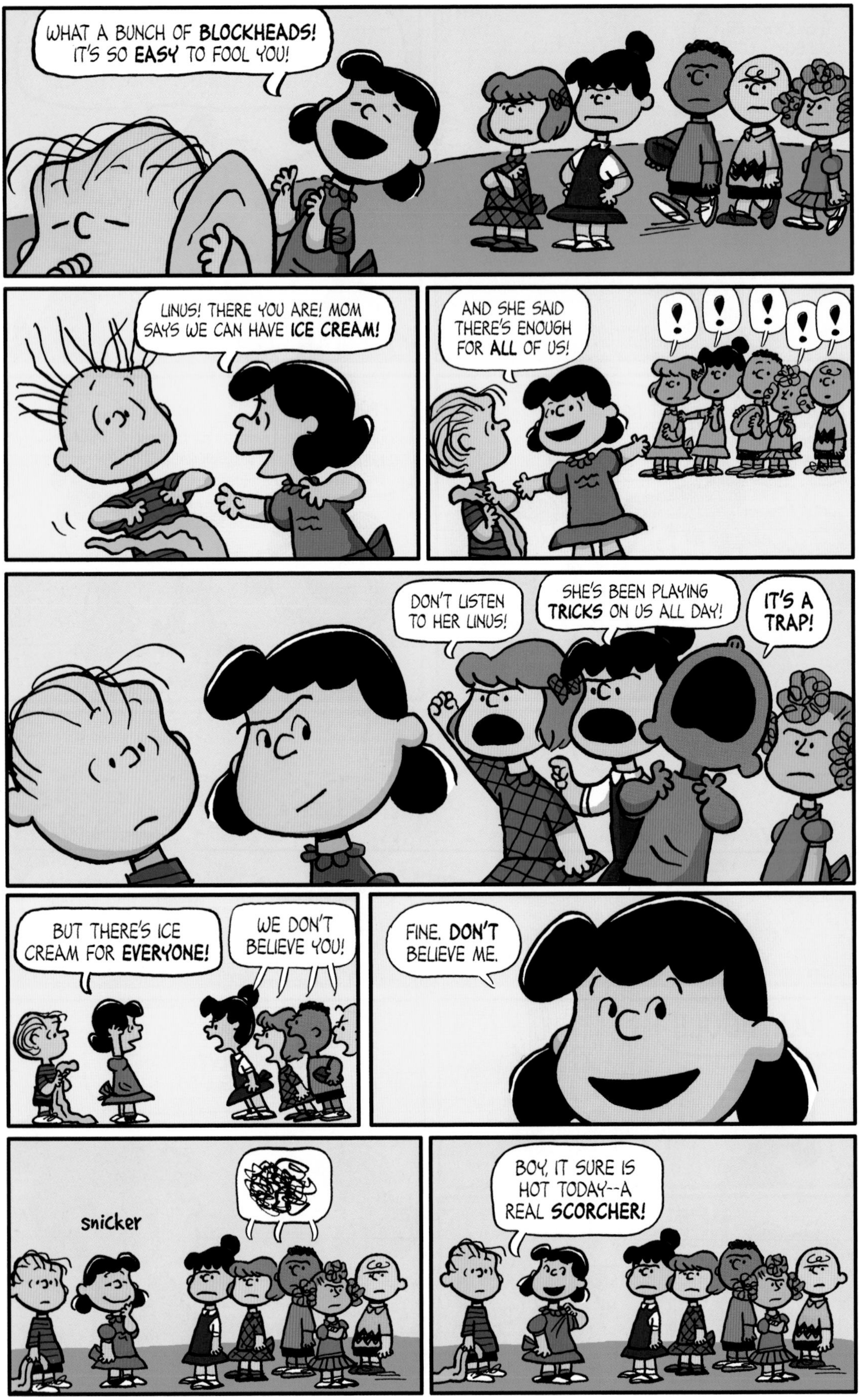

WHAT A BUNCH OF BLOCKHEADS! IT'S SO EASY TO FOOL YOU!
LINUS! THERE YOU ARE! MOM SAYS WE CAN HAVE ICE CREAM!
AND SHE SAID THERE'S ENOUGH FOR ALL OF US!
!
!
!
!
!
DON'T LISTEN TO HER LINUS!
SHE'S BEEN PLAYING TRICKS ON US ALL DAY!
IT'S A TRAP!
BUT THERE'S ICE CREAM FOR EVERYONE!
WE DON'T BELIEVE YOU!
FINE. DON'T BELIEVE ME.
snicker
BOY, IT SURE IS HOT TODAY--A REAL SCORCHER!

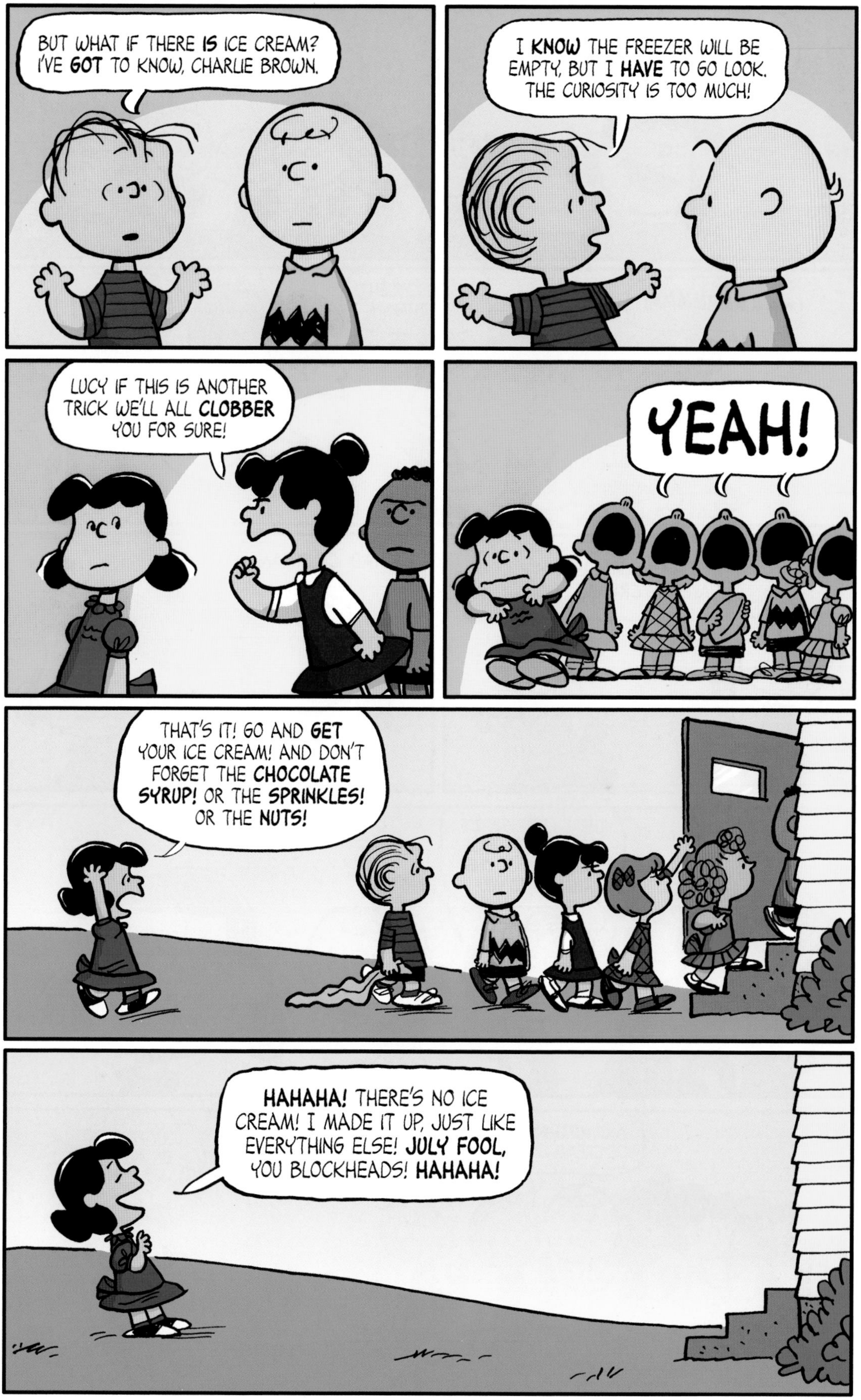
BUT WHAT IF THERE **IS** ICE CREAM? I'VE **GOT** TO KNOW, CHARLIE BROWN.
I **KNOW** THE FREEZER WILL BE EMPTY, BUT I **HAVE** TO GO LOOK. THE CURIOSITY IS TOO MUCH!
LUCY IF THIS IS ANOTHER TRICK WE'LL ALL **CLOBBER** YOU FOR SURE!
YEAH!
THAT'S IT! GO AND **GET** YOUR ICE CREAM! AND DON'T FORGET THE **CHOCOLATE SYRUP!** OR THE **SPRINKLES!** OR THE **NUTS!**
HAHAHA! THERE'S NO ICE CREAM! I MADE IT UP, JUST LIKE EVERYTHING ELSE! **JULY FOOL,** YOU BLOCKHEADS! **HAHAHA!**

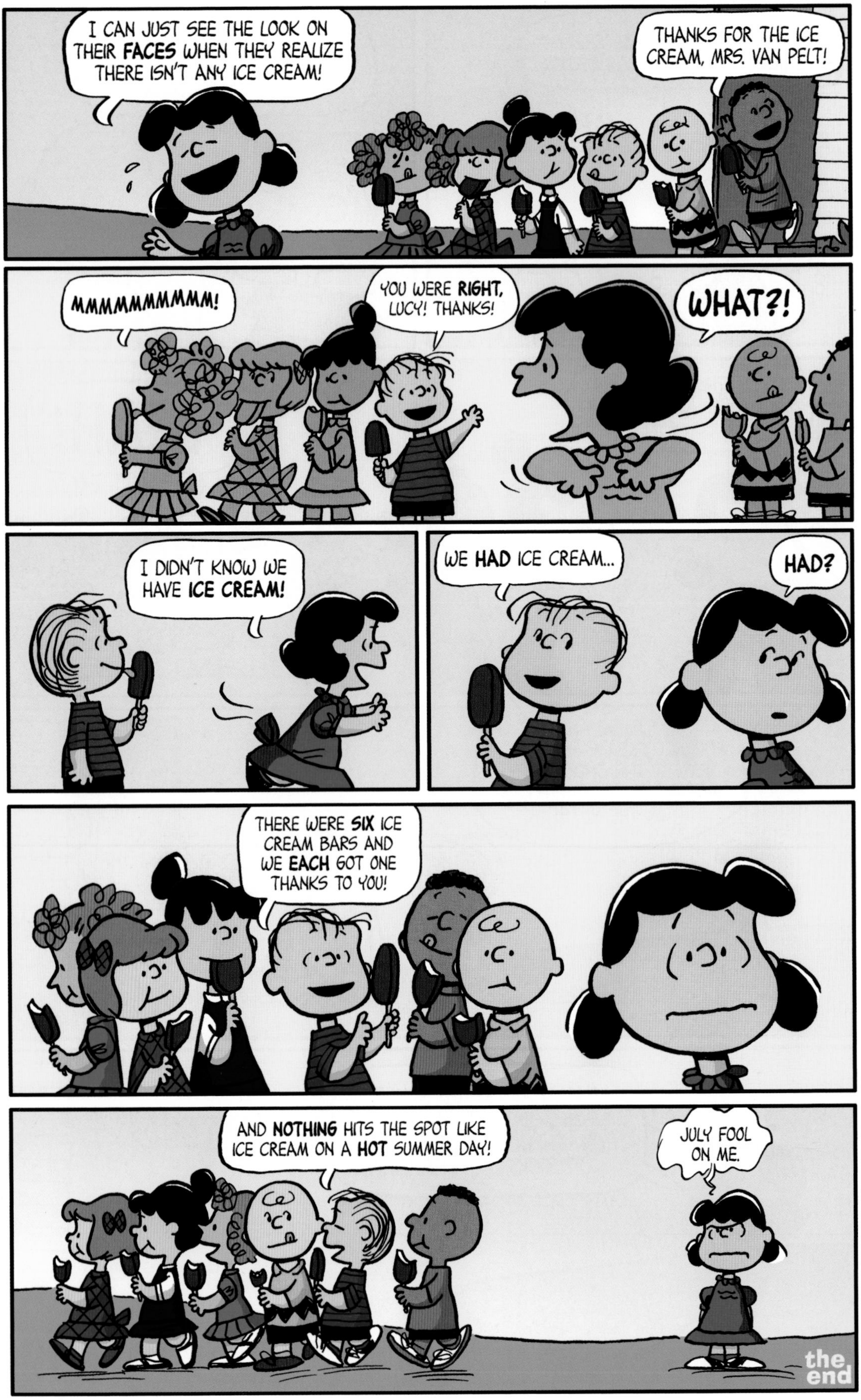
I CAN JUST SEE THE LOOK ON THEIR FACES WHEN THEY REALIZE THERE ISN'T ANY ICE CREAM!
THANKS FOR THE ICE CREAM, MRS. VAN PELT!
MMMMMMMMMM!
YOU WERE RIGHT, LUCY! THANKS!
WHAT?!
I DIDN'T KNOW WE HAVE ICE CREAM!
WE HAD ICE CREAM...
HAD?
THERE WERE SIX ICE CREAM BARS AND WE EACH GOT ONE THANKS TO YOU!
AND NOTHING HITS THE SPOT LIKE ICE CREAM ON A HOT SUMMER DAY!
JULY FOOL ON ME.
the end

From the Drawing Board

> " *I still think that my function is just to draw a little picture, whether it's on a scrap of paper or in a national magazine or in a comic strip which runs in seventeen-hundred newspapers.*

But there's some-thing about writing a letter to a friend, or illustrating a point with a little cartoon, or having a child come up to you and say, "Will you draw me a Snoopy?" and right before their eyes a Snoopy appears and his or her eyes grow big with delight and I've drawn them a Snoopy and I've given that person a brief moment of happiness.

And what more can a person ask? "

—Charles M. Schulz

THE DOGTOR IS IN

PSYCHIATRIC HELP 5¢

THE DOCTOR IS IN

HELP 5

HI, LUCY. I HAVE A PROBLEM AND WAS HOPING YOU COULD HELP...

THE DOCTOR IS IN

OH MY...LOOK AT THE **TIME!**

E DOCTOR

SORRY, CHARLIE BROWN, BUT MY FAMILY IS LEAVING FOR VACATION TODAY.

OUT

BUT DON'T WORRY...I HAVE A VERY ABLE **ASSISTANT** WHO WILL BE FILLING IN FOR ME WHILE I'M GONE...

THE DOCTOR IS

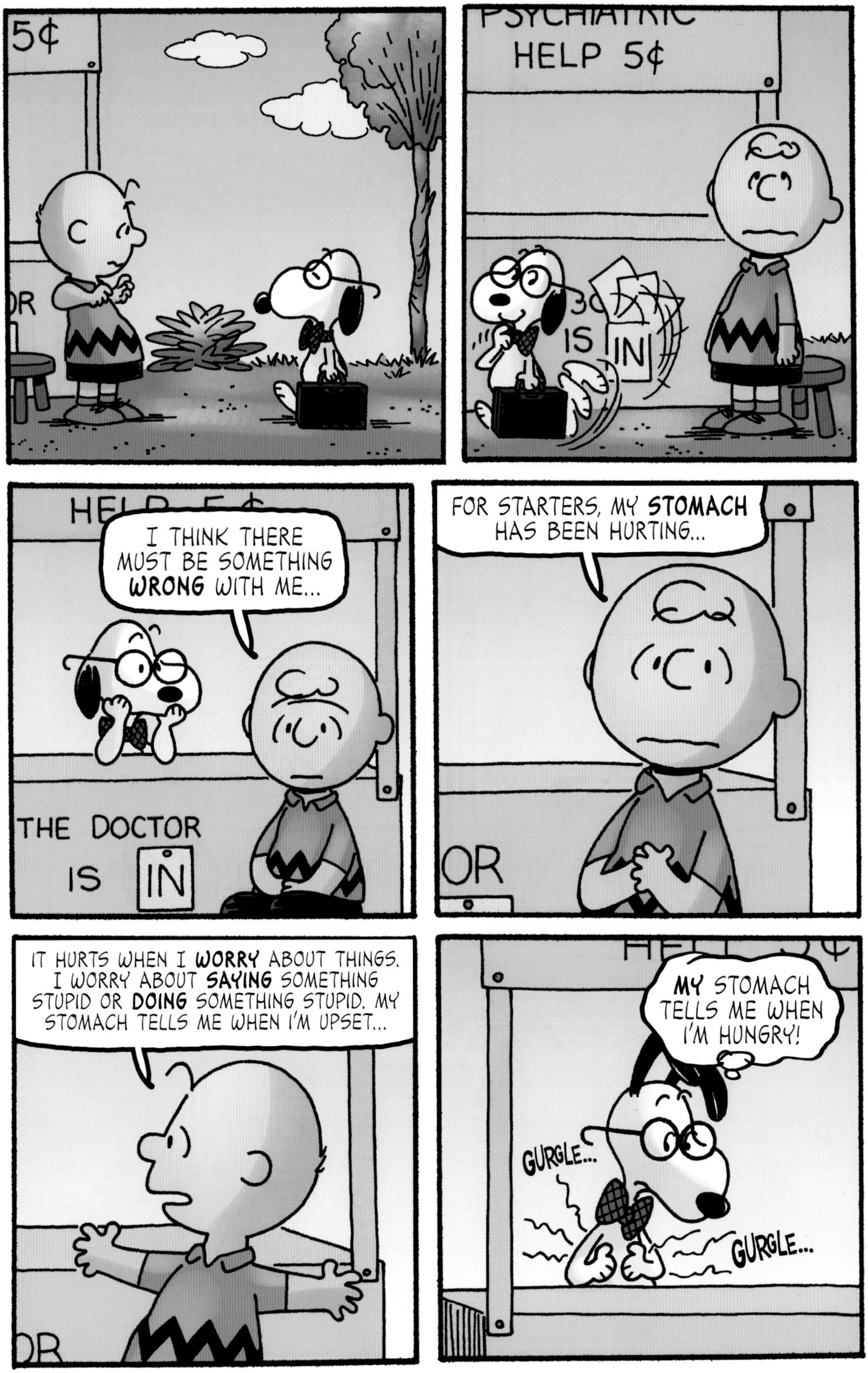
5¢
PSYCHIATRIC
HELP 5¢
IS IN
I THINK THERE MUST BE SOMETHING WRONG WITH ME...
THE DOCTOR
IS IN
FOR STARTERS, MY STOMACH HAS BEEN HURTING...
IT HURTS WHEN I WORRY ABOUT THINGS. I WORRY ABOUT SAYING SOMETHING STUPID OR DOING SOMETHING STUPID. MY STOMACH TELLS ME WHEN I'M UPSET...
MY STOMACH TELLS ME WHEN I'M HUNGRY!
GURGLE...
GURGLE...

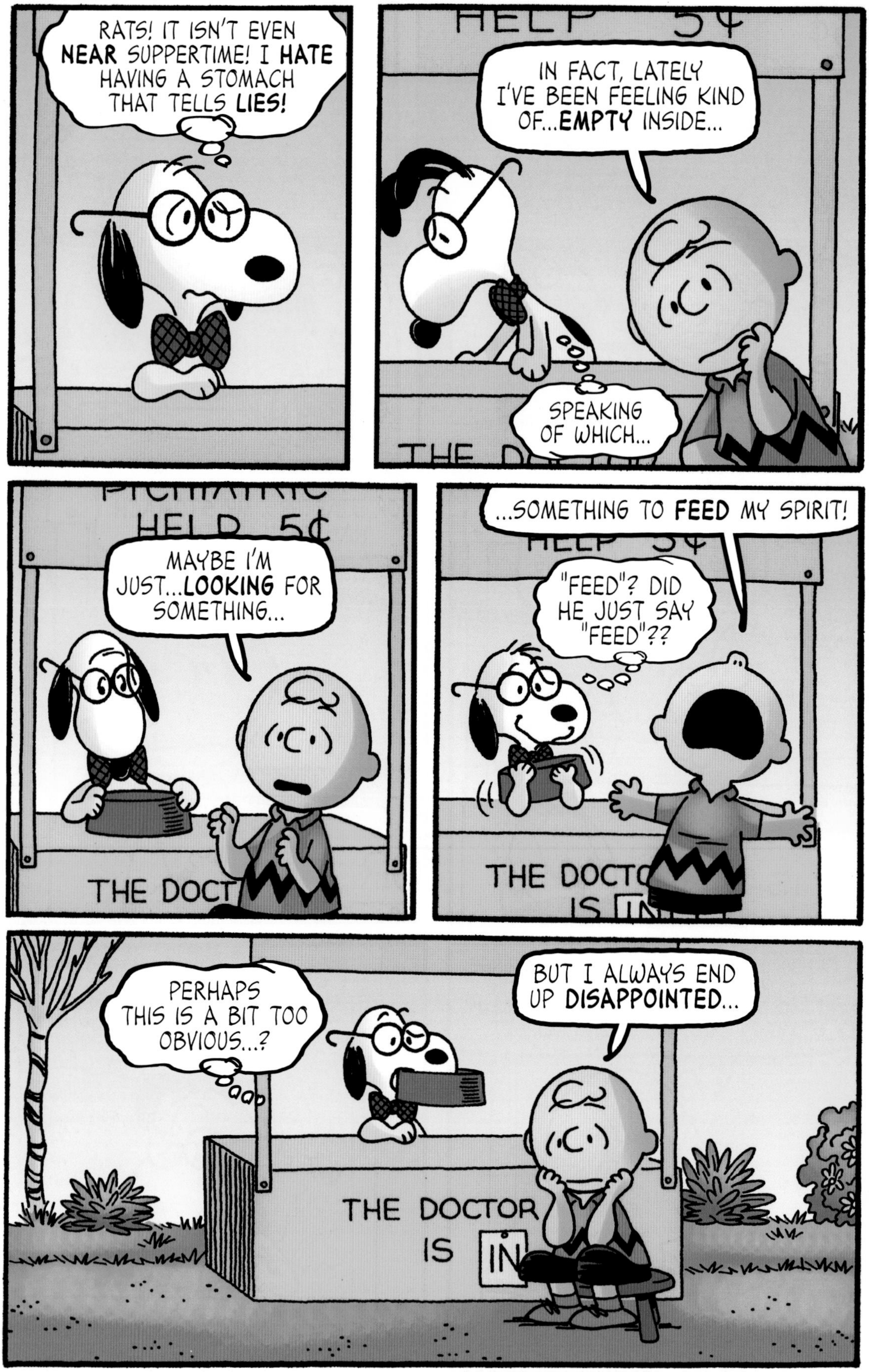
RATS! IT ISN'T EVEN NEAR SUPPERTIME! I HATE HAVING A STOMACH THAT TELLS LIES!
HELP 5¢
IN FACT, LATELY I'VE BEEN FEELING KIND OF...EMPTY INSIDE...
SPEAKING OF WHICH...
HELP 5¢
MAYBE I'M JUST...LOOKING FOR SOMETHING...
THE DOCT
...SOMETHING TO FEED MY SPIRIT!
"FEED"? DID HE JUST SAY "FEED"??
THE DOCTO
PERHAPS THIS IS A BIT TOO OBVIOUS...?
BUT I ALWAYS END UP DISAPPOINTED...
THE DOCTOR IS IN

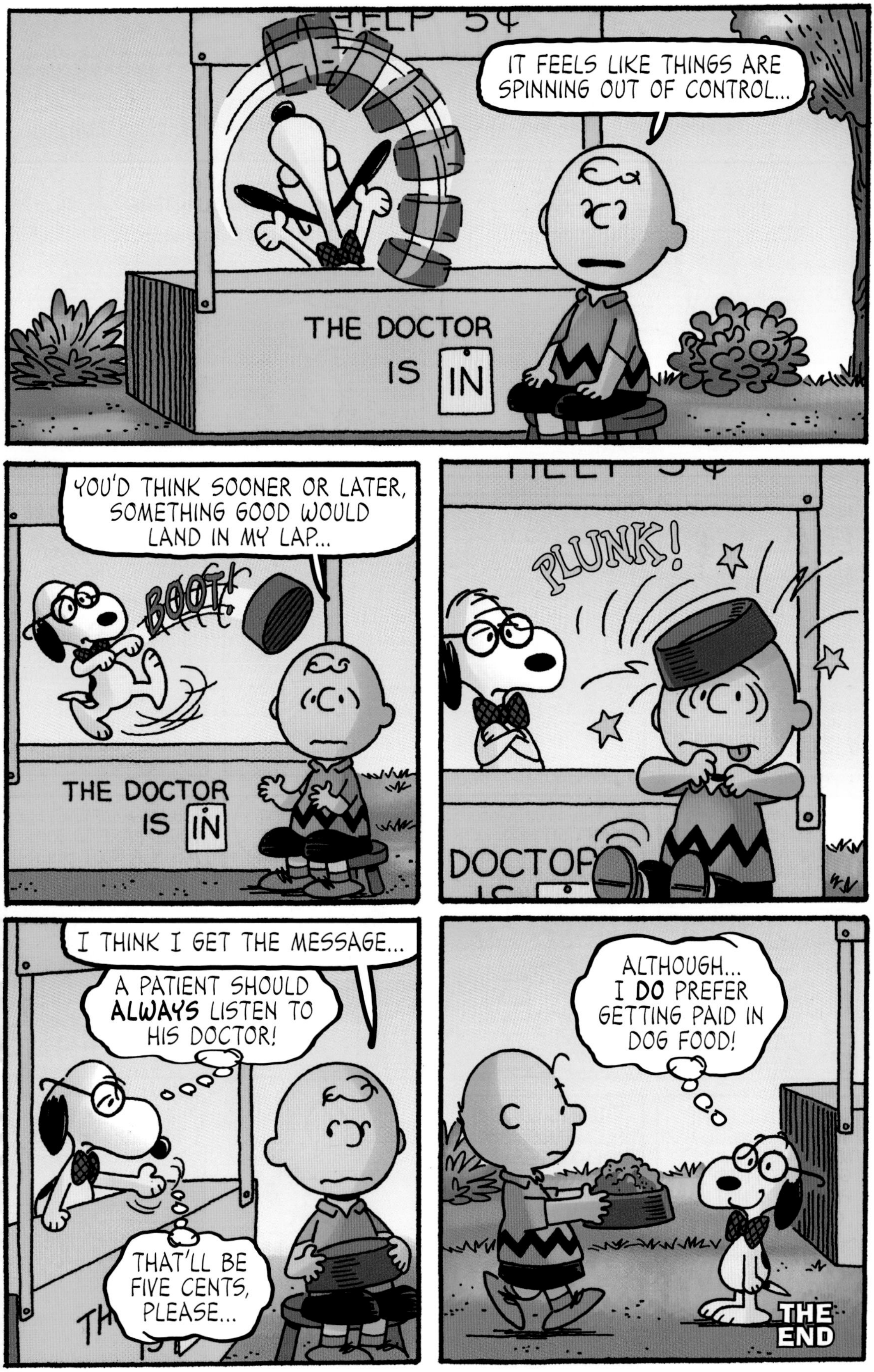

HELP 5¢
IT FEELS LIKE THINGS ARE SPINNING OUT OF CONTROL...
THE DOCTOR IS IN
YOU'D THINK SOONER OR LATER, SOMETHING GOOD WOULD LAND IN MY LAP...
BOOT!
THE DOCTOR IS IN
PLUNK!
DOCTOR
I THINK I GET THE MESSAGE...
A PATIENT SHOULD **ALWAYS** LISTEN TO HIS DOCTOR!
THAT'LL BE FIVE CENTS, PLEASE...
ALTHOUGH... I **DO** PREFER GETTING PAID IN DOG FOOD!
THE END

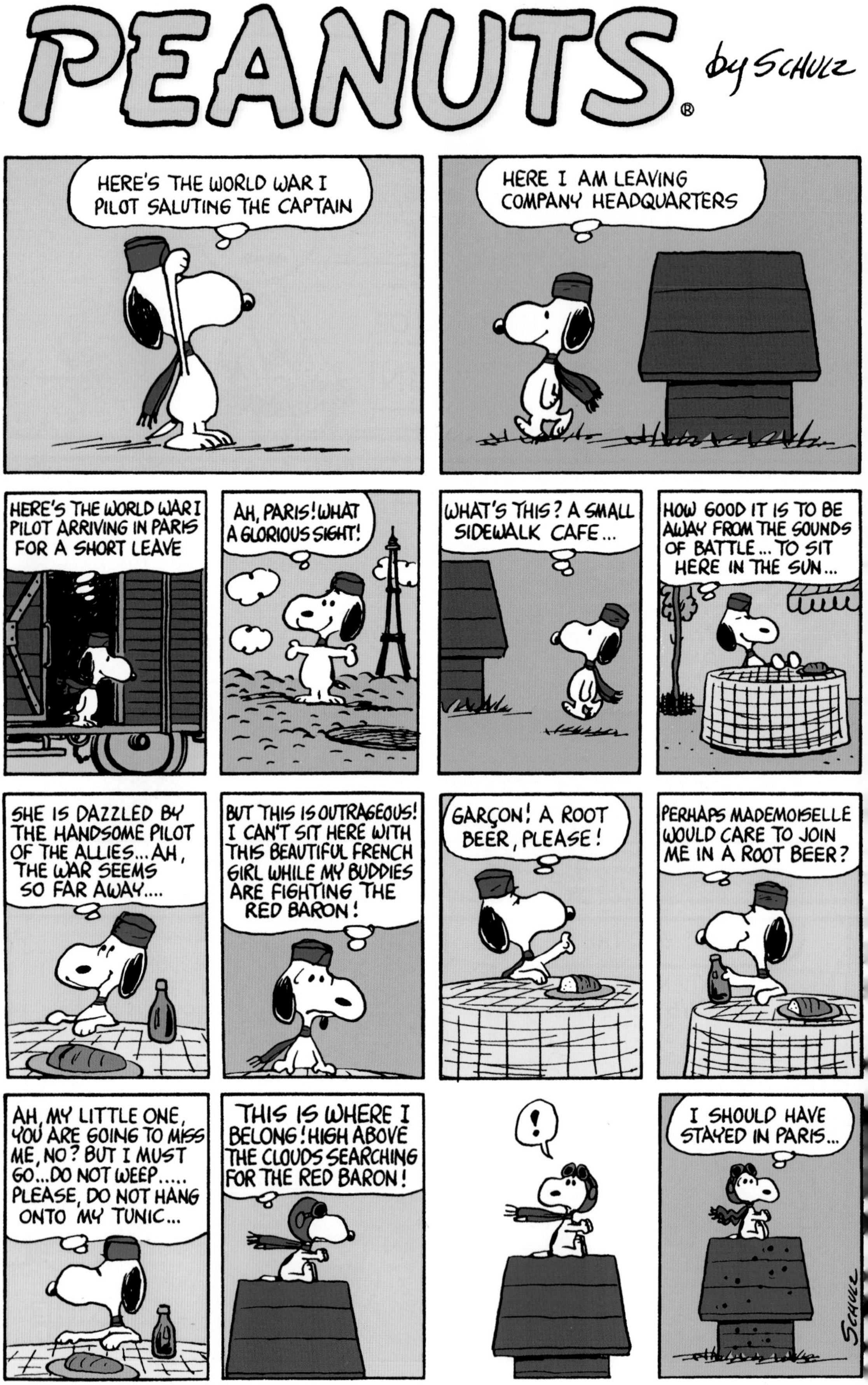
PEANUTS
by SCHULZ
HERE'S THE WORLD WAR I PILOT SALUTING THE CAPTAIN
HERE I AM LEAVING COMPANY HEADQUARTERS
HERE'S THE WORLD WAR I PILOT ARRIVING IN PARIS FOR A SHORT LEAVE
AH, PARIS! WHAT A GLORIOUS SIGHT!
WHAT'S THIS? A SMALL SIDEWALK CAFE...
HOW GOOD IT IS TO BE AWAY FROM THE SOUNDS OF BATTLE... TO SIT HERE IN THE SUN...
SHE IS DAZZLED BY THE HANDSOME PILOT OF THE ALLIES... AH, THE WAR SEEMS SO FAR AWAY....
BUT THIS IS OUTRAGEOUS! I CAN'T SIT HERE WITH THIS BEAUTIFUL FRENCH GIRL WHILE MY BUDDIES ARE FIGHTING THE RED BARON!
GARÇON! A ROOT BEER, PLEASE!
PERHAPS MADEMOISELLE WOULD CARE TO JOIN ME IN A ROOT BEER?
AH, MY LITTLE ONE, YOU ARE GOING TO MISS ME, NO? BUT I MUST GO... DO NOT WEEP..... PLEASE, DO NOT HANG ONTO MY TUNIC...
THIS IS WHERE I BELONG! HIGH ABOVE THE CLOUDS SEARCHING FOR THE RED BARON!
!
I SHOULD HAVE STAYED IN PARIS...
SCHULZ

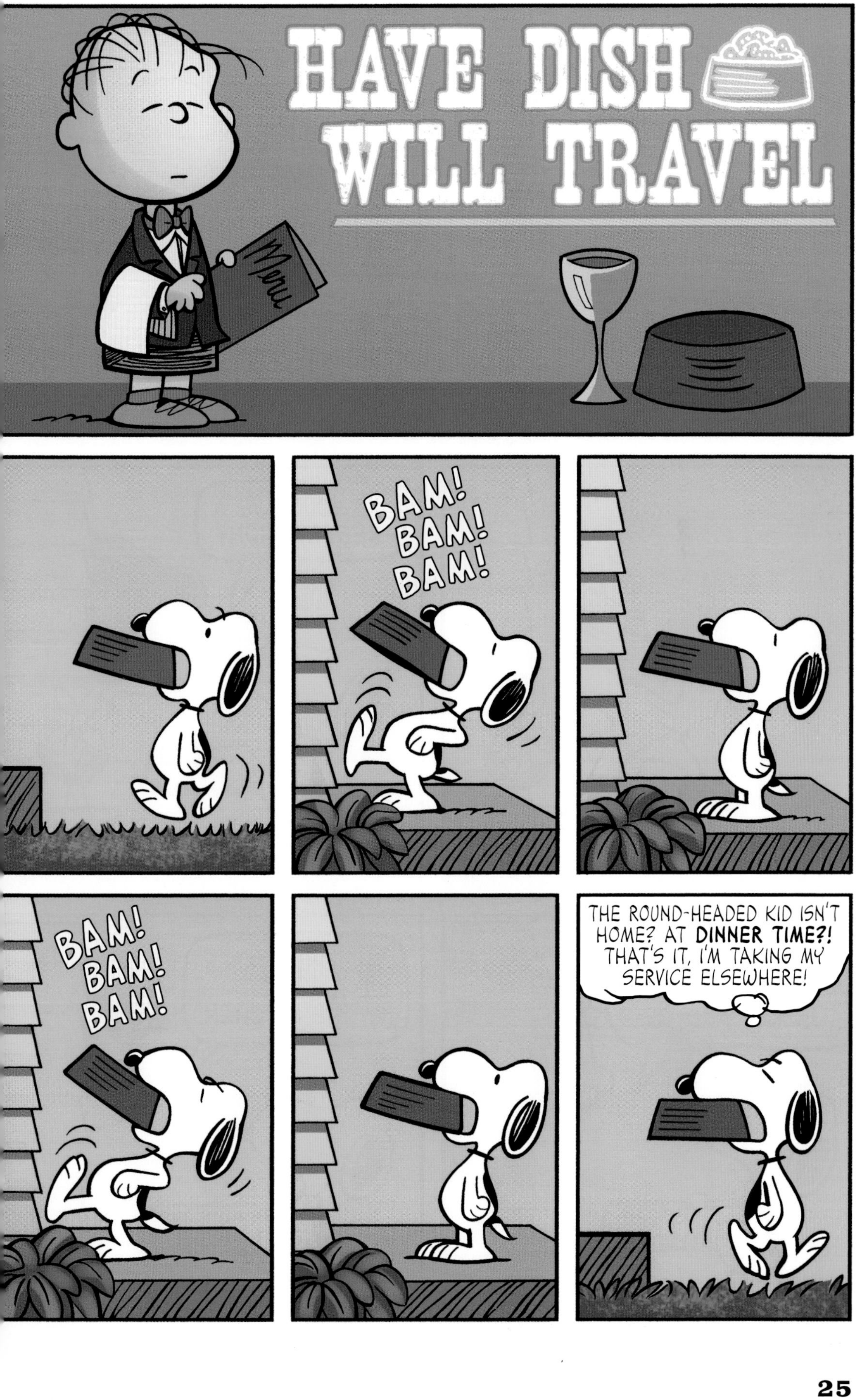
HAVE DISH WILL TRAVEL
Menu
BAM! BAM! BAM!
BAM! BAM! BAM!
THE ROUND-HEADED KID ISN'T HOME? AT **DINNER TIME?!** THAT'S IT, I'M TAKING MY SERVICE ELSEWHERE!

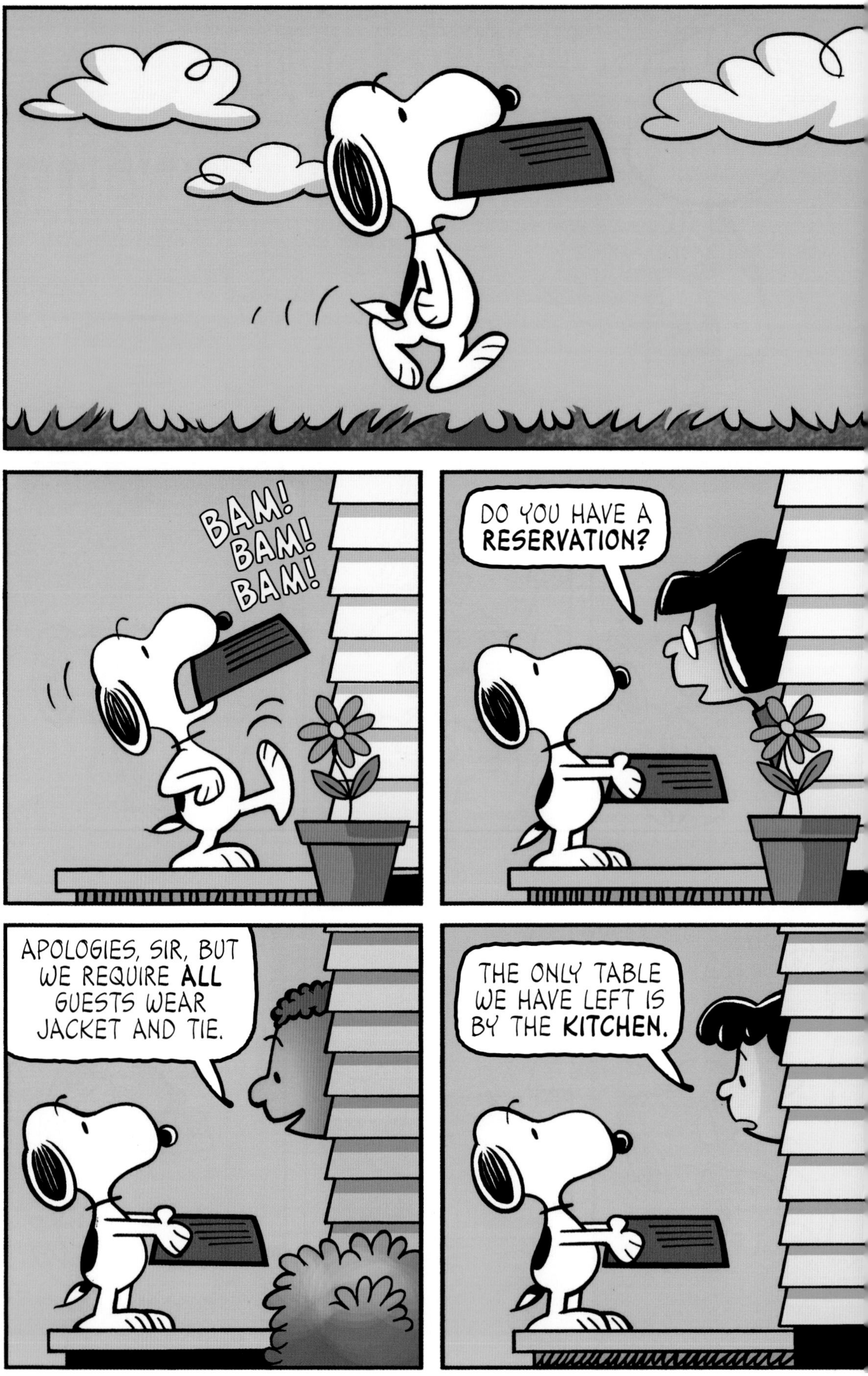
BAM! BAM! BAM!
DO YOU HAVE A RESERVATION?
APOLOGIES, SIR, BUT WE REQUIRE ALL GUESTS WEAR JACKET AND TIE.
THE ONLY TABLE WE HAVE LEFT IS BY THE KITCHEN.

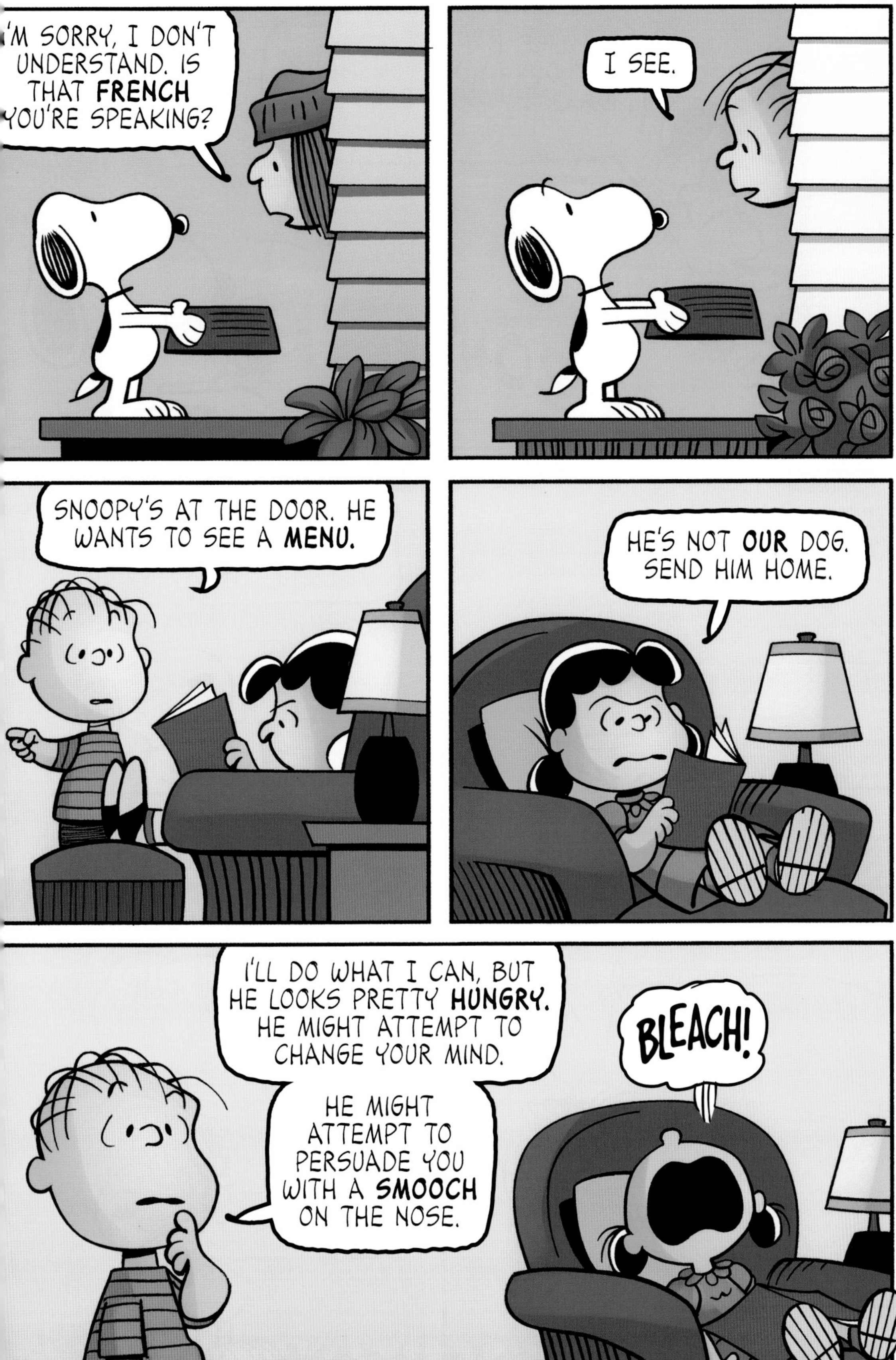
I'M SORRY, I DON'T UNDERSTAND. IS THAT FRENCH YOU'RE SPEAKING?
I SEE.
SNOOPY'S AT THE DOOR. HE WANTS TO SEE A MENU.
HE'S NOT OUR DOG. SEND HIM HOME.
I'LL DO WHAT I CAN, BUT HE LOOKS PRETTY HUNGRY. HE MIGHT ATTEMPT TO CHANGE YOUR MIND.
HE MIGHT ATTEMPT TO PERSUADE YOU WITH A SMOOCH ON THE NOSE.
BLEACH!

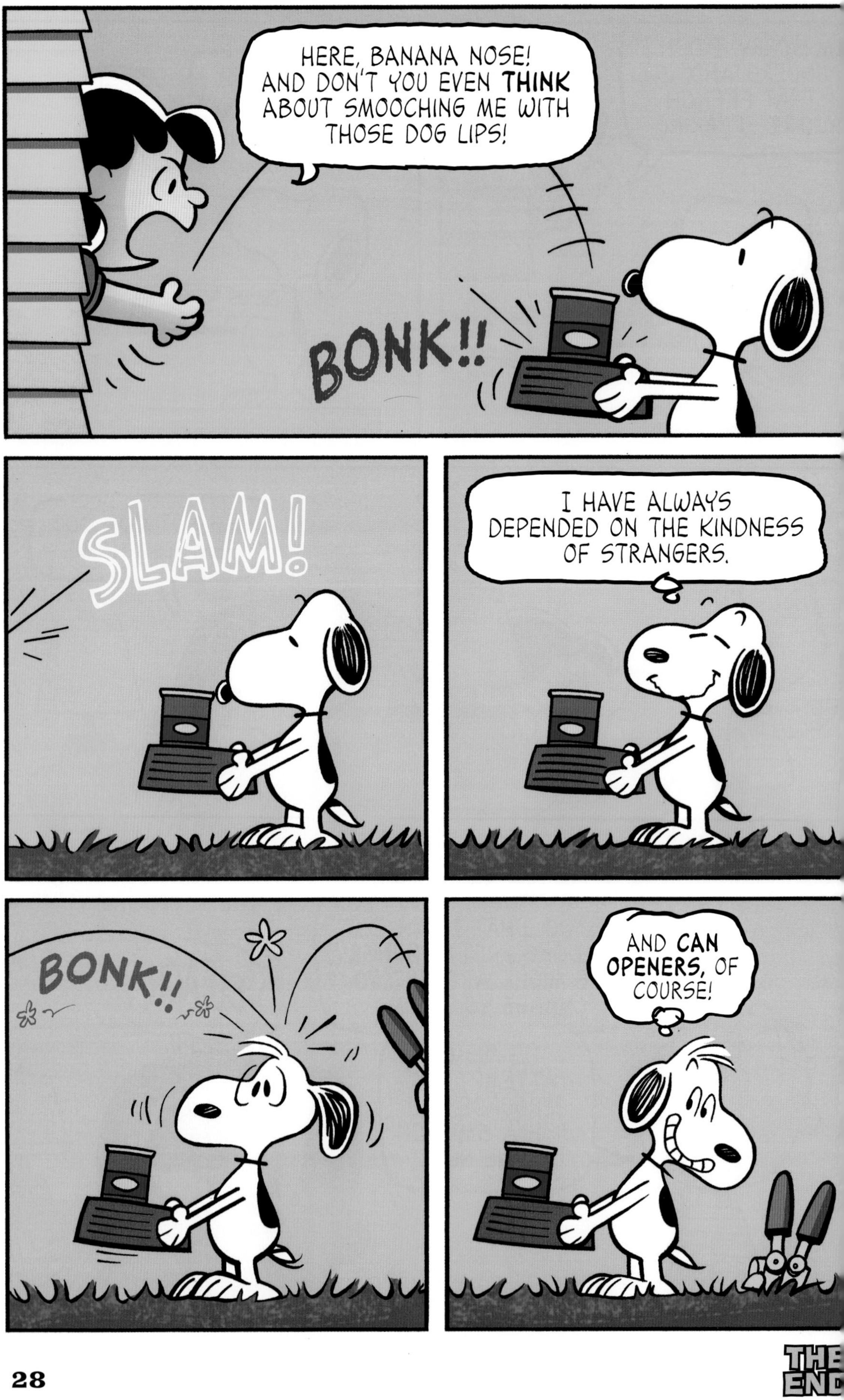
HERE, BANANA NOSE! AND DON'T YOU EVEN THINK ABOUT SMOOCHING ME WITH THOSE DOG LIPS!
BONK!!
SLAM!
I HAVE ALWAYS DEPENDED ON THE KINDNESS OF STRANGERS.
BONK!!
AND CAN OPENERS, OF COURSE!
THE END

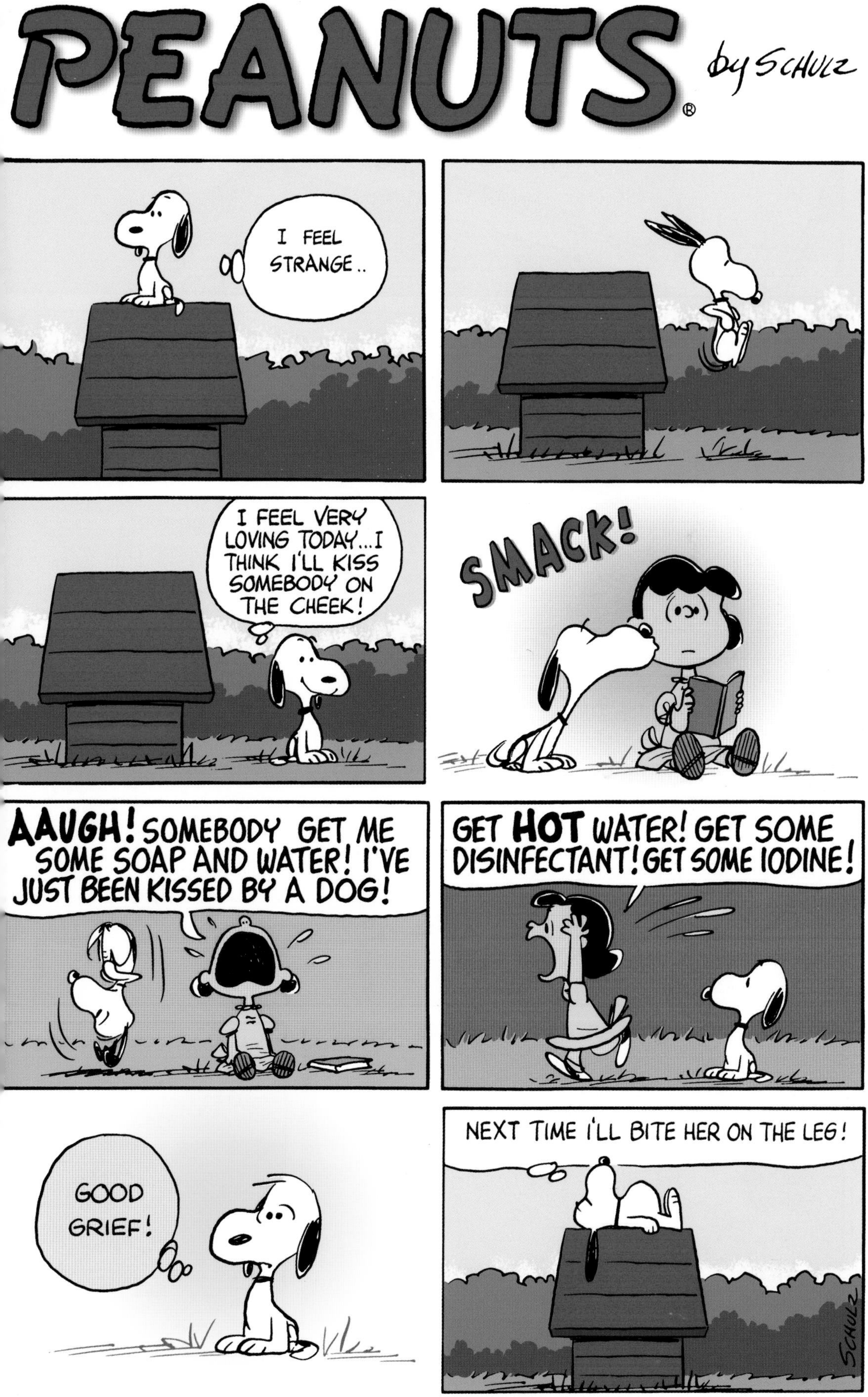
PEANUTS
by SCHULZ
I FEEL STRANGE..
I FEEL VERY LOVING TODAY...I THINK I'LL KISS SOMEBODY ON THE CHEEK!
SMACK!
AAUGH! SOMEBODY GET ME SOME SOAP AND WATER! I'VE JUST BEEN KISSED BY A DOG!
GET HOT WATER! GET SOME DISINFECTANT! GET SOME IODINE!
GOOD GRIEF!
NEXT TIME I'LL BITE HER ON THE LEG!
SCHULZ

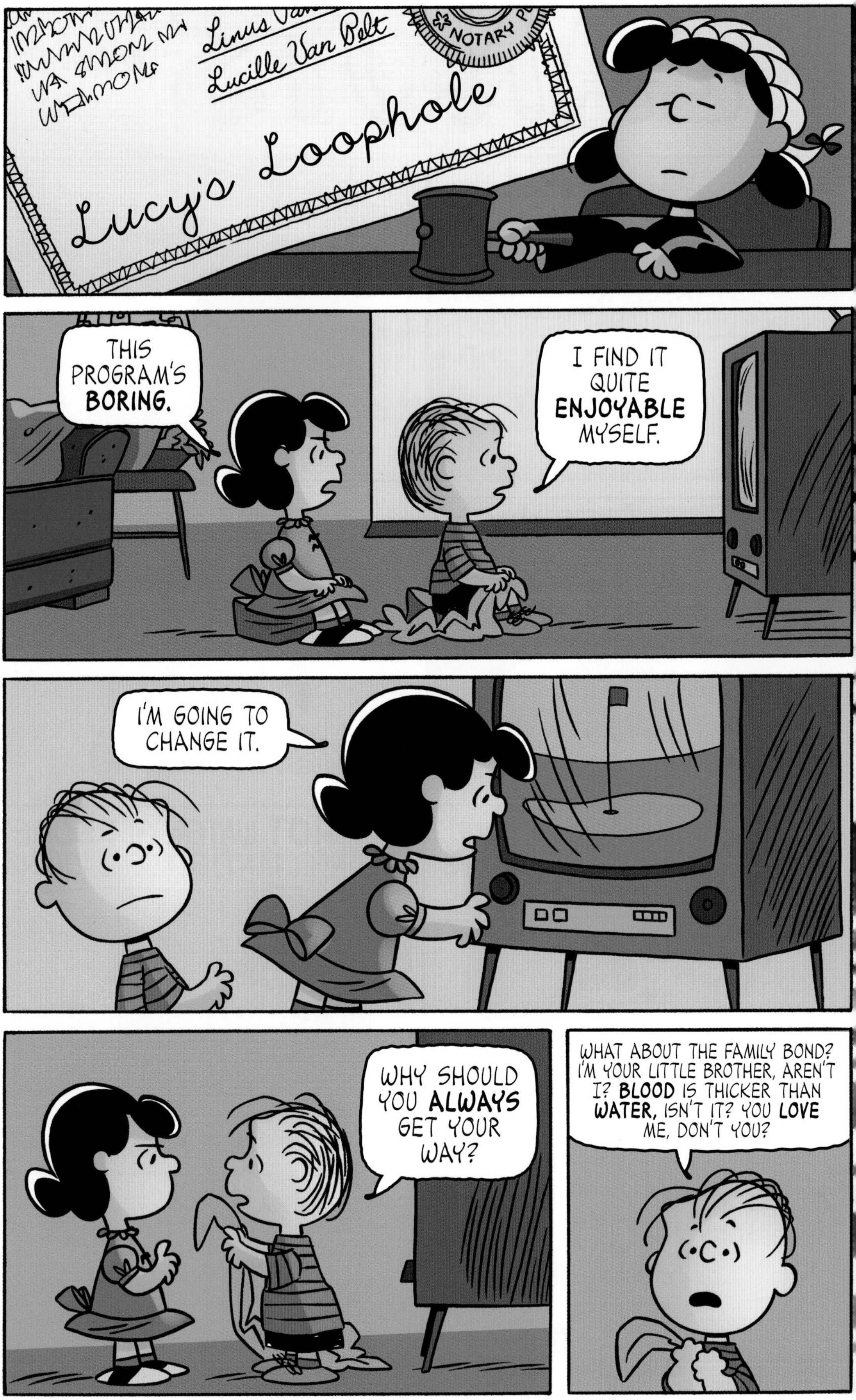
Linus Van
Lucille Van Pelt
NOTARY
Lucy's Loophole
THIS PROGRAM'S BORING.
I FIND IT QUITE ENJOYABLE MYSELF.
I'M GOING TO CHANGE IT.
WHY SHOULD YOU ALWAYS GET YOUR WAY?
WHAT ABOUT THE FAMILY BOND? I'M YOUR LITTLE BROTHER, AREN'T I? BLOOD IS THICKER THAN WATER, ISN'T IT? YOU LOVE ME, DON'T YOU?

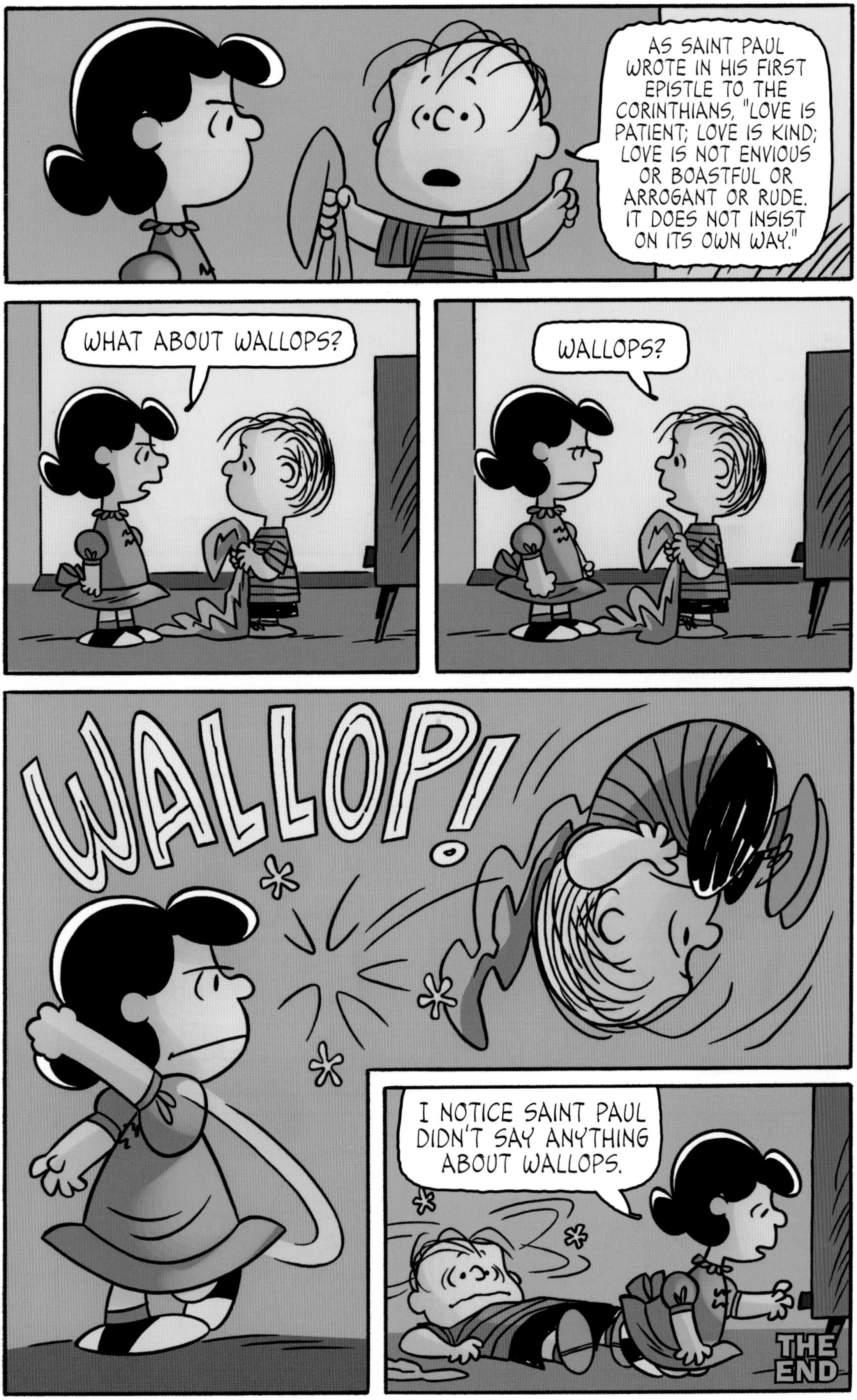
AS SAINT PAUL WROTE IN HIS FIRST EPISTLE TO THE CORINTHIANS, "LOVE IS PATIENT; LOVE IS KIND; LOVE IS NOT ENVIOUS OR BOASTFUL OR ARROGANT OR RUDE. IT DOES NOT INSIST ON ITS OWN WAY."
WHAT ABOUT WALLOPS?
WALLOPS?
WALLOP!
I NOTICE SAINT PAUL DIDN'T SAY ANYTHING ABOUT WALLOPS.
THE END

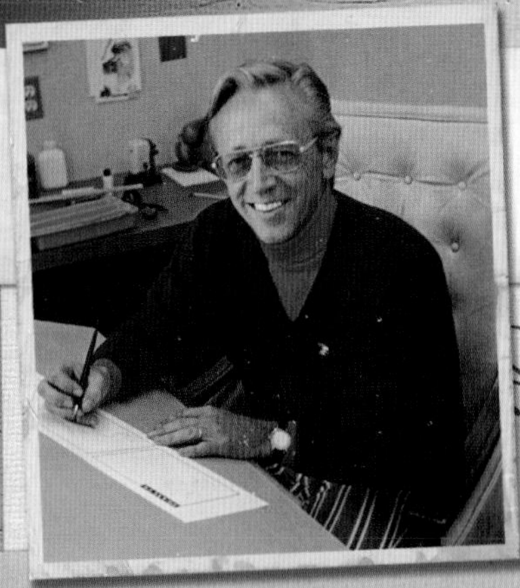

From the Drawing Board

"If you have to define happiness in one little phrase, I defy you to define it in a better way than 'happiness is a warm puppy'.

That says a lot."

–Charles M. Schulz

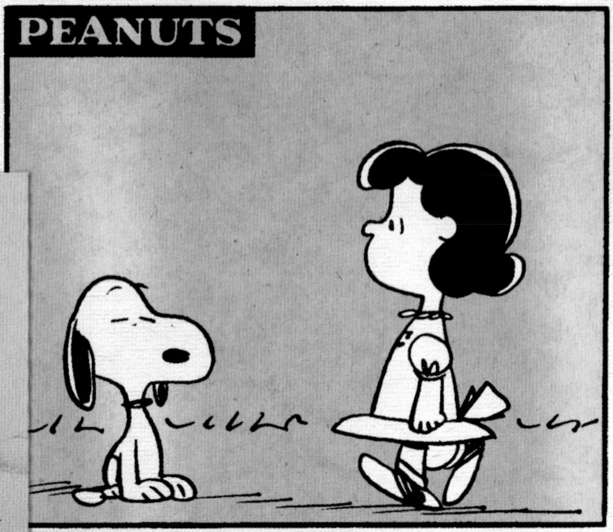
PEANUTS

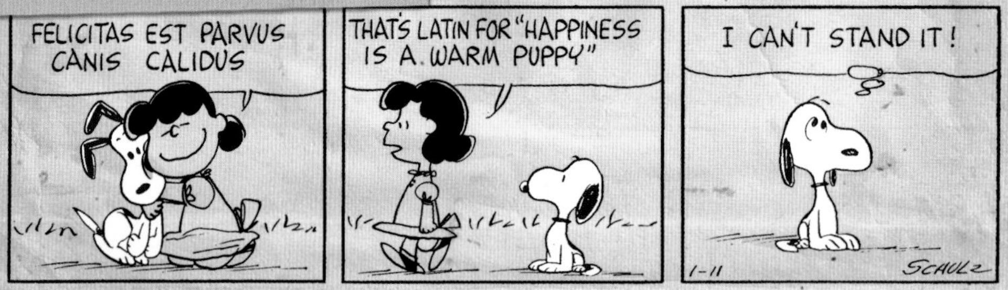
FELICITAS EST PARVUS CANIS CALIDUS
THAT'S LATIN FOR "HAPPINESS IS A WARM PUPPY"
I CAN'T STAND IT!
1-11
SCHULZ

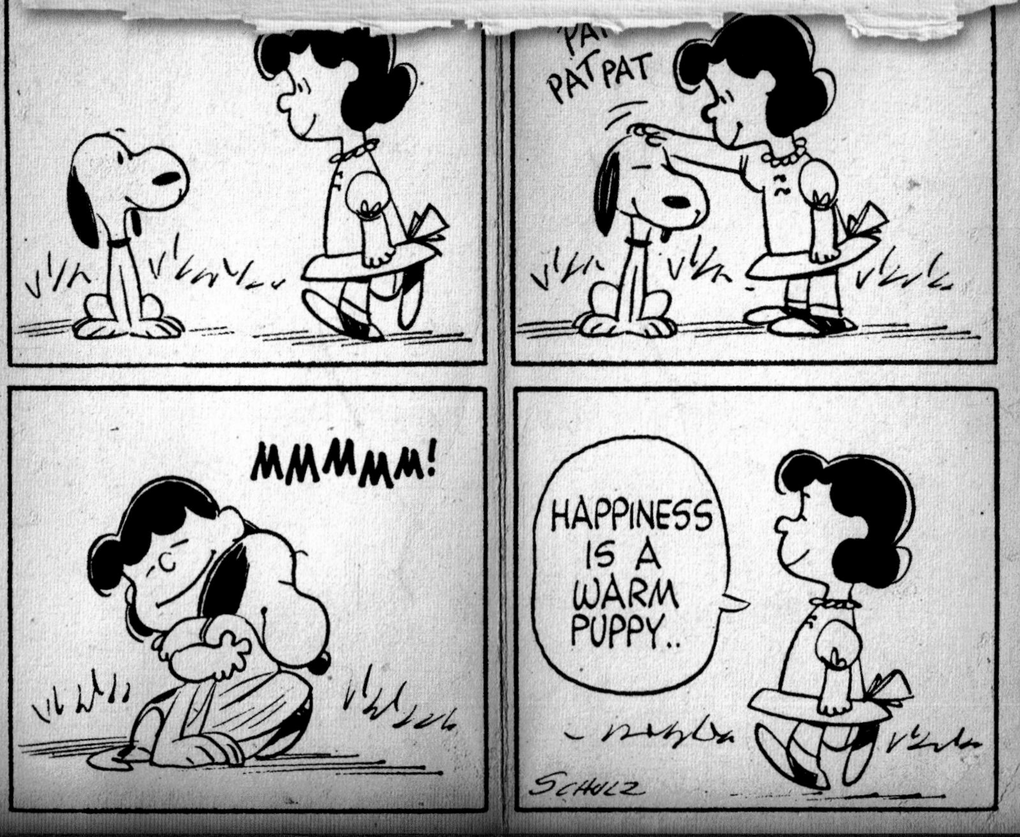
PAT PAT PAT
MMMMM!
HAPPINESS IS A WARM PUPPY..
SCHULZ

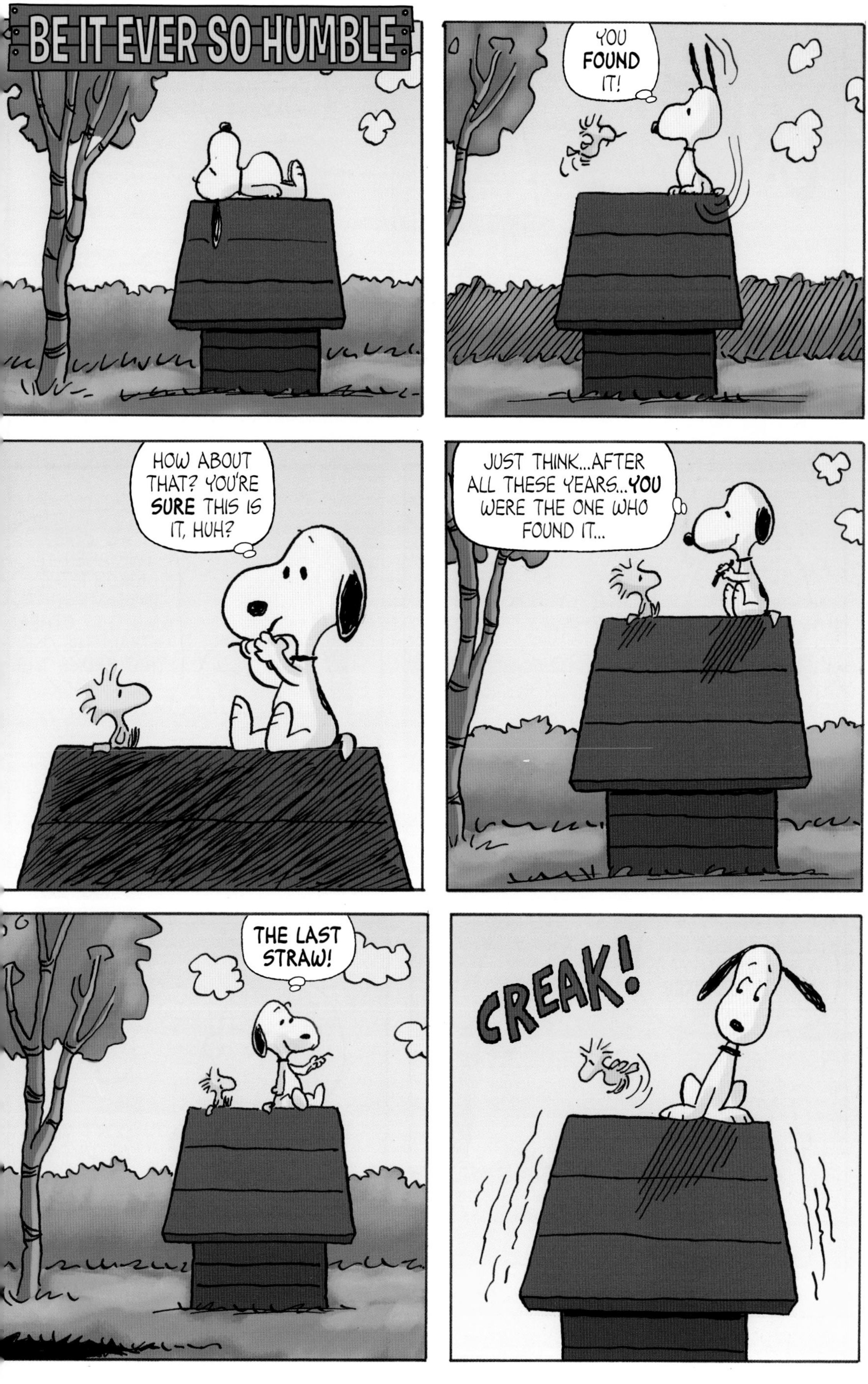
BE IT EVER SO HUMBLE
YOU FOUND IT!
HOW ABOUT THAT? YOU'RE SURE THIS IS IT, HUH?
JUST THINK...AFTER ALL THESE YEARS...YOU WERE THE ONE WHO FOUND IT...
THE LAST STRAW!
CREAK!

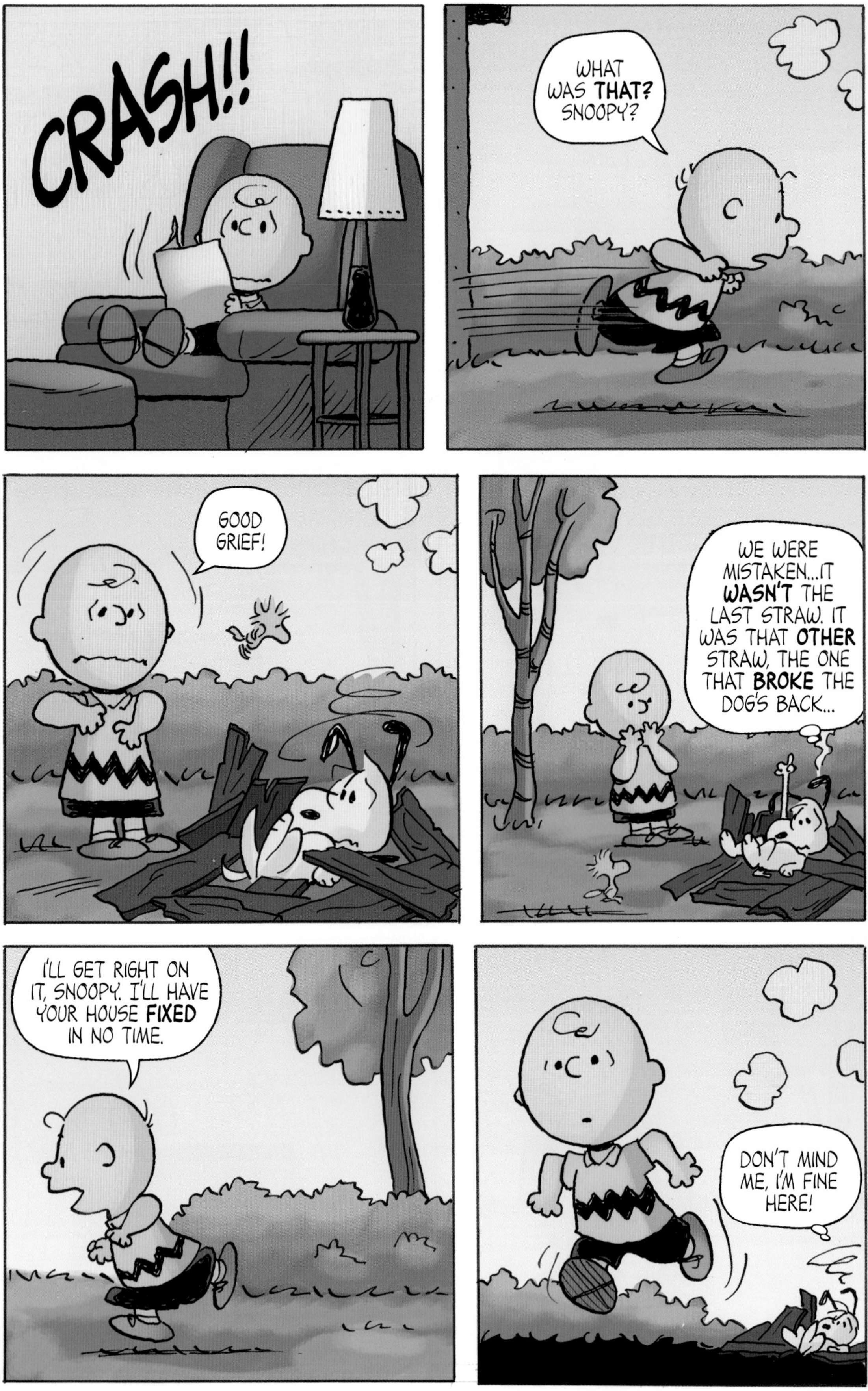
CRASH!!
WHAT WAS **THAT?** SNOOPY?
GOOD GRIEF!
WE WERE MISTAKEN...IT **WASN'T** THE LAST STRAW. IT WAS THAT **OTHER** STRAW, THE ONE THAT **BROKE** THE DOG'S BACK...
I'LL GET RIGHT ON IT, SNOOPY. I'LL HAVE YOUR HOUSE **FIXED** IN NO TIME.
DON'T MIND ME, I'M FINE HERE!

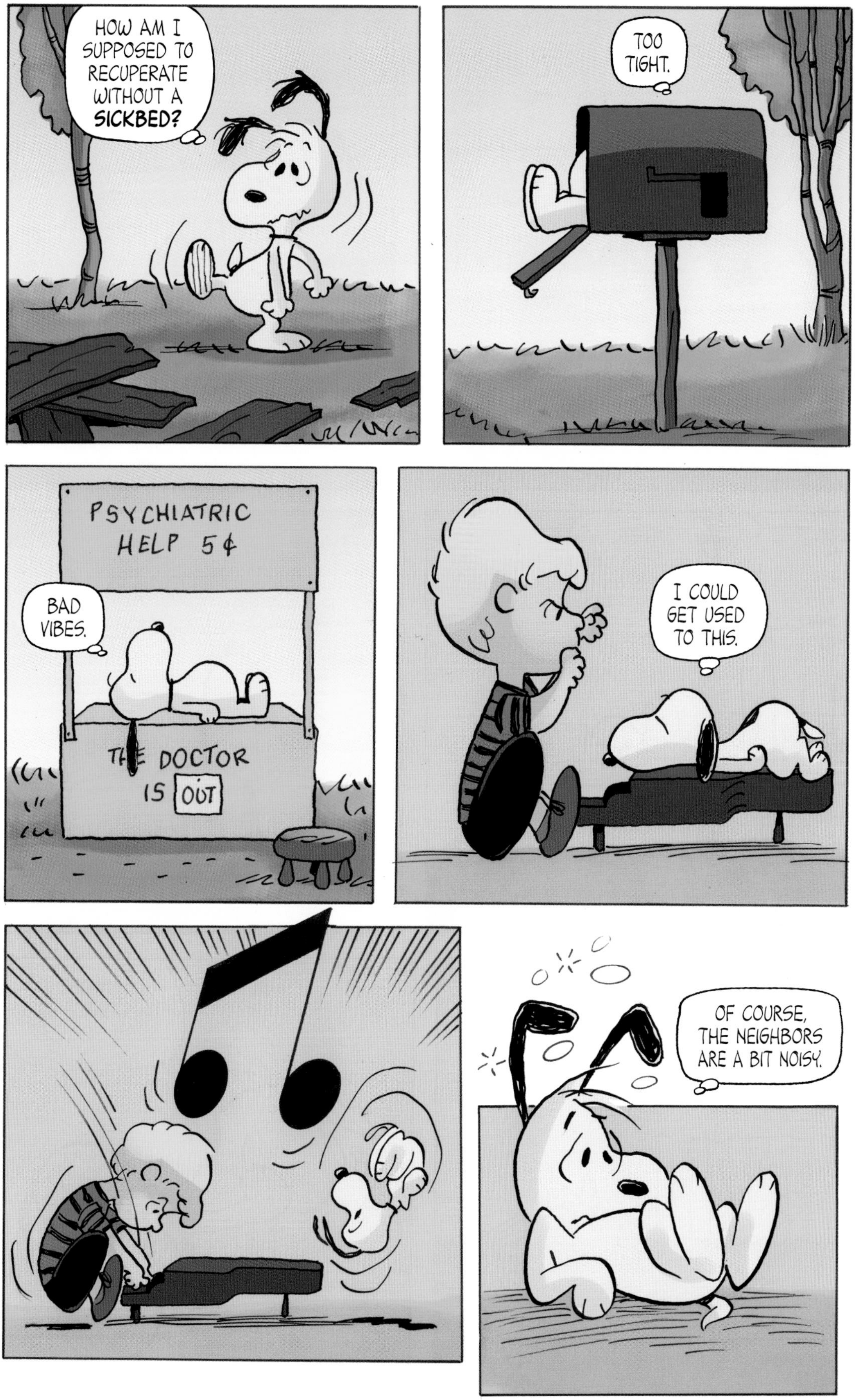

HOW AM I SUPPOSED TO RECUPERATE WITHOUT A SICKBED?
TOO TIGHT.
PSYCHIATRIC HELP 5¢
BAD VIBES.
THE DOCTOR IS OUT
I COULD GET USED TO THIS.
OF COURSE, THE NEIGHBORS ARE A BIT NOISY.

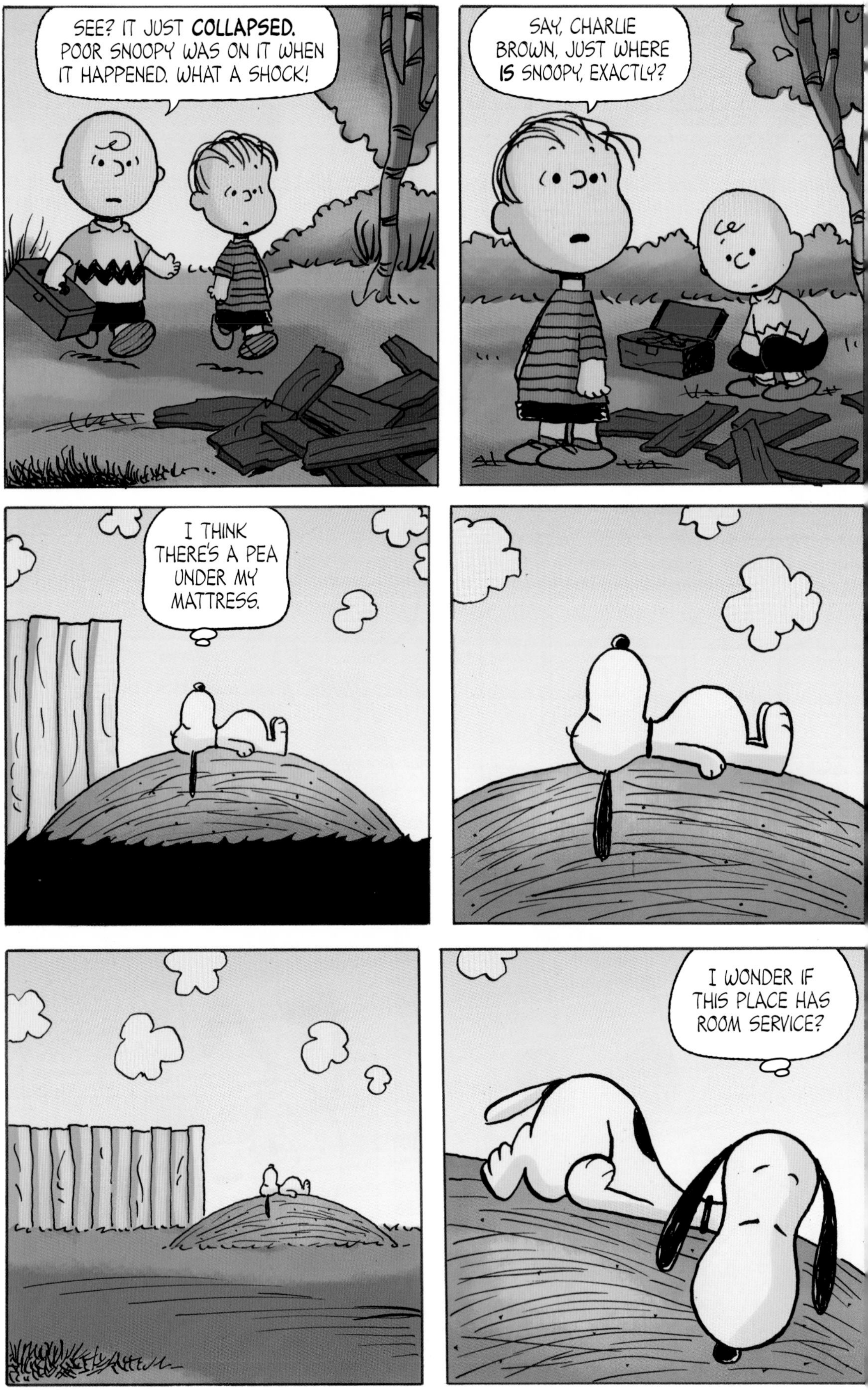
SEE? IT JUST **COLLAPSED.** POOR SNOOPY WAS ON IT WHEN IT HAPPENED. WHAT A SHOCK!
SAY, CHARLIE BROWN, JUST WHERE **IS** SNOOPY, EXACTLY?
I THINK THERE'S A PEA UNDER MY MATTRESS.
I WONDER IF THIS PLACE HAS ROOM SERVICE?

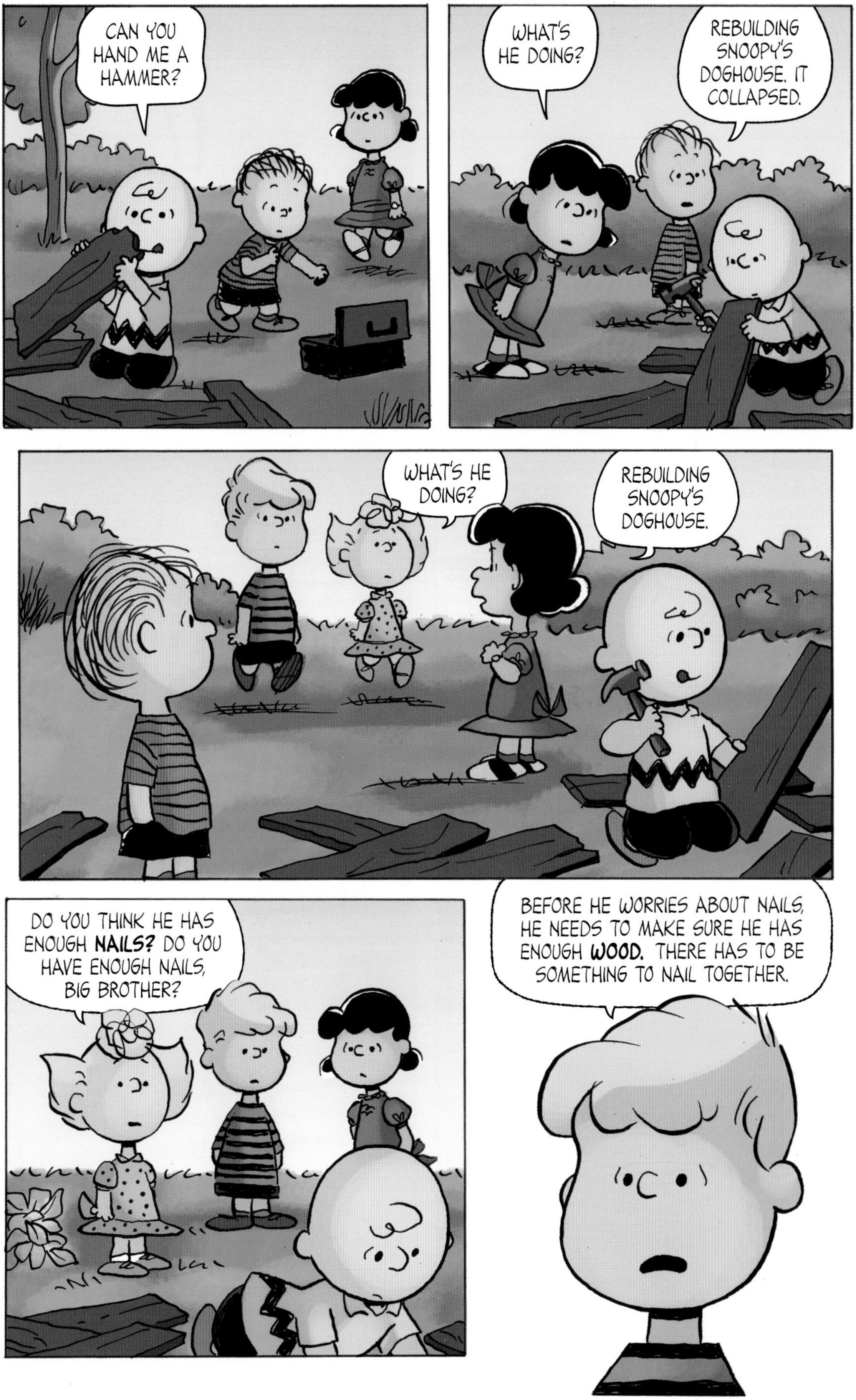
CAN YOU HAND ME A HAMMER?
WHAT'S HE DOING?
REBUILDING SNOOPY'S DOGHOUSE. IT COLLAPSED.
WHAT'S HE DOING?
REBUILDING SNOOPY'S DOGHOUSE.
DO YOU THINK HE HAS ENOUGH **NAILS?** DO YOU HAVE ENOUGH NAILS, BIG BROTHER?
BEFORE HE WORRIES ABOUT NAILS, HE NEEDS TO MAKE SURE HE HAS ENOUGH **WOOD.** THERE HAS TO BE SOMETHING TO NAIL TOGETHER.

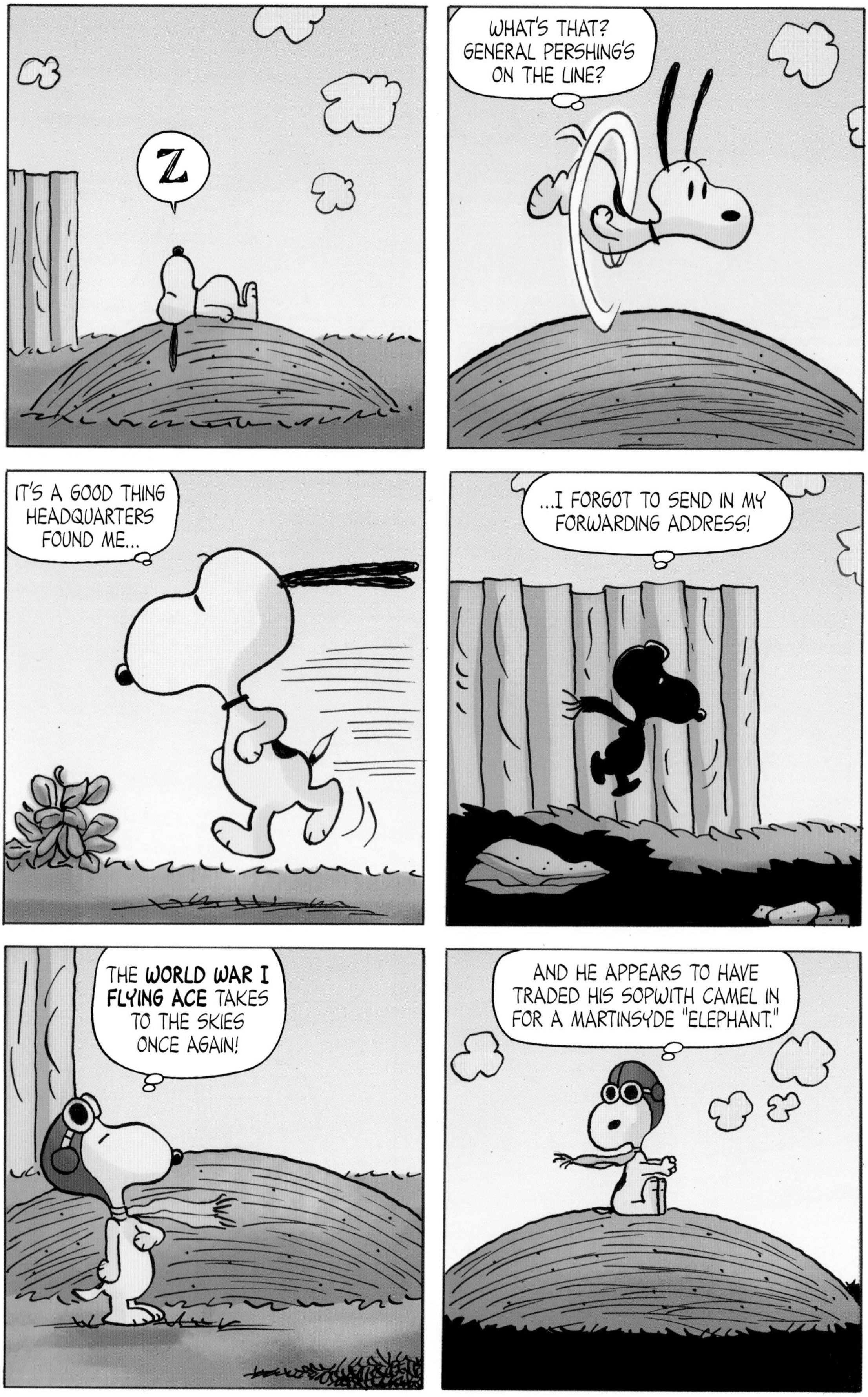
Z
WHAT'S THAT? GENERAL PERSHING'S ON THE LINE?
IT'S A GOOD THING HEADQUARTERS FOUND ME...
...I FORGOT TO SEND IN MY FORWARDING ADDRESS!
THE WORLD WAR I FLYING ACE TAKES TO THE SKIES ONCE AGAIN!
AND HE APPEARS TO HAVE TRADED HIS SOPWITH CAMEL IN FOR A MARTINSYDE "ELEPHANT."

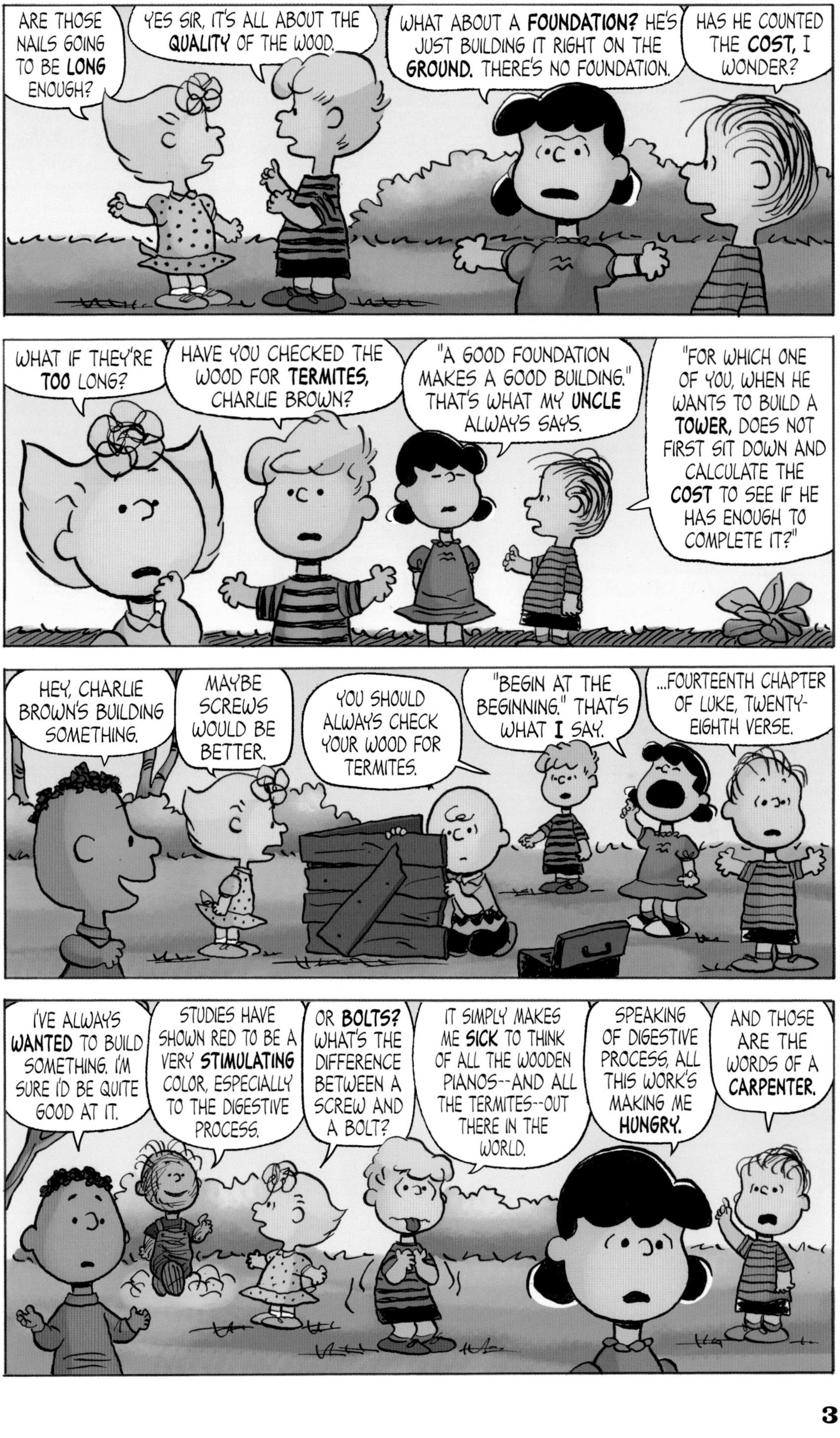
ARE THOSE NAILS GOING TO BE **LONG** ENOUGH?
YES SIR, IT'S ALL ABOUT THE **QUALITY** OF THE WOOD.
WHAT ABOUT A **FOUNDATION?** HE'S JUST BUILDING IT RIGHT ON THE **GROUND.** THERE'S NO FOUNDATION.
HAS HE COUNTED THE **COST,** I WONDER?
WHAT IF THEY'RE **TOO** LONG?
HAVE YOU CHECKED THE WOOD FOR **TERMITES,** CHARLIE BROWN?
"A GOOD FOUNDATION MAKES A GOOD BUILDING." THAT'S WHAT MY **UNCLE** ALWAYS SAYS.
"FOR WHICH ONE OF YOU, WHEN HE WANTS TO BUILD A **TOWER,** DOES NOT FIRST SIT DOWN AND CALCULATE THE **COST** TO SEE IF HE HAS ENOUGH TO COMPLETE IT?"
HEY, CHARLIE BROWN'S BUILDING SOMETHING.
MAYBE SCREWS WOULD BE BETTER.
YOU SHOULD ALWAYS CHECK YOUR WOOD FOR TERMITES.
"BEGIN AT THE BEGINNING." THAT'S WHAT **I** SAY.
...FOURTEENTH CHAPTER OF LUKE, TWENTY-EIGHTH VERSE.
I'VE ALWAYS **WANTED** TO BUILD SOMETHING. I'M SURE I'D BE QUITE GOOD AT IT.
STUDIES HAVE SHOWN RED TO BE A VERY **STIMULATING** COLOR, ESPECIALLY TO THE DIGESTIVE PROCESS.
OR **BOLTS?** WHAT'S THE DIFFERENCE BETWEEN A SCREW AND A BOLT?
IT SIMPLY MAKES ME **SICK** TO THINK OF ALL THE WOODEN PIANOS--AND ALL THE TERMITES--OUT THERE IN THE WORLD.
SPEAKING OF DIGESTIVE PROCESS, ALL THIS WORK'S MAKING ME **HUNGRY.**
AND THOSE ARE THE WORDS OF A **CARPENTER.**

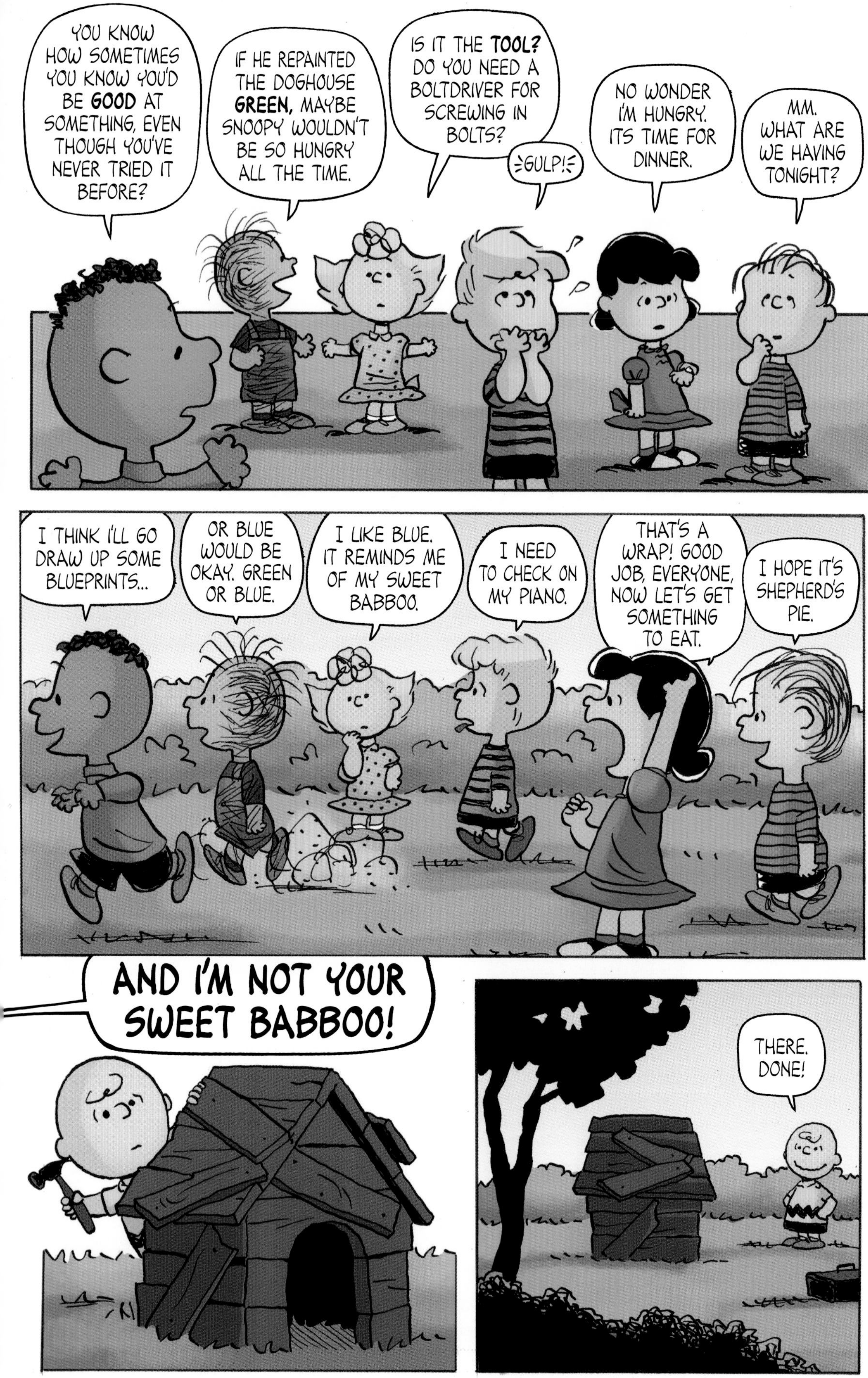
YOU KNOW HOW SOMETIMES YOU KNOW YOU'D BE **GOOD** AT SOMETHING, EVEN THOUGH YOU'VE NEVER TRIED IT BEFORE?
IF HE REPAINTED THE DOGHOUSE **GREEN,** MAYBE SNOOPY WOULDN'T BE SO HUNGRY ALL THE TIME.
IS IT THE **TOOL?** DO YOU NEED A BOLTDRIVER FOR SCREWING IN BOLTS?
GULP!
NO WONDER I'M HUNGRY. ITS TIME FOR DINNER.
MM. WHAT ARE WE HAVING TONIGHT?
I THINK I'LL GO DRAW UP SOME BLUEPRINTS...
OR BLUE WOULD BE OKAY. GREEN OR BLUE.
I LIKE BLUE. IT REMINDS ME OF MY SWEET BABBOO.
I NEED TO CHECK ON MY PIANO.
THAT'S A WRAP! GOOD JOB, EVERYONE, NOW LET'S GET SOMETHING TO EAT.
I HOPE IT'S SHEPHERD'S PIE.
AND I'M NOT YOUR SWEET BABBOO!
THERE. DONE!

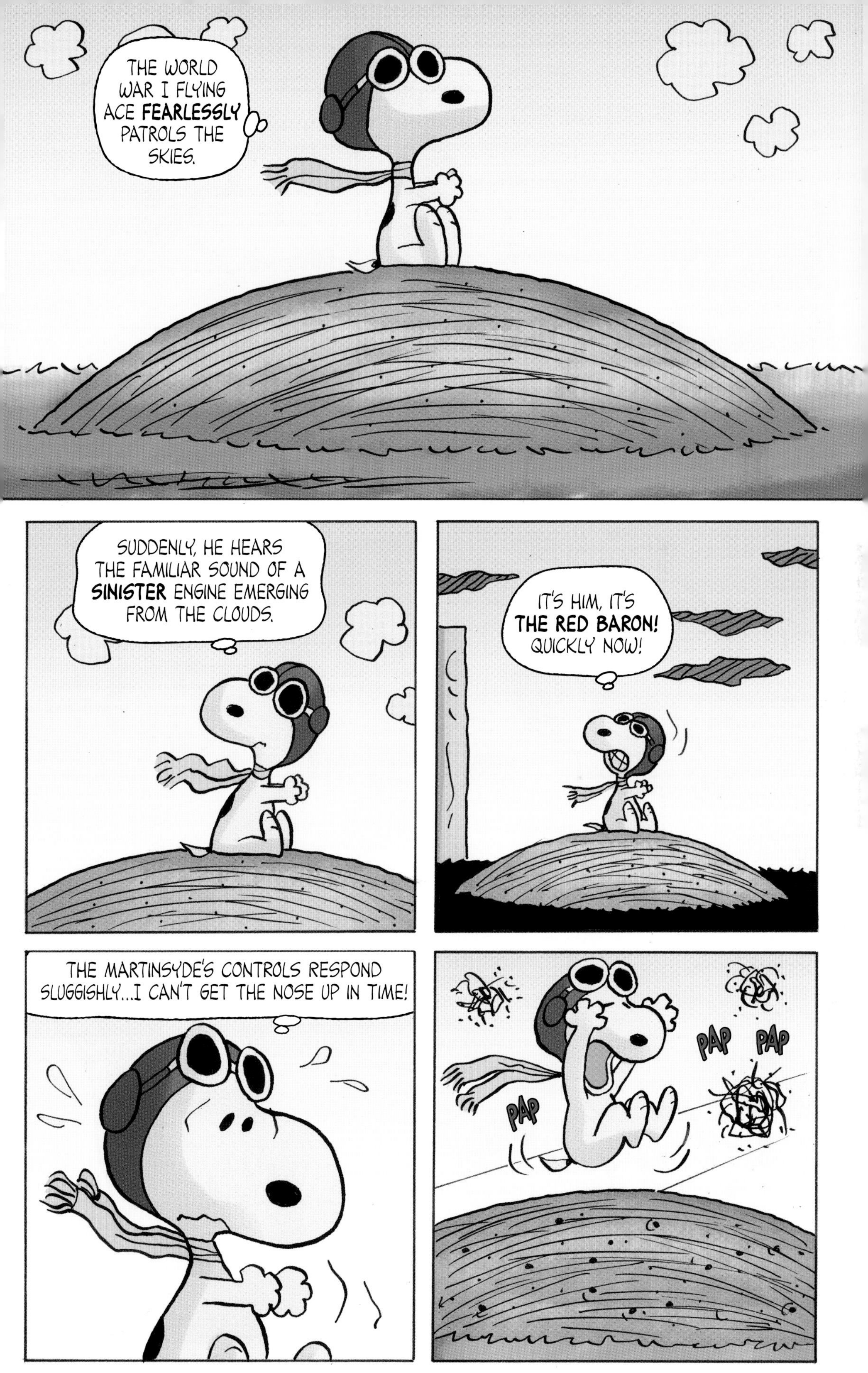
THE WORLD WAR I FLYING ACE **FEARLESSLY** PATROLS THE SKIES.
SUDDENLY, HE HEARS THE FAMILIAR SOUND OF A **SINISTER** ENGINE EMERGING FROM THE CLOUDS.
IT'S HIM, IT'S **THE RED BARON!** QUICKLY NOW!
THE MARTINSYDE'S CONTROLS RESPOND SLUGGISHLY...I CAN'T GET THE NOSE UP IN TIME!
PAP
PAP
PAP

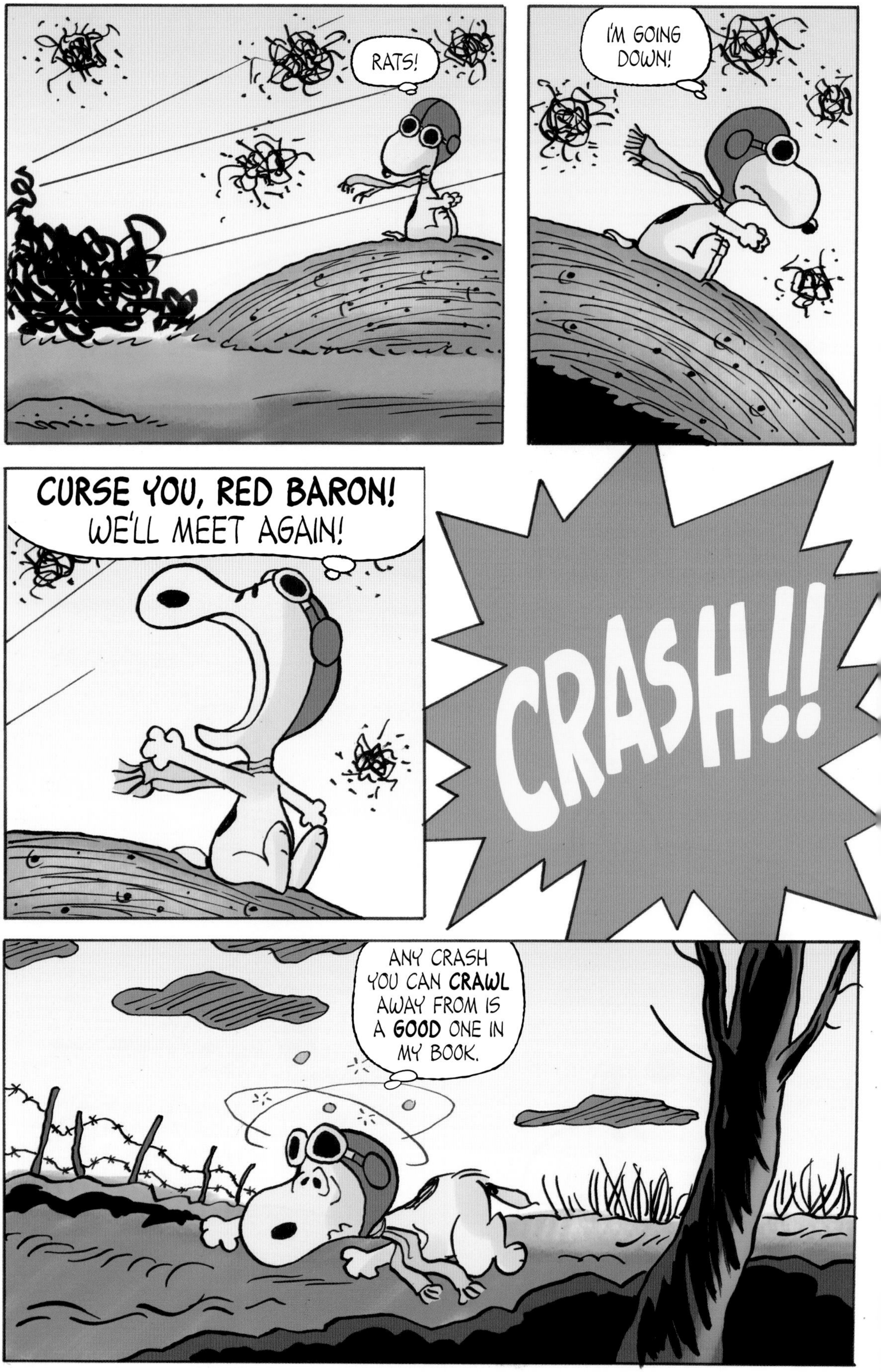
RATS!
I'M GOING DOWN!
CURSE YOU, RED BARON!
WE'LL MEET AGAIN!
CRASH!!
ANY CRASH YOU CAN CRAWL AWAY FROM IS A GOOD ONE IN MY BOOK.

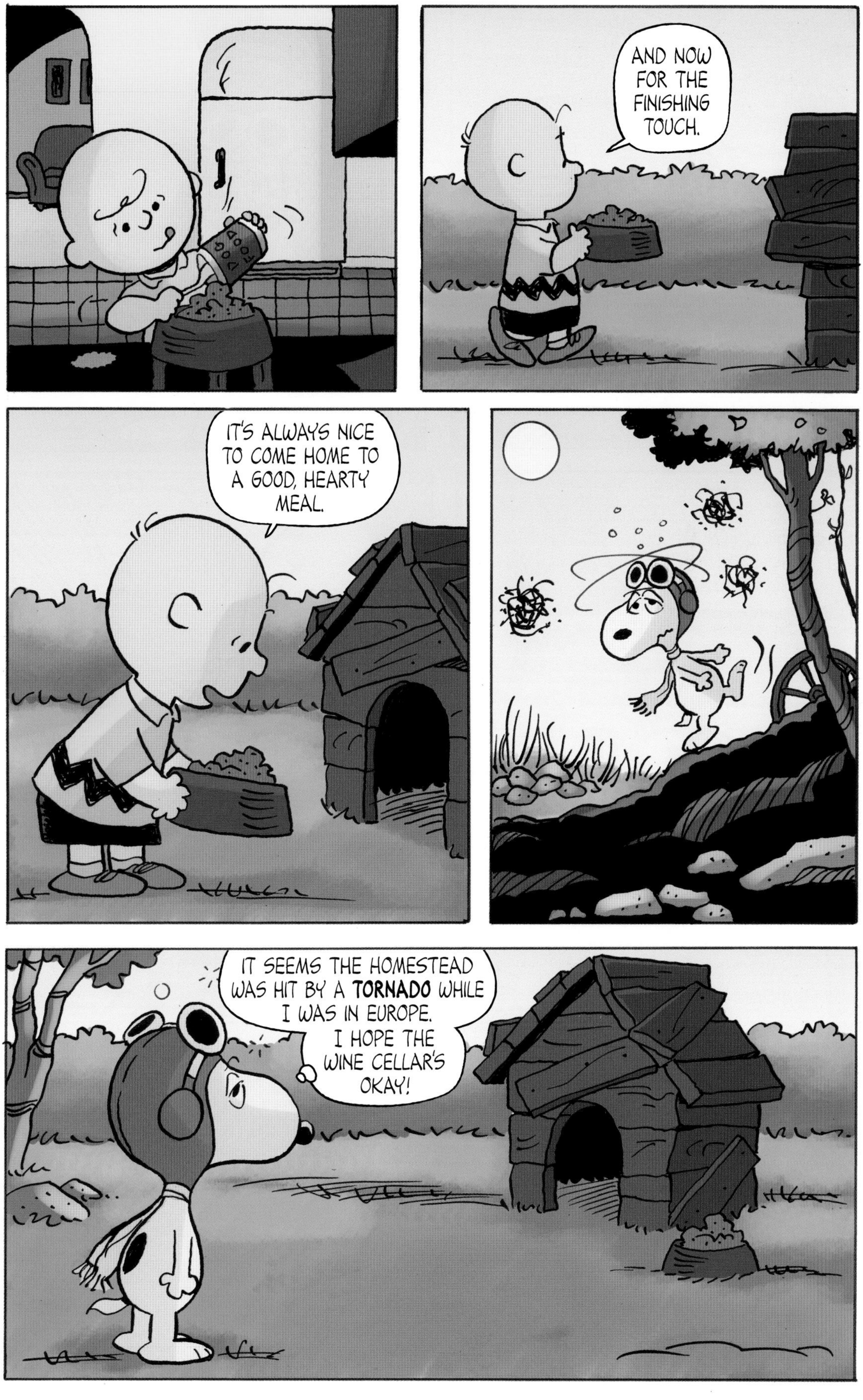
AND NOW FOR THE FINISHING TOUCH.
IT'S ALWAYS NICE TO COME HOME TO A GOOD, HEARTY MEAL.
IT SEEMS THE HOMESTEAD WAS HIT BY A **TORNADO** WHILE I WAS IN EUROPE.
I HOPE THE WINE CELLAR'S OKAY!

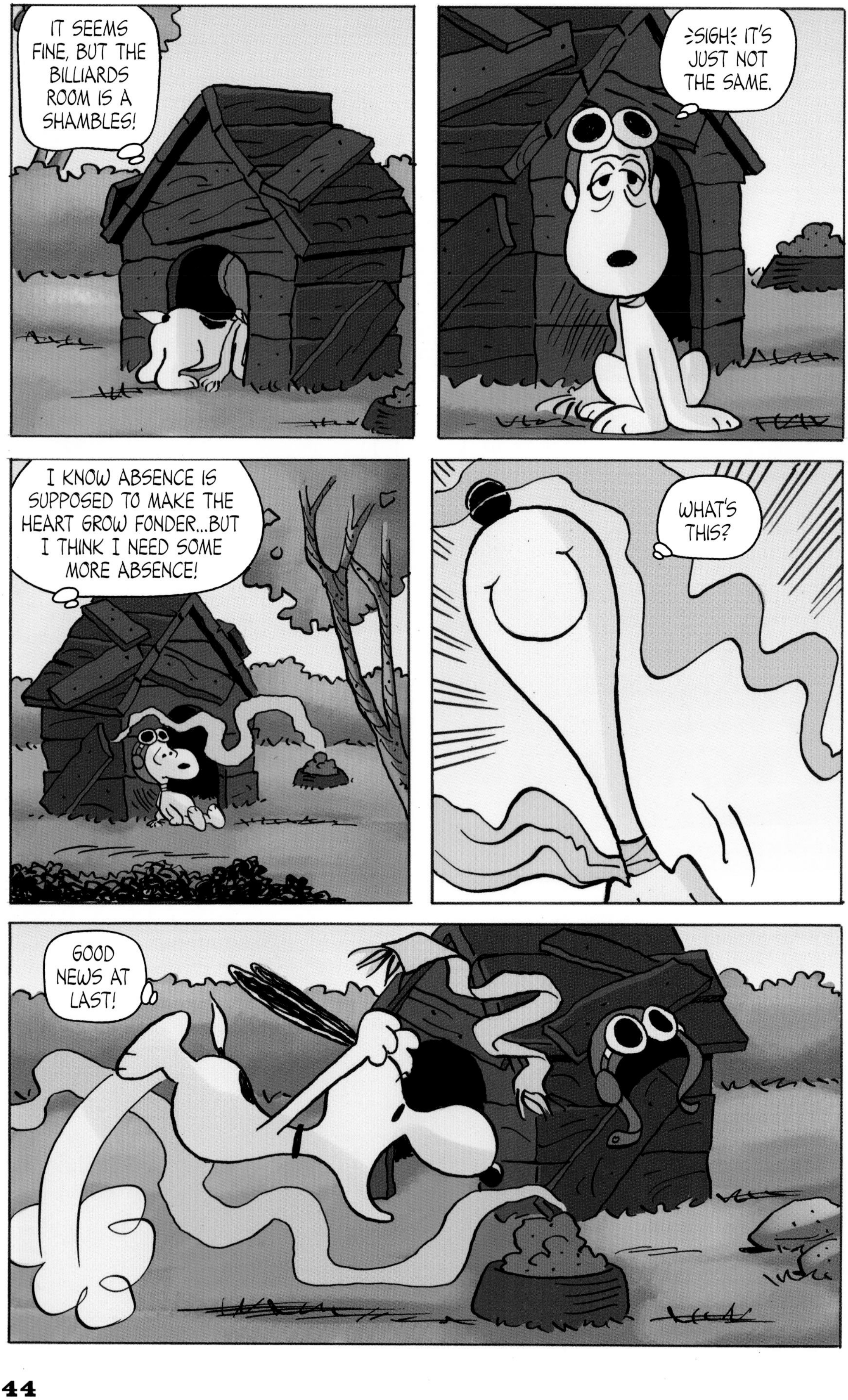
IT SEEMS FINE, BUT THE BILLIARDS ROOM IS A SHAMBLES!
⁼SIGH⁼ IT'S JUST NOT THE SAME.
I KNOW ABSENCE IS SUPPOSED TO MAKE THE HEART GROW FONDER...BUT I THINK I NEED SOME MORE ABSENCE!
WHAT'S THIS?
GOOD NEWS AT LAST!

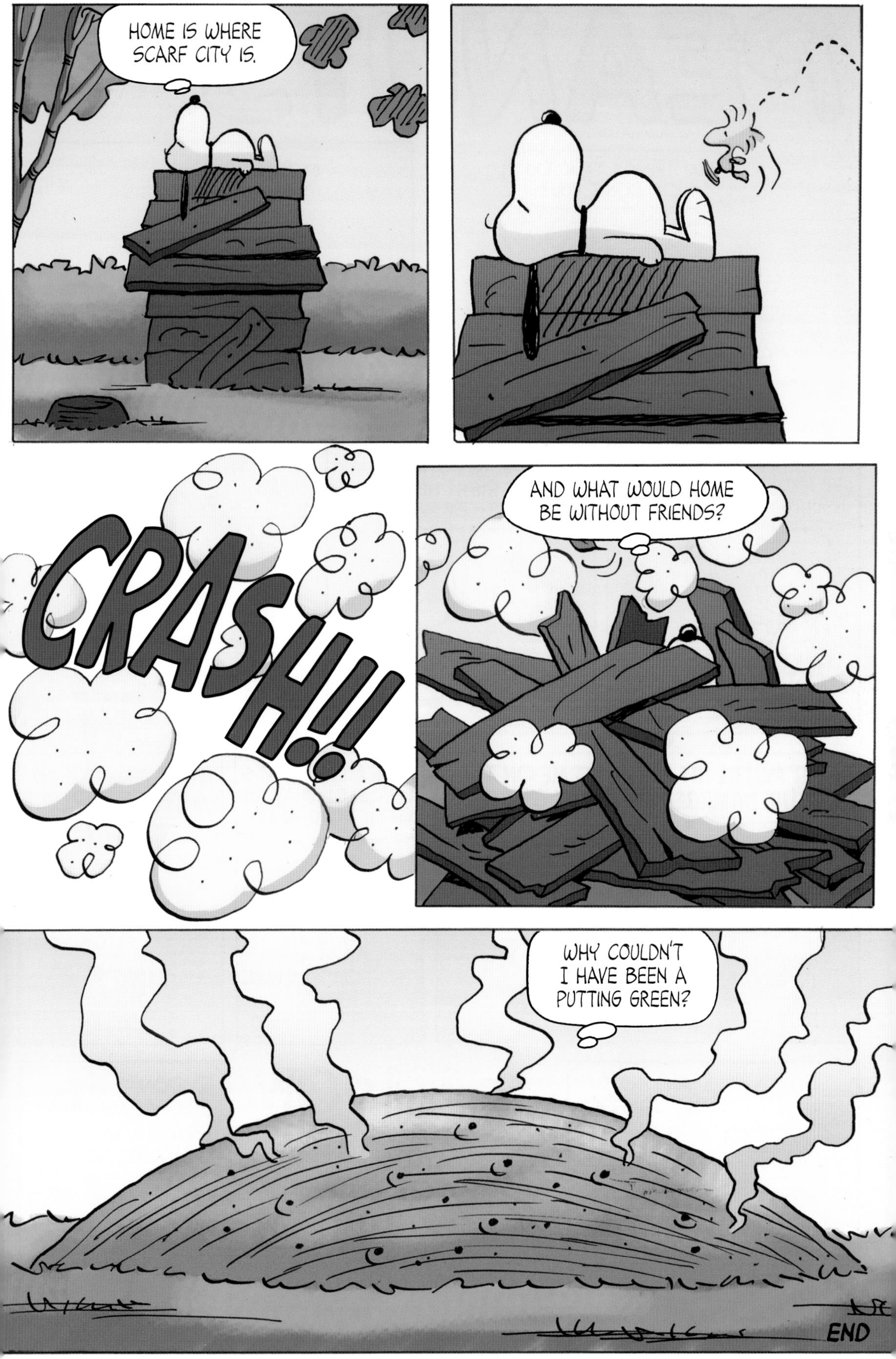
HOME IS WHERE SCARF CITY IS.
CRASH!!!
AND WHAT WOULD HOME BE WITHOUT FRIENDS?
WHY COULDN'T I HAVE BEEN A PUTTING GREEN?
END

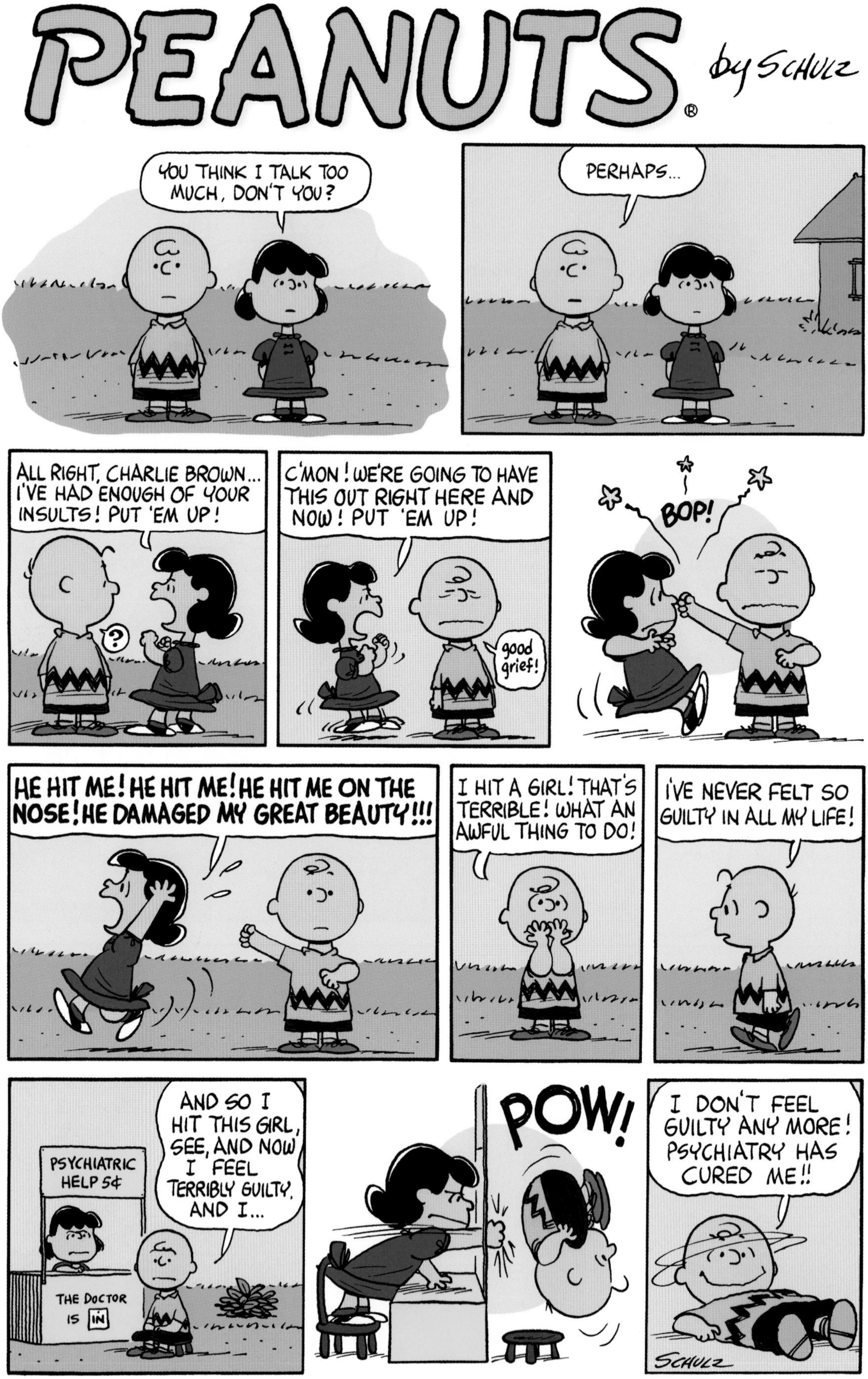
PEANUTS
by SCHULZ
YOU THINK I TALK TOO MUCH, DON'T YOU?
PERHAPS...
ALL RIGHT, CHARLIE BROWN... I'VE HAD ENOUGH OF YOUR INSULTS! PUT 'EM UP!
?
C'MON! WE'RE GOING TO HAVE THIS OUT RIGHT HERE AND NOW! PUT 'EM UP!
good grief!
BOP!
HE HIT ME! HE HIT ME! HE HIT ME ON THE NOSE! HE DAMAGED MY GREAT BEAUTY!!!
I HIT A GIRL! THAT'S TERRIBLE! WHAT AN AWFUL THING TO DO!
I'VE NEVER FELT SO GUILTY IN ALL MY LIFE!
PSYCHIATRIC HELP 5¢
THE DOCTOR IS IN
AND SO I HIT THIS GIRL, SEE, AND NOW I FEEL TERRIBLY GUILTY, AND I...
POW!
I DON'T FEEL GUILTY ANY MORE! PSYCHIATRY HAS CURED ME!!
SCHULZ

twinklethinkle

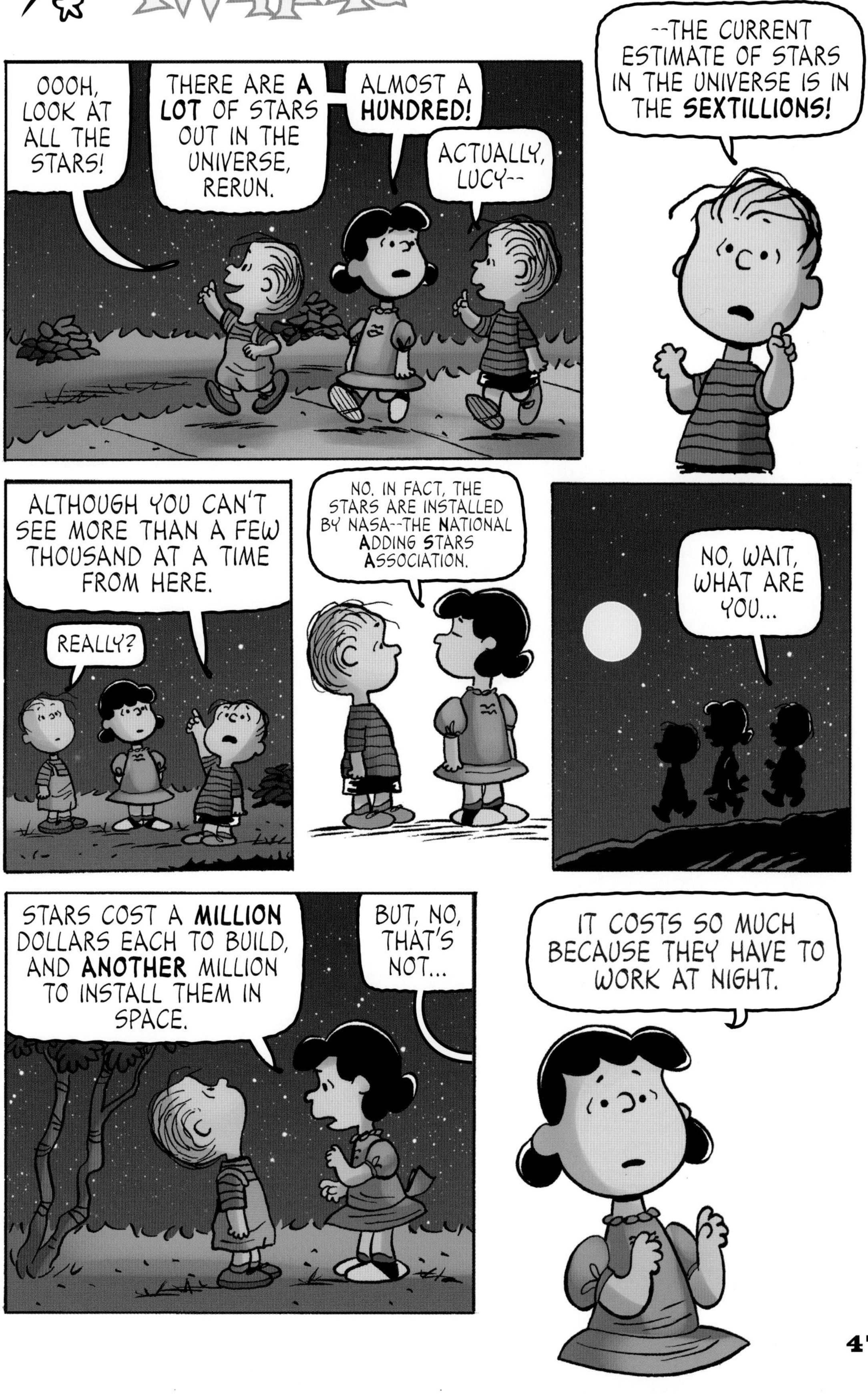

OOOH, LOOK AT ALL THE STARS!
THERE ARE A LOT OF STARS OUT IN THE UNIVERSE, RERUN.
ALMOST A HUNDRED!
ACTUALLY, LUCY--
--THE CURRENT ESTIMATE OF STARS IN THE UNIVERSE IS IN THE SEXTILLIONS!
ALTHOUGH YOU CAN'T SEE MORE THAN A FEW THOUSAND AT A TIME FROM HERE.
REALLY?
NO. IN FACT, THE STARS ARE INSTALLED BY NASA--THE NATIONAL ADDING STARS ASSOCIATION.
NO, WAIT, WHAT ARE YOU...
STARS COST A MILLION DOLLARS EACH TO BUILD, AND ANOTHER MILLION TO INSTALL THEM IN SPACE.
BUT, NO, THAT'S NOT...
IT COSTS SO MUCH BECAUSE THEY HAVE TO WORK AT NIGHT.

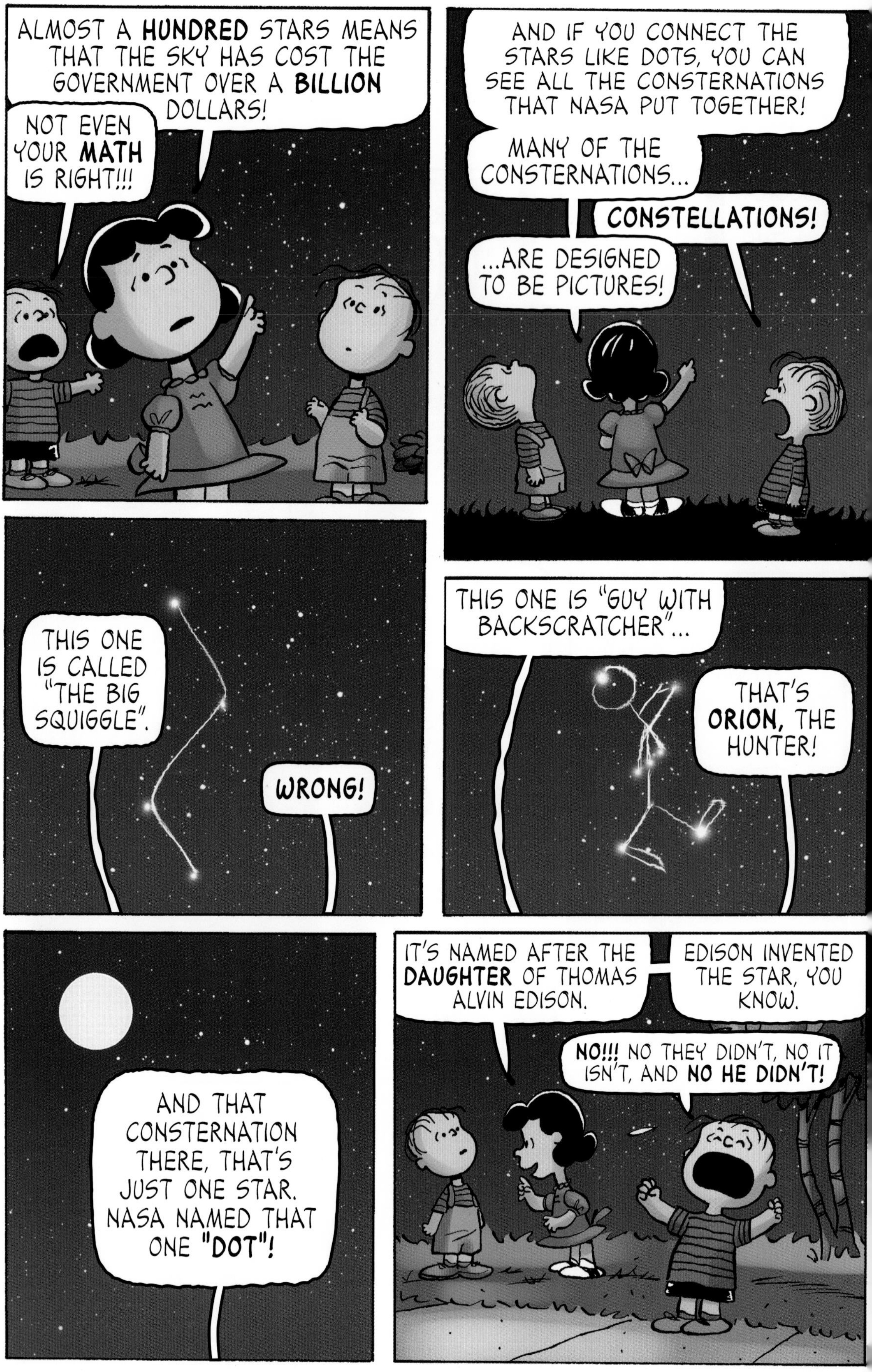
ALMOST A **HUNDRED** STARS MEANS THAT THE SKY HAS COST THE GOVERNMENT OVER A **BILLION** DOLLARS!
NOT EVEN YOUR **MATH** IS RIGHT!!!
AND IF YOU CONNECT THE STARS LIKE DOTS, YOU CAN SEE ALL THE CONSTERNATIONS THAT NASA PUT TOGETHER!
MANY OF THE CONSTERNATIONS...
CONSTELLATIONS!
...ARE DESIGNED TO BE PICTURES!
THIS ONE IS CALLED "THE BIG SQUIGGLE".
WRONG!
THIS ONE IS "GUY WITH BACKSCRATCHER"...
THAT'S **ORION,** THE HUNTER!
AND THAT CONSTERNATION THERE, THAT'S JUST ONE STAR. NASA NAMED THAT ONE "**DOT**"!
IT'S NAMED AFTER THE **DAUGHTER** OF THOMAS ALVIN EDISON.
EDISON INVENTED THE STAR, YOU KNOW.
NO!!! NO THEY DIDN'T, NO IT ISN'T, AND **NO HE DIDN'T!**

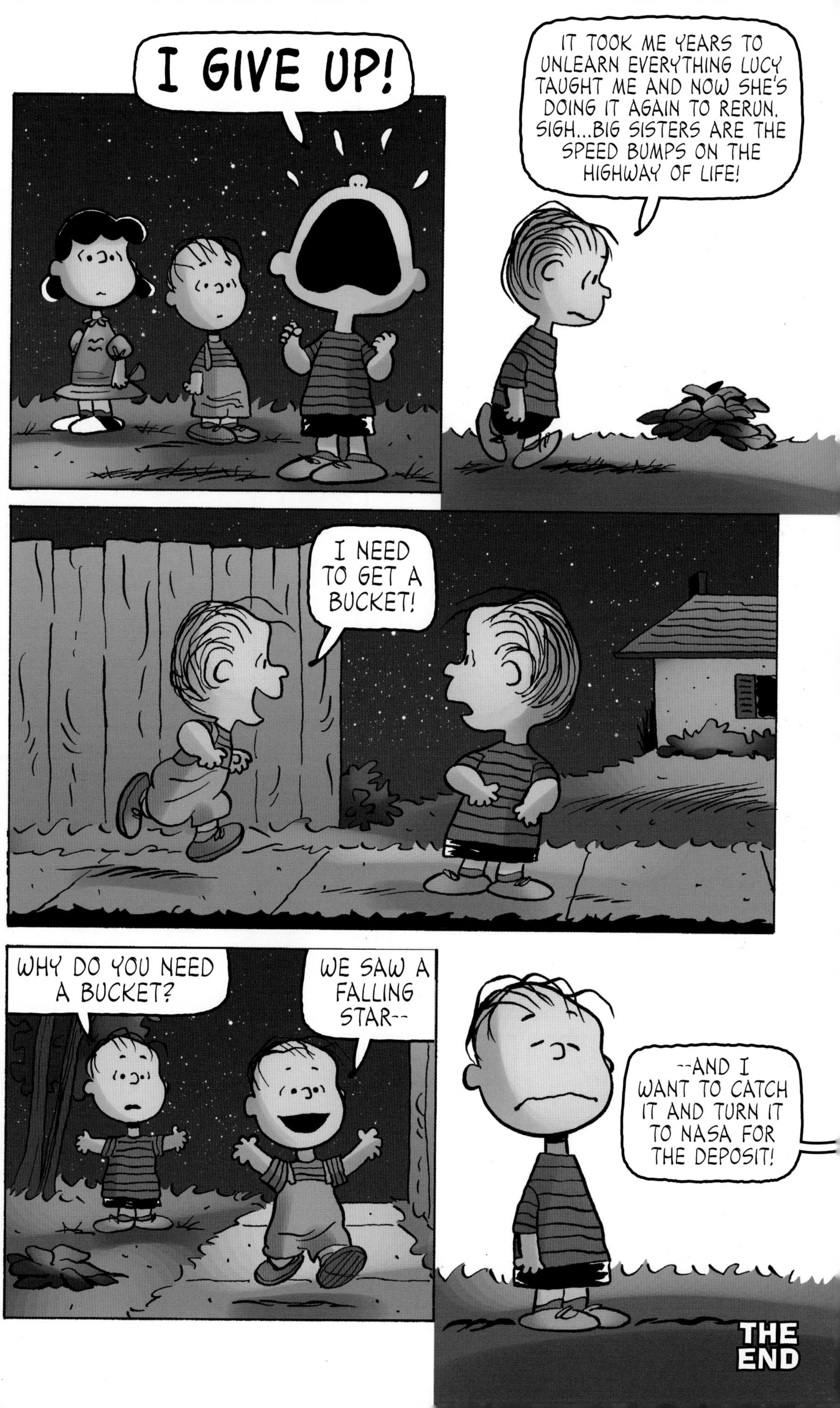
I GIVE UP!
IT TOOK ME YEARS TO UNLEARN EVERYTHING LUCY TAUGHT ME AND NOW SHE'S DOING IT AGAIN TO RERUN. SIGH...BIG SISTERS ARE THE SPEED BUMPS ON THE HIGHWAY OF LIFE!
I NEED TO GET A BUCKET!
WHY DO YOU NEED A BUCKET?
WE SAW A FALLING STAR--
--AND I WANT TO CATCH IT AND TURN IT TO NASA FOR THE DEPOSIT!
THE END

PEANUTS
by SCHULZ
SIGH
I LIKE YOU, LINUS... I LIKE YOU, AND I ADMIRE YOU, BUT I COULD LIKE YOU EVEN MORE IF YOU'D GIVE UP THAT BLANKET...
I DON'T REALLY CARE IF YOU LIKE ME OR NOT...
I LOOK FORWARD TO THE DAY WHEN I'LL UNDERSTAND GIRLS..
SCHULZ

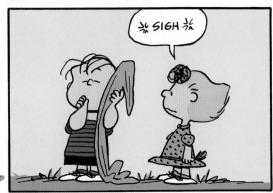

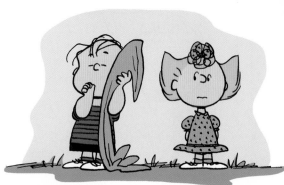

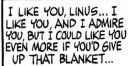

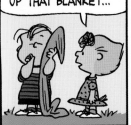

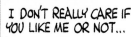

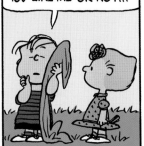

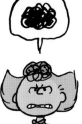

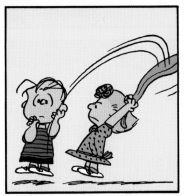

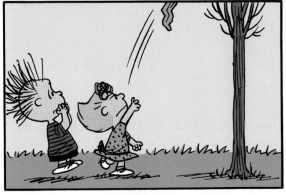

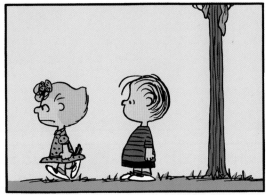

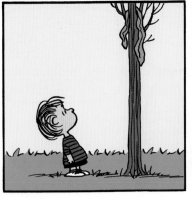

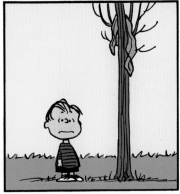

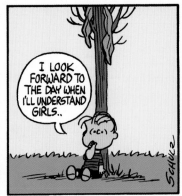

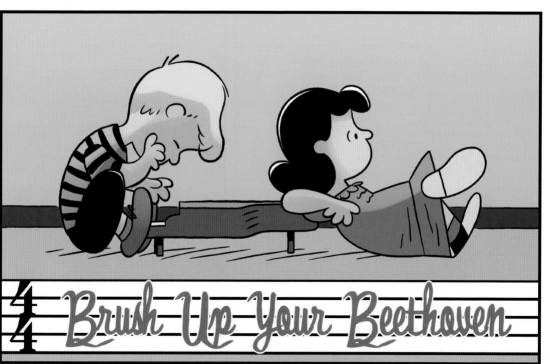

Brush Up Your Beethoven

HOW COME BEETHOVEN NEVER WROTE ANY **SONGS?**

WHAT ARE YOU **TALKING** ABOUT? HE WROTE **ALL KINDS** OF SONGS!

HE WROTE **NINE** SYMPHONIES, **NINE** CONCERTOS, **138** OPUSES, **TWELVE** PIANO TRIOS, **THIRTY-TWO** CELEBRATED SONATAS AND OVER **THIRTY** BAGATELLES!

HE SPENT HIS **WHOLE LIFE** WRITING SONGS!

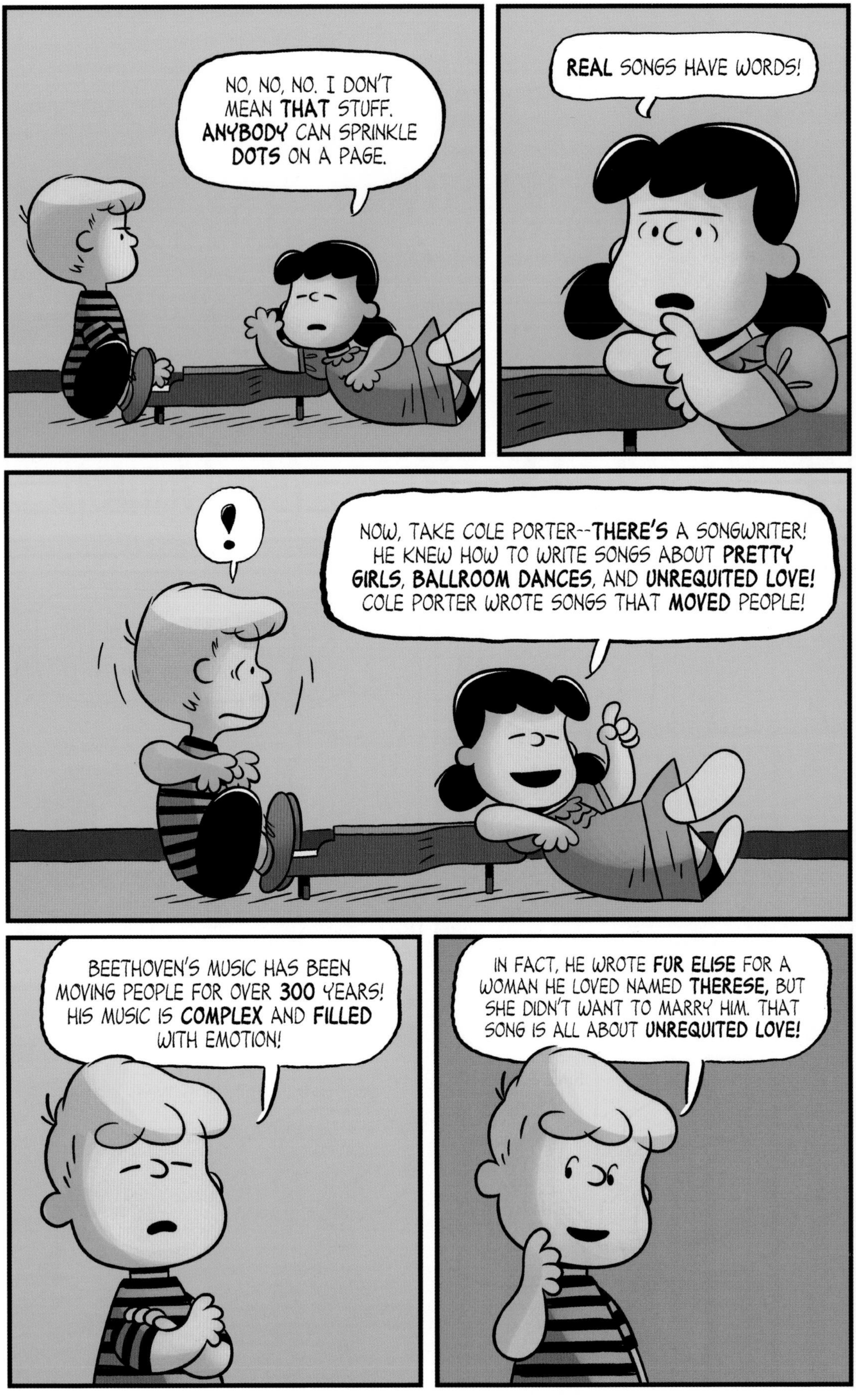
NO, NO, NO. I DON'T MEAN **THAT** STUFF. **ANYBODY** CAN SPRINKLE **DOTS** ON A PAGE.
REAL SONGS HAVE WORDS!
!
NOW, TAKE COLE PORTER--**THERE'S** A SONGWRITER! HE KNEW HOW TO WRITE SONGS ABOUT **PRETTY GIRLS**, **BALLROOM DANCES**, AND **UNREQUITED LOVE!** COLE PORTER WROTE SONGS THAT **MOVED** PEOPLE!
BEETHOVEN'S MUSIC HAS BEEN MOVING PEOPLE FOR OVER **300** YEARS! HIS MUSIC IS **COMPLEX** AND **FILLED** WITH EMOTION!
IN FACT, HE WROTE **FUR ELISE** FOR A WOMAN HE LOVED NAMED **THERESE,** BUT SHE DIDN'T WANT TO MARRY HIM. THAT SONG IS ALL ABOUT **UNREQUITED LOVE!**

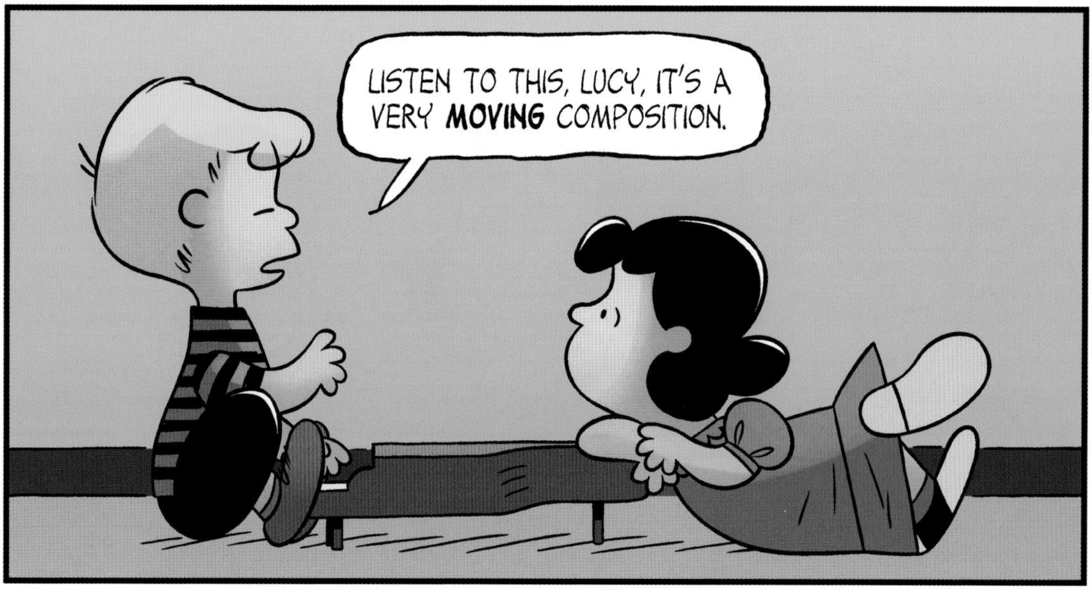
LISTEN TO THIS, LUCY, IT'S A VERY **MOVING** COMPOSITION.

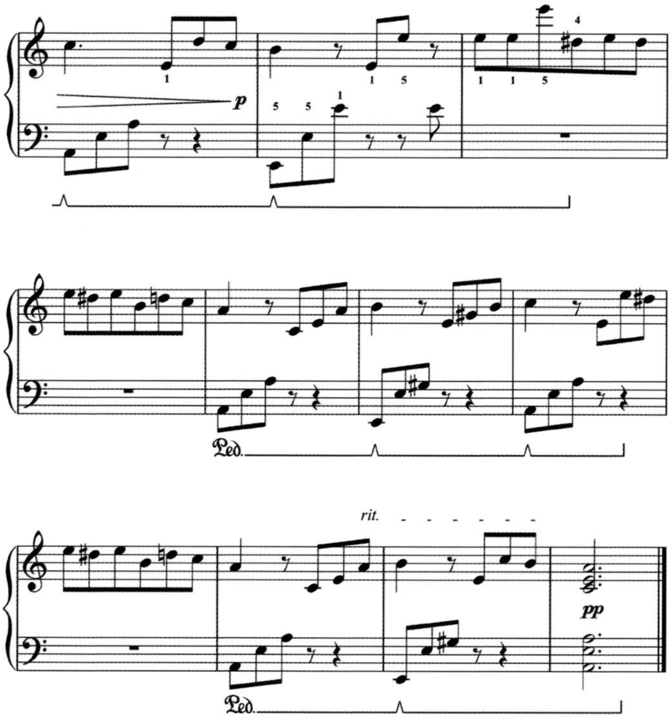
p
Ped.
rit.
pp
Ped.

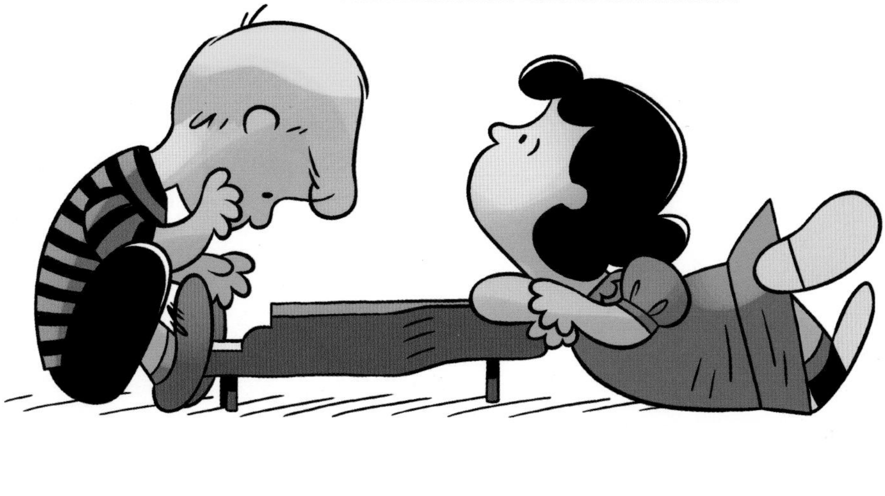

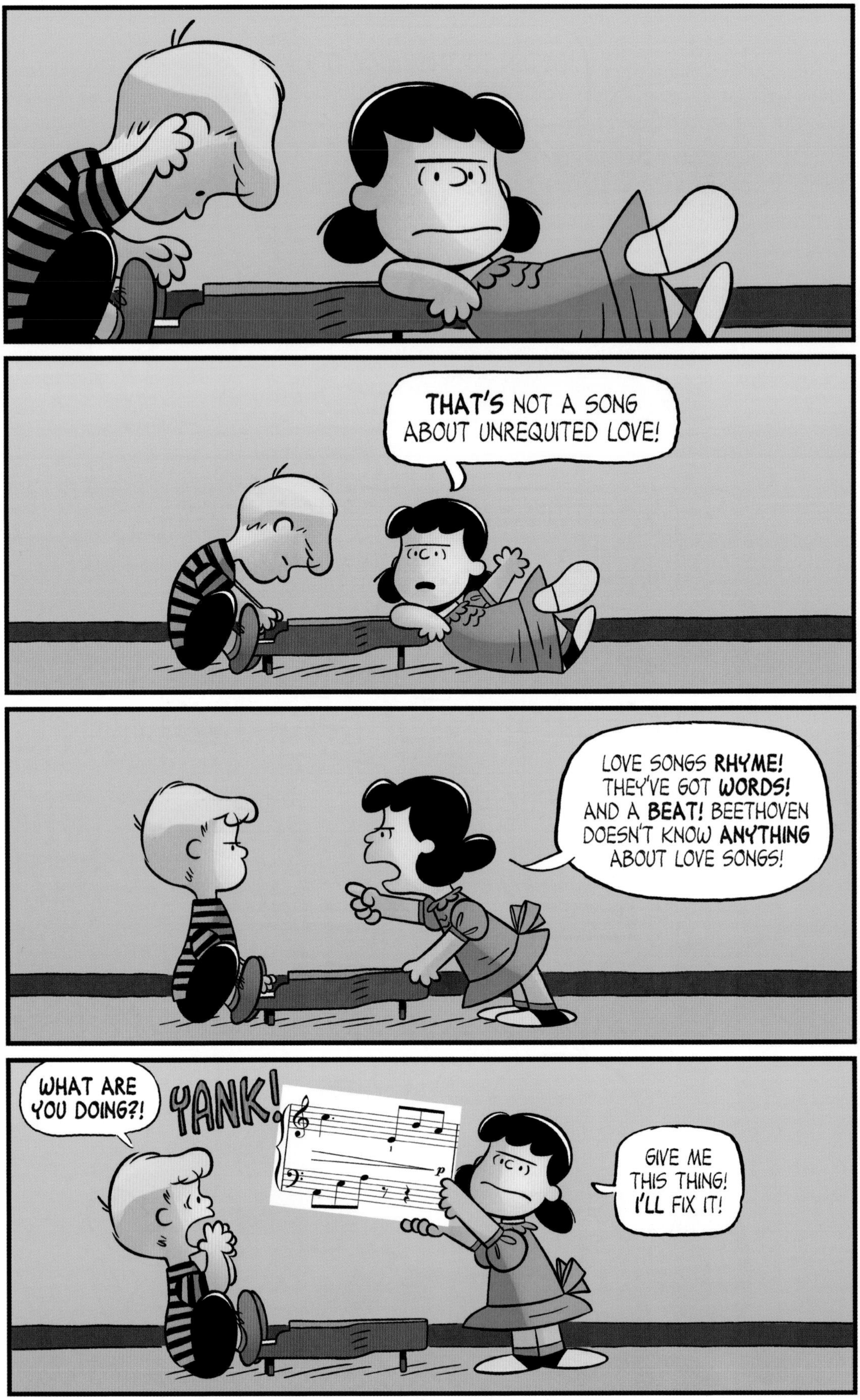
THAT'S NOT A SONG ABOUT UNREQUITED LOVE!
LOVE SONGS RHYME! THEY'VE GOT WORDS! AND A BEAT! BEETHOVEN DOESN'T KNOW ANYTHING ABOUT LOVE SONGS!
WHAT ARE YOU DOING?!
YANK!
GIVE ME THIS THING! I'LL FIX IT!

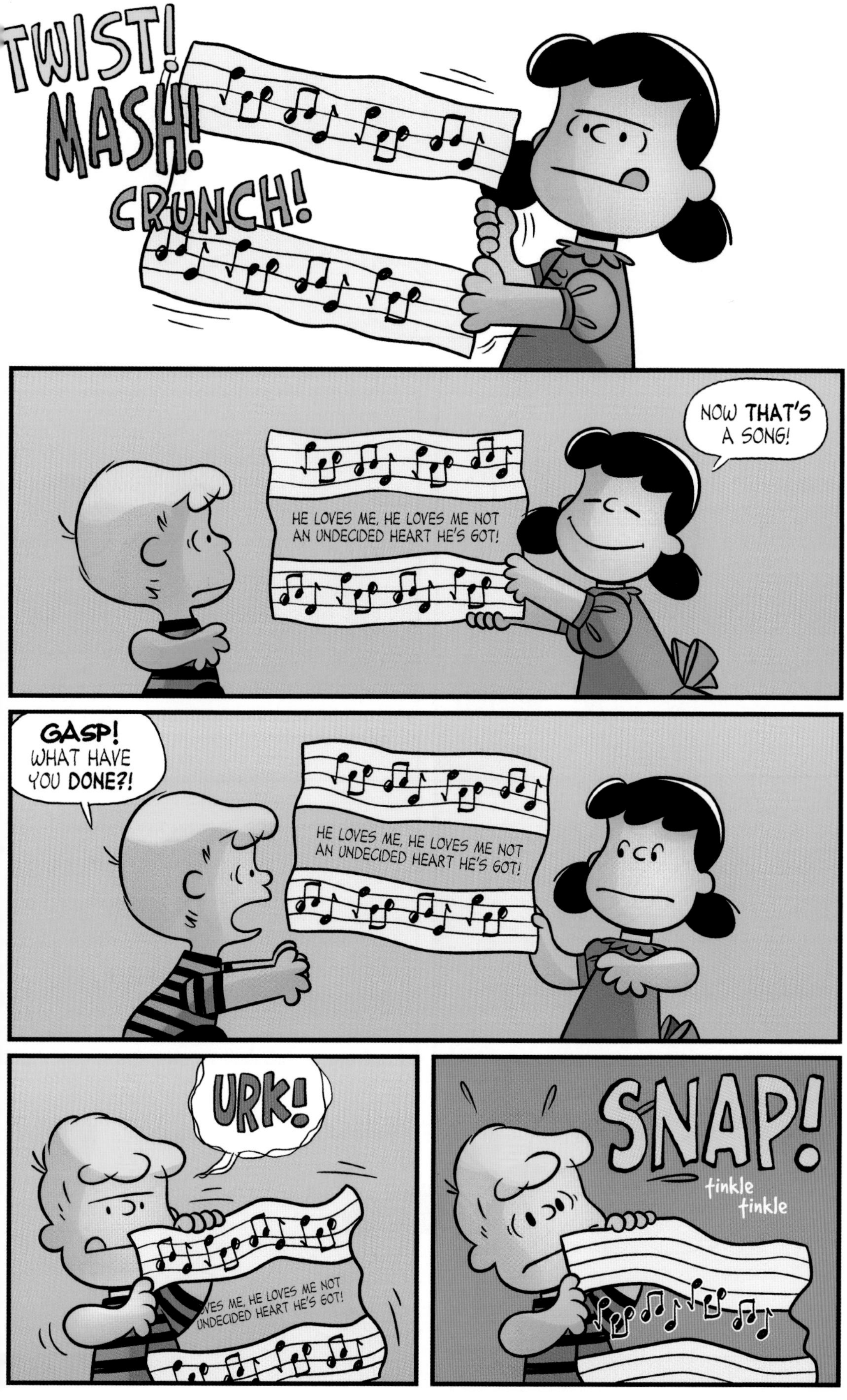
TWIST!
MASH!
CRUNCH!
NOW THAT'S A SONG!
HE LOVES ME, HE LOVES ME NOT
AN UNDECIDED HEART HE'S GOT!
GASP! WHAT HAVE YOU DONE?!
HE LOVES ME, HE LOVES ME NOT
AN UNDECIDED HEART HE'S GOT!
URK!
VES ME, HE LOVES ME NOT
UNDECIDED HEART HE'S GOT!
SNAP!
tinkle
tinkle

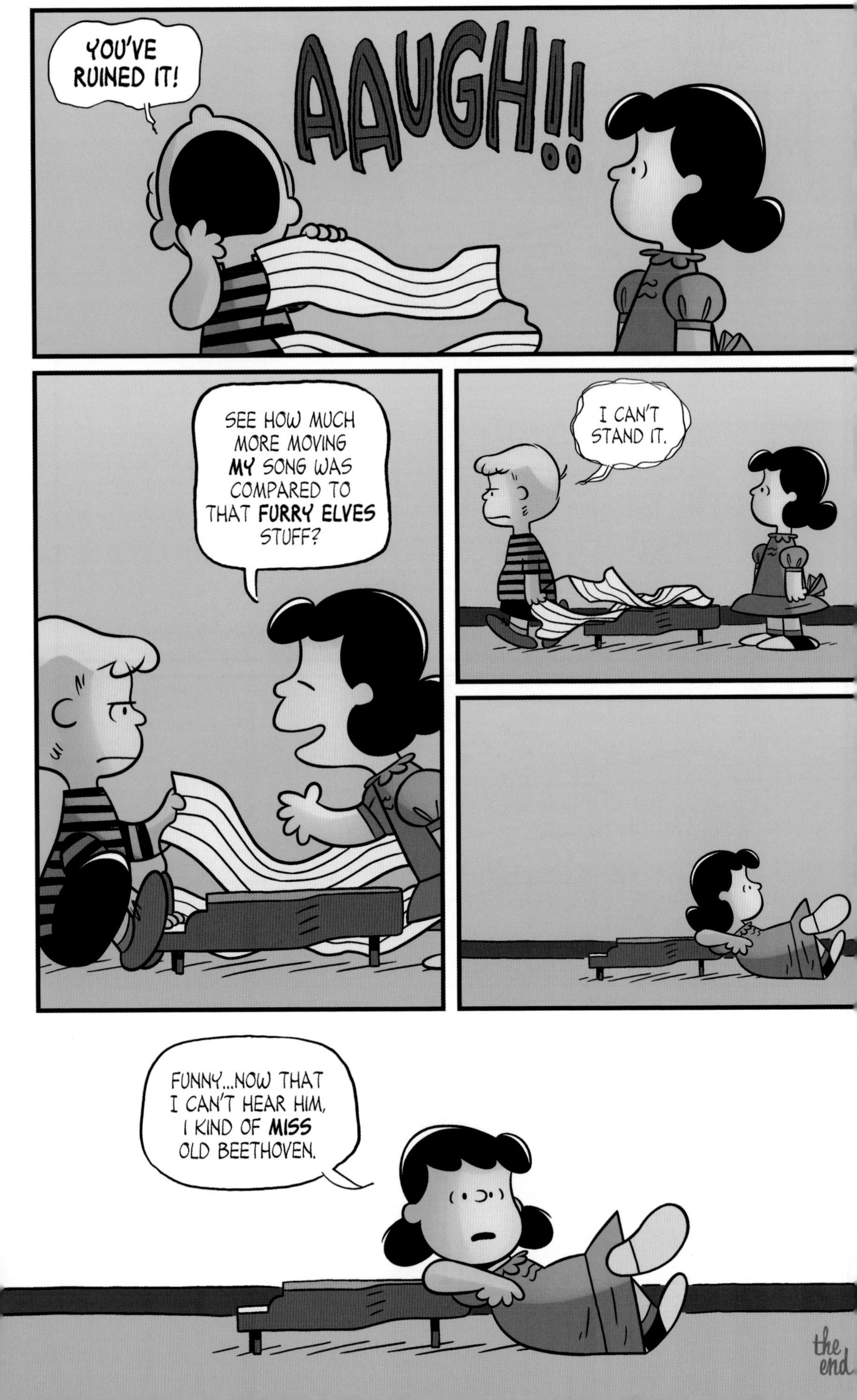

YOU'VE RUINED IT!
AAUGH!!
SEE HOW MUCH MORE MOVING MY SONG WAS COMPARED TO THAT FURRY ELVES STUFF?
I CAN'T STAND IT.
FUNNY...NOW THAT I CAN'T HEAR HIM, I KIND OF MISS OLD BEETHOVEN.
the end

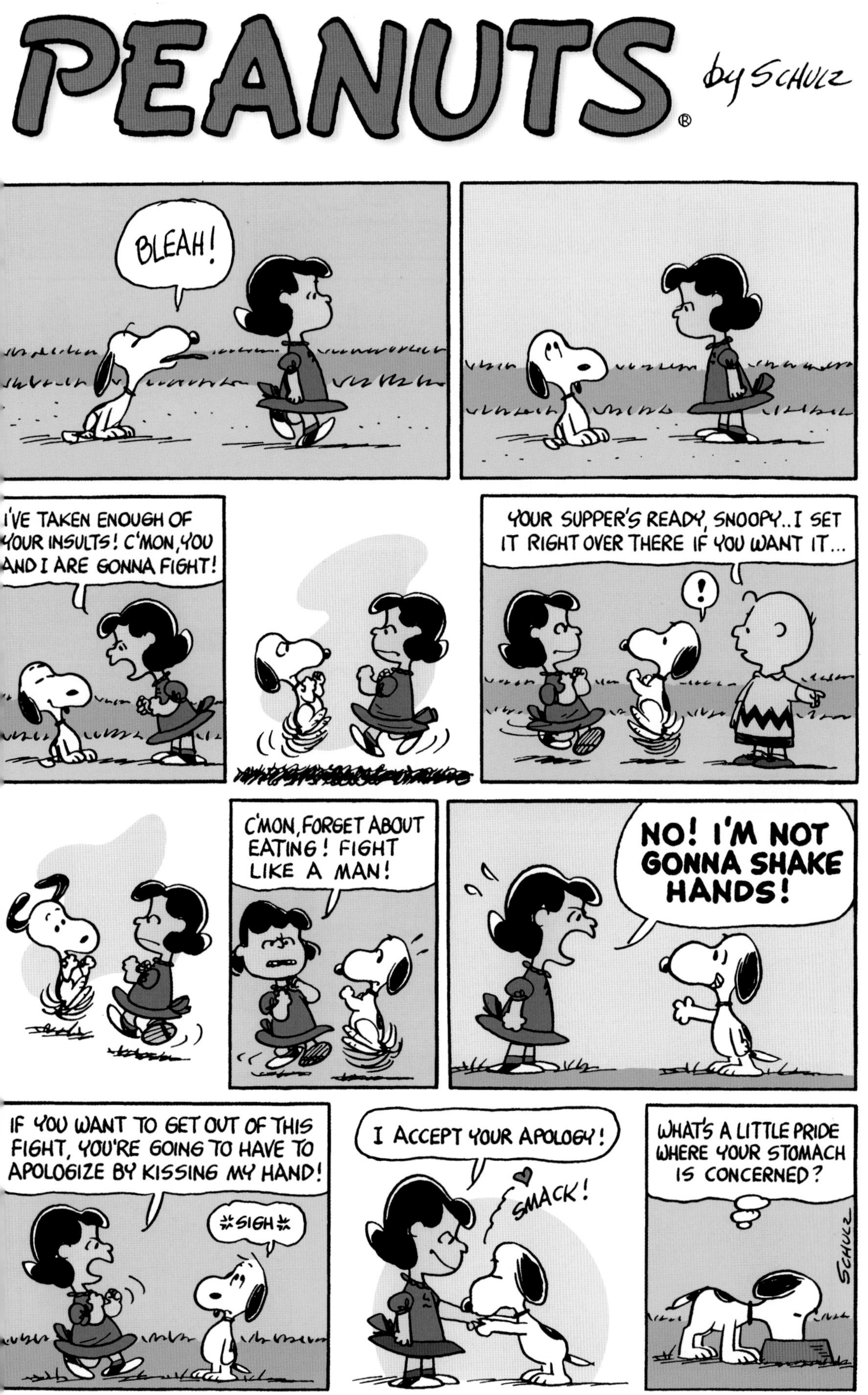
PEANUTS
by SCHULZ
BLEAH!
I'VE TAKEN ENOUGH OF YOUR INSULTS! C'MON, YOU AND I ARE GONNA FIGHT!
YOUR SUPPER'S READY, SNOOPY..I SET IT RIGHT OVER THERE IF YOU WANT IT...
!
C'MON, FORGET ABOUT EATING! FIGHT LIKE A MAN!
NO! I'M NOT GONNA SHAKE HANDS!
IF YOU WANT TO GET OUT OF THIS FIGHT, YOU'RE GOING TO HAVE TO APOLOGIZE BY KISSING MY HAND!
SIGH
I ACCEPT YOUR APOLOGY!
SMACK!
WHAT'S A LITTLE PRIDE WHERE YOUR STOMACH IS CONCERNED?
SCHULZ

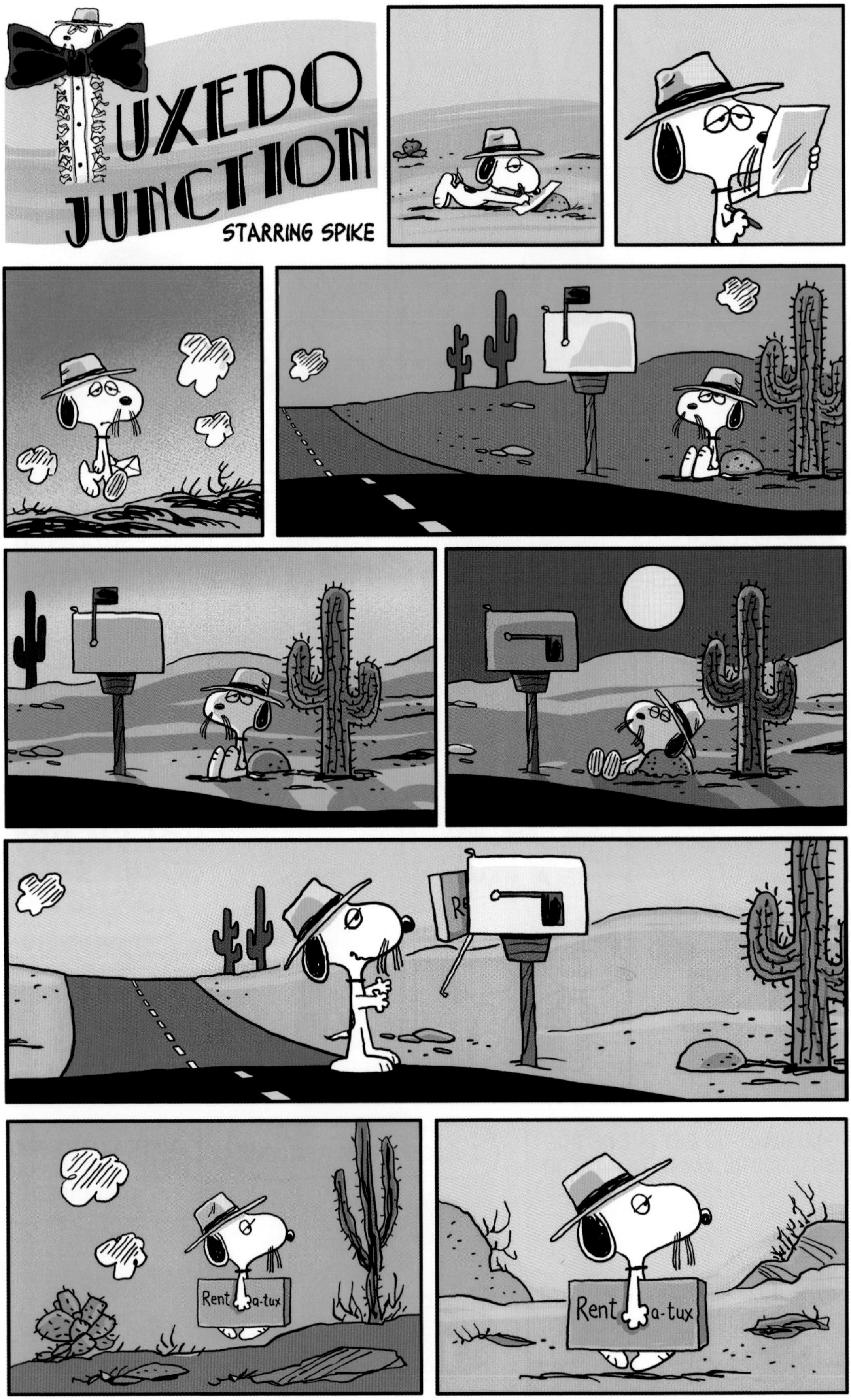
TUXEDO JUNCTION
STARRING SPIKE
Rent a-tux
Rent a-tux

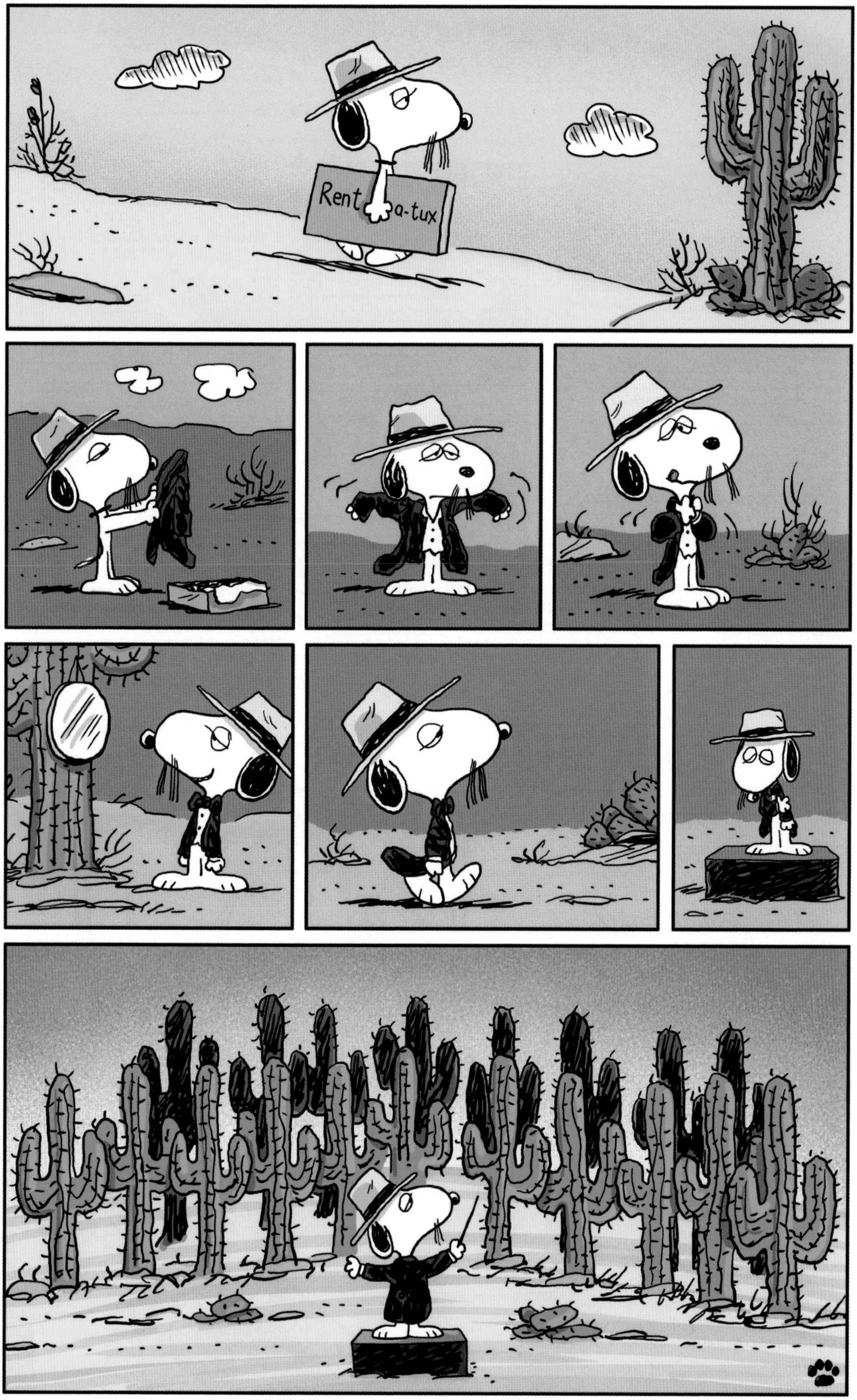
Rent-a-tux

From the Drawing Board

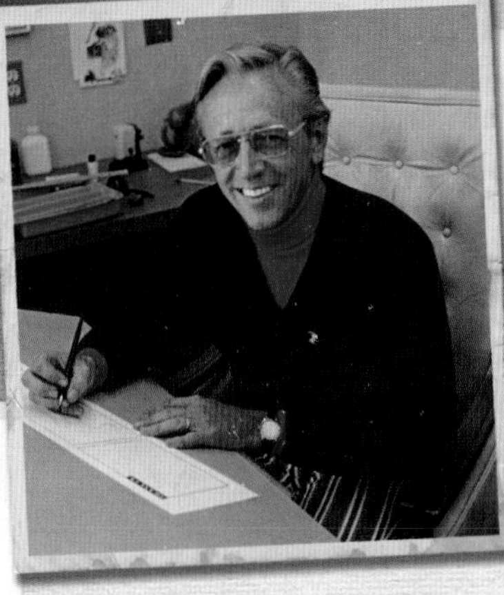

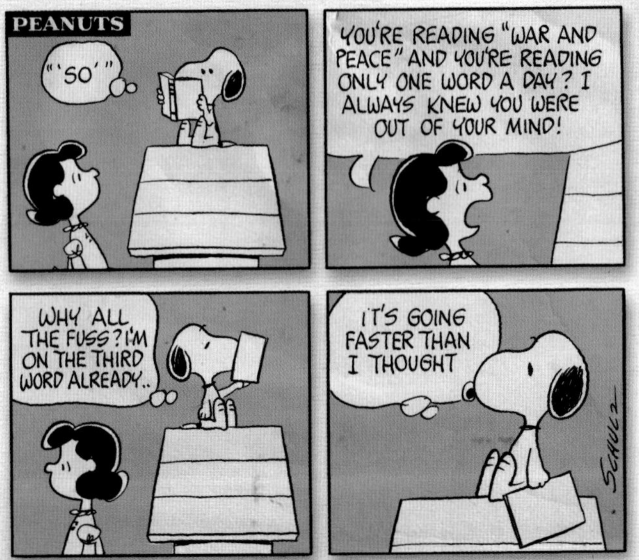

PEANUTS
"'SO'"
YOU'RE READING "WAR AND PEACE" AND YOU'RE READING ONLY ONE WORD A DAY? I ALWAYS KNEW YOU WERE OUT OF YOUR MIND!
WHY ALL THE FUSS? I'M ON THE THIRD WORD ALREADY..
IT'S GOING FASTER THAN I THOUGHT
SCHULZ

"I'm not dealing with major problems—Leo Tolstoy dealt with the major problems—I'm only dealing with why we all have the feeling that people don't like us, this is Charlie Brown's problem.

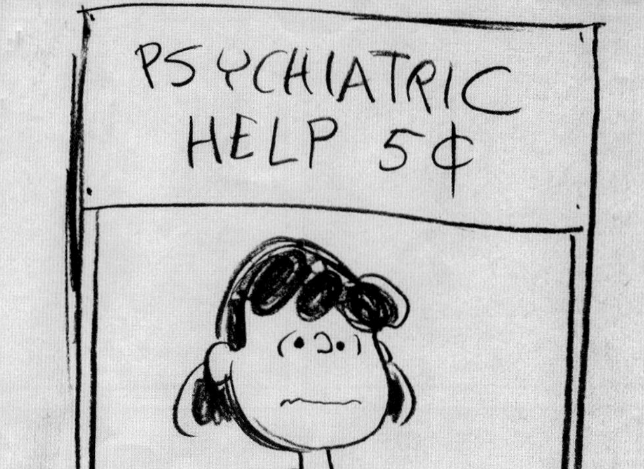

PSYCHIATRIC HELP 5¢
THE DOCTOR IS REAL IN
SCHULZ

A cartoonist is a lot like Lucy's psychiatric stand, she said once that she only points out the problems, she doesn't try to solve them and I think this is what a cartoonist does.

I like to think that I come up with some solutions now and then I suppose that one of the solutions is, as Charlie Brown, just to keep on trying.

He never gives up.

And if anybody should give up, he should."

–Charles M. Schulz

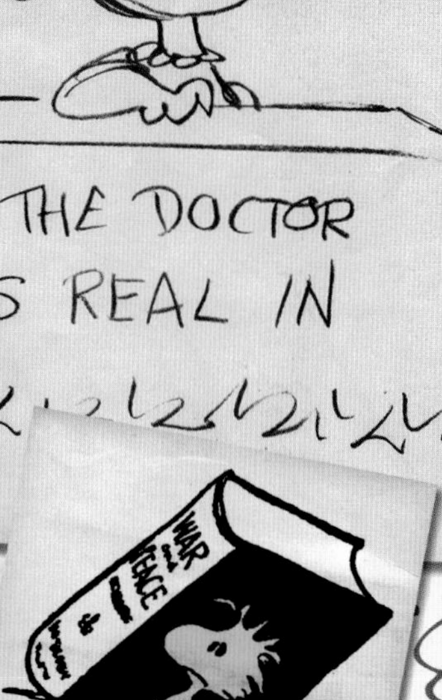

WAR
PEACE

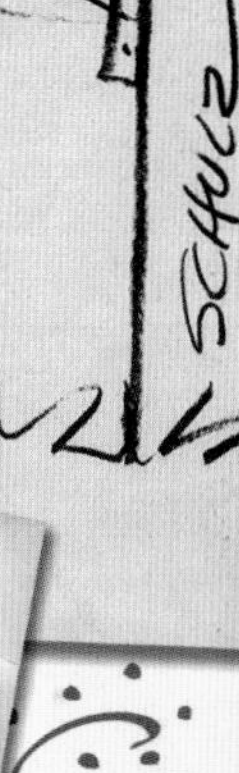

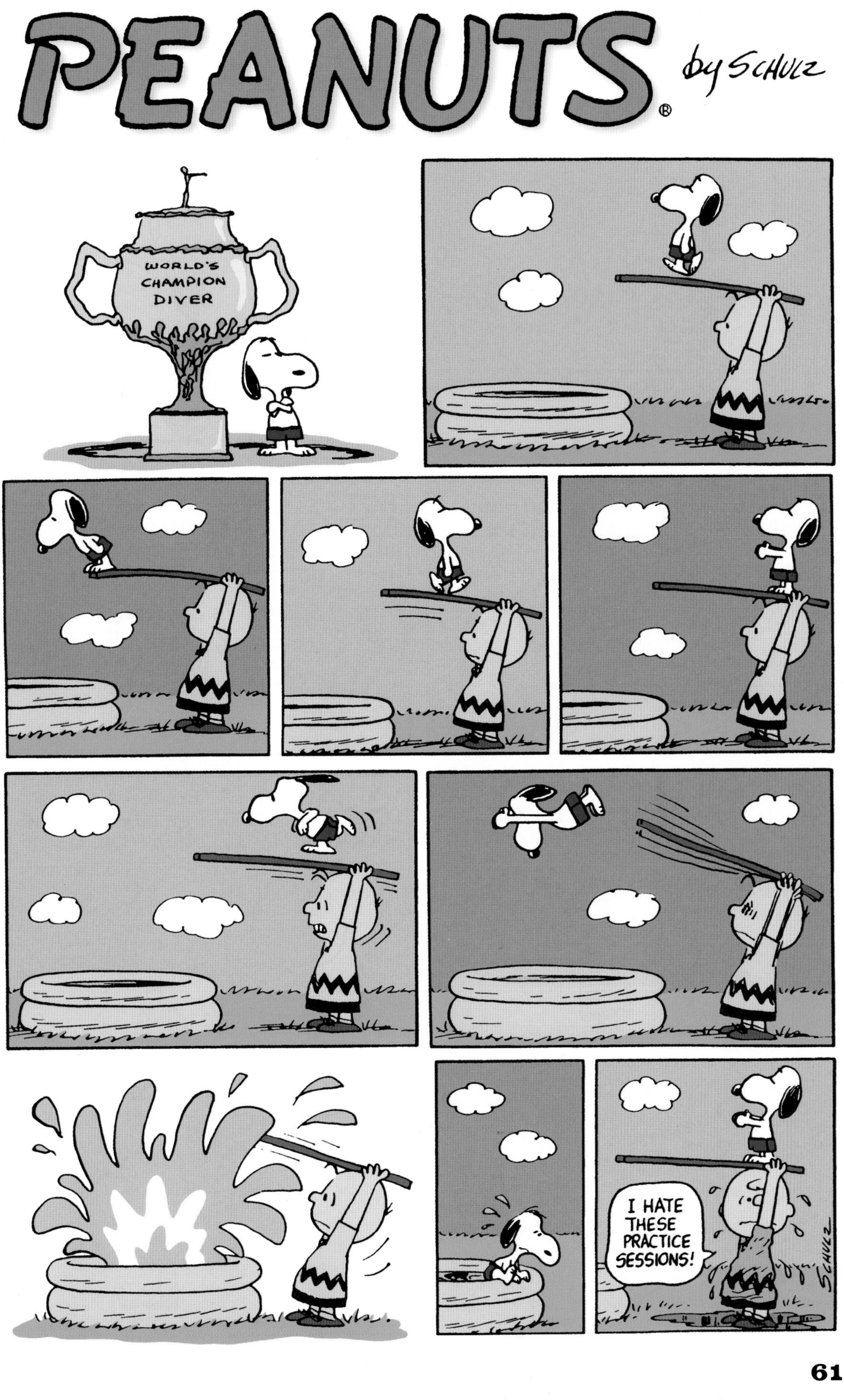
PEANUTS
by SCHULZ
WORLD'S CHAMPION DIVER
I HATE THESE PRACTICE SESSIONS!
SCHULZ

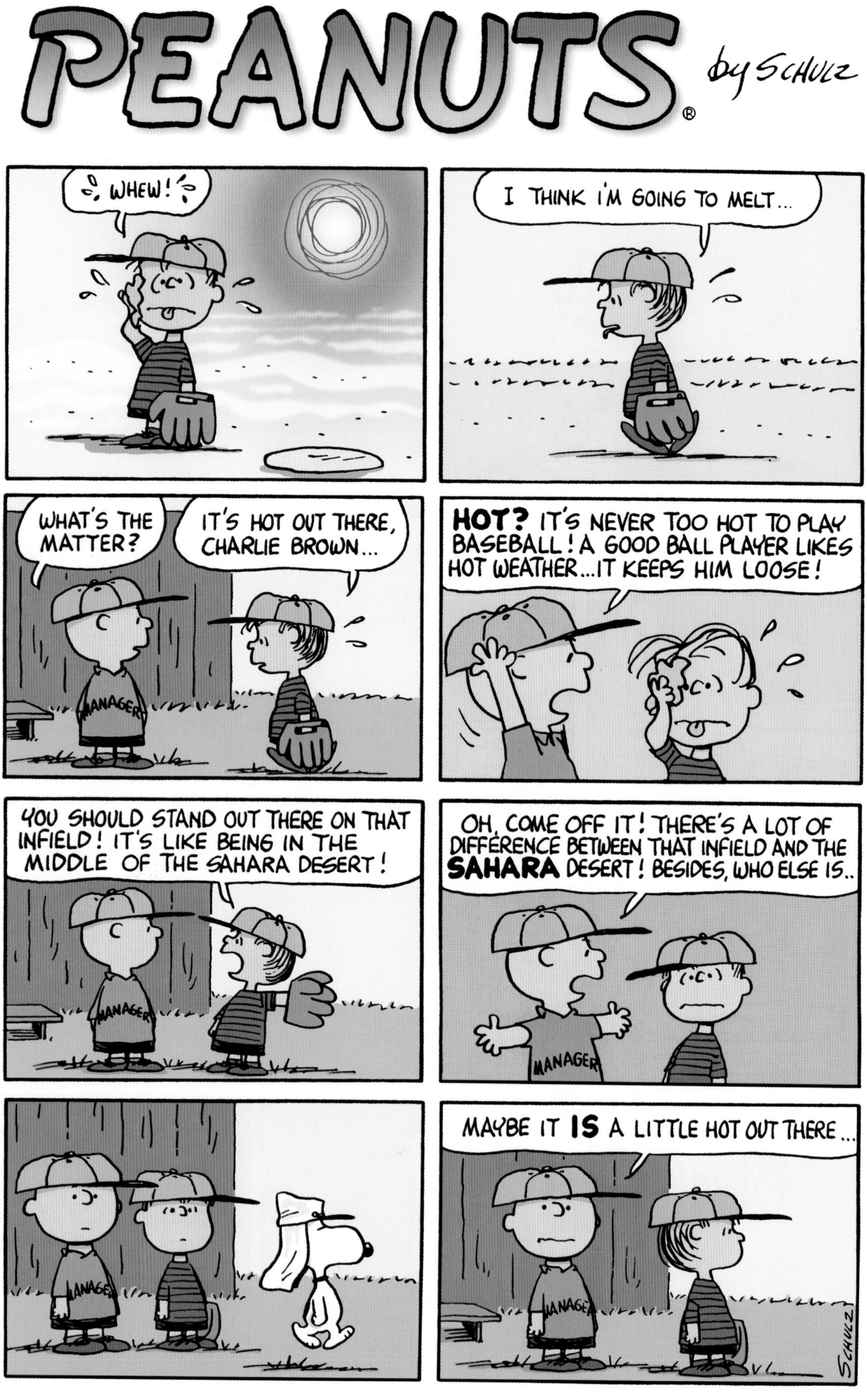
PEANUTS
by SCHULZ
WHEW!
I THINK I'M GOING TO MELT...
WHAT'S THE MATTER?
IT'S HOT OUT THERE, CHARLIE BROWN...
MANAGER
HOT? IT'S NEVER TOO HOT TO PLAY BASEBALL! A GOOD BALL PLAYER LIKES HOT WEATHER...IT KEEPS HIM LOOSE!
YOU SHOULD STAND OUT THERE ON THAT INFIELD! IT'S LIKE BEING IN THE MIDDLE OF THE SAHARA DESERT!
MANAGER
OH, COME OFF IT! THERE'S A LOT OF DIFFERENCE BETWEEN THAT INFIELD AND THE SAHARA DESERT! BESIDES, WHO ELSE IS..
MANAGER
MAYBE IT IS A LITTLE HOT OUT THERE...
SCHULZ

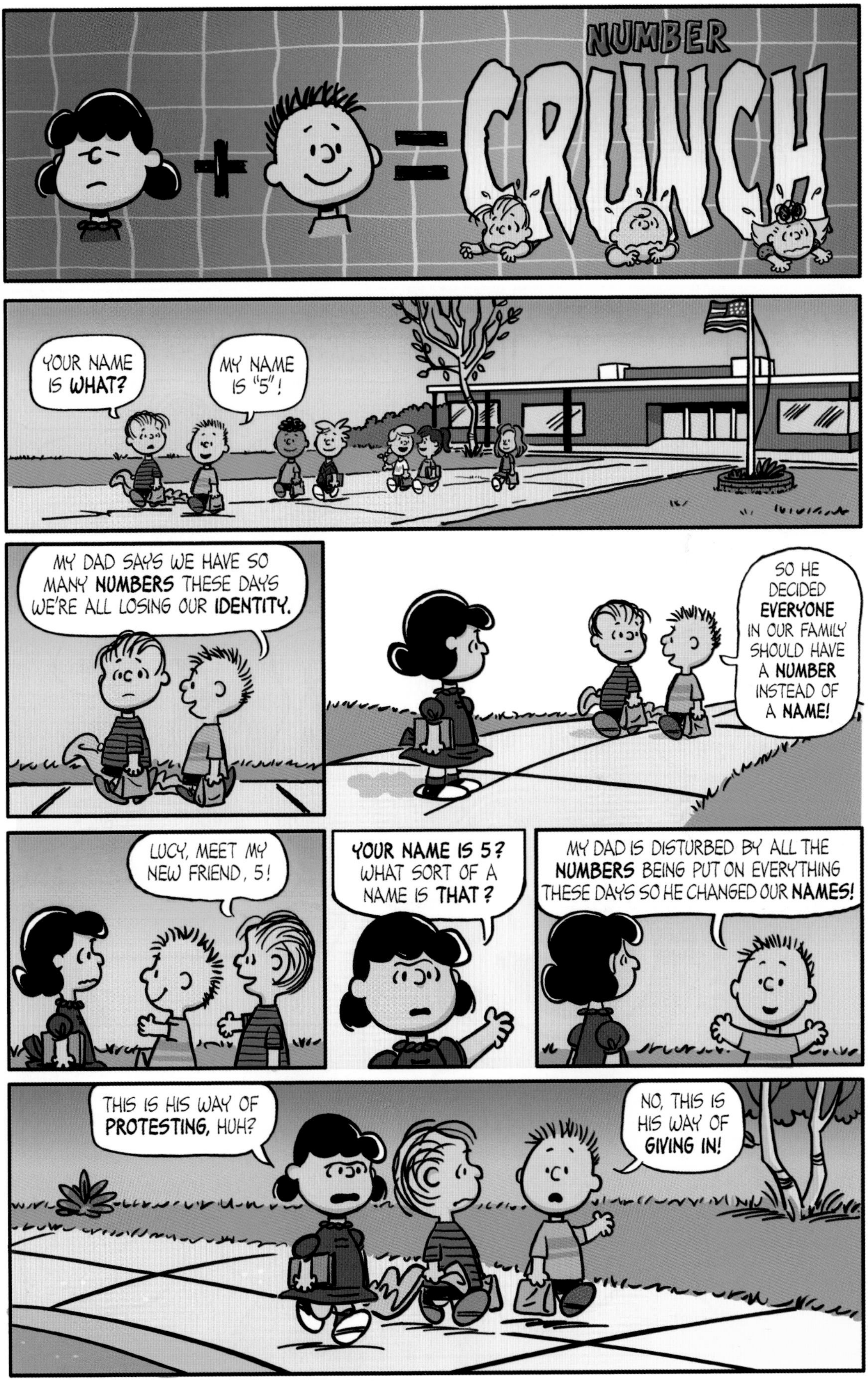
NUMBER CRUNCH
YOUR NAME IS WHAT?
MY NAME IS "5"!
MY DAD SAYS WE HAVE SO MANY NUMBERS THESE DAYS WE'RE ALL LOSING OUR IDENTITY.
SO HE DECIDED EVERYONE IN OUR FAMILY SHOULD HAVE A NUMBER INSTEAD OF A NAME!
LUCY, MEET MY NEW FRIEND, 5!
YOUR NAME IS 5? WHAT SORT OF A NAME IS THAT?
MY DAD IS DISTURBED BY ALL THE NUMBERS BEING PUT ON EVERYTHING THESE DAYS SO HE CHANGED OUR NAMES!
THIS IS HIS WAY OF PROTESTING, HUH?
NO, THIS IS HIS WAY OF GIVING IN!

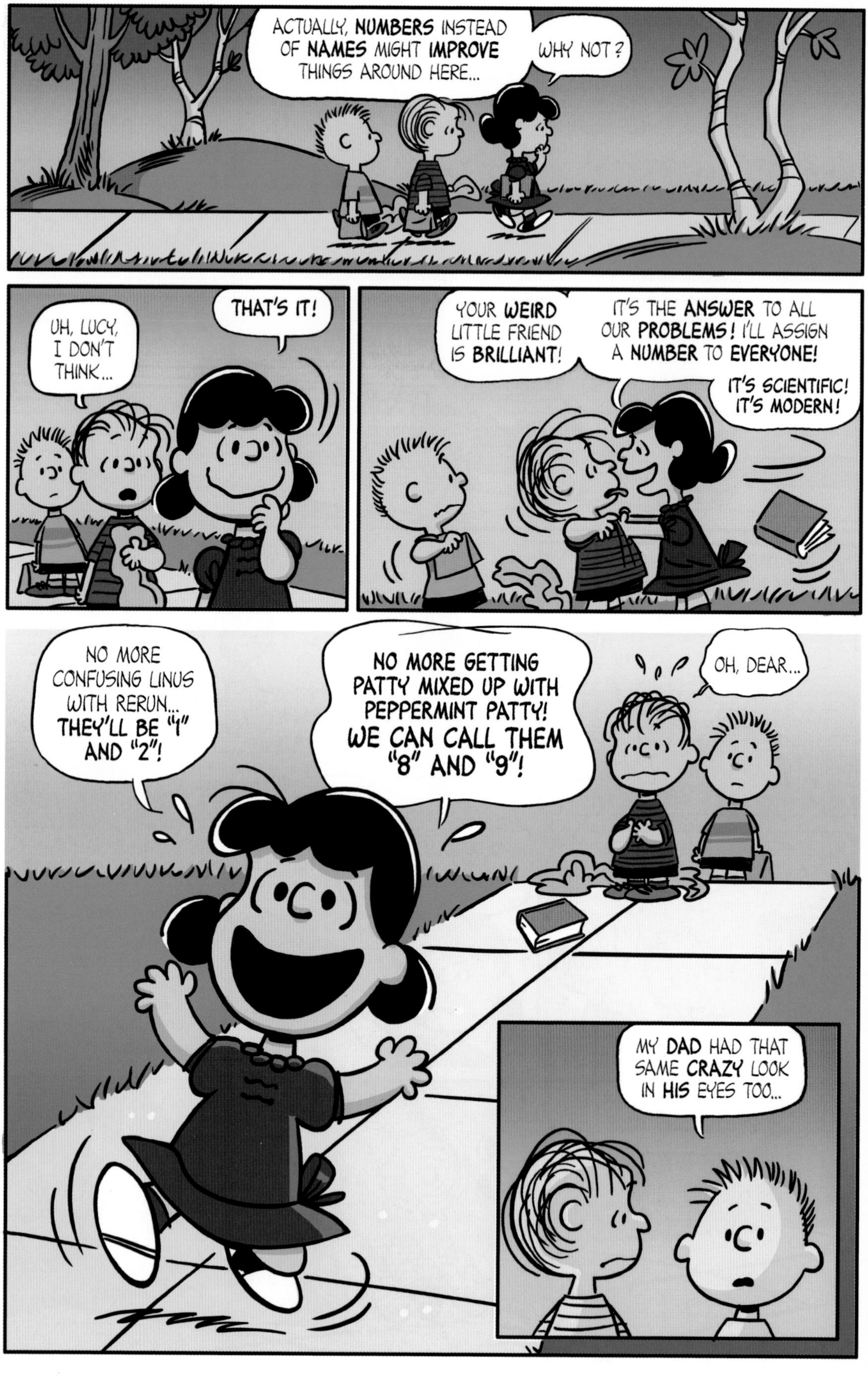

ACTUALLY, NUMBERS INSTEAD OF NAMES MIGHT IMPROVE THINGS AROUND HERE...
WHY NOT?
UH, LUCY, I DON'T THINK...
THAT'S IT!
YOUR WEIRD LITTLE FRIEND IS BRILLIANT!
IT'S THE ANSWER TO ALL OUR PROBLEMS! I'LL ASSIGN A NUMBER TO EVERYONE!
IT'S SCIENTIFIC! IT'S MODERN!
NO MORE CONFUSING LINUS WITH RERUN... THEY'LL BE "1" AND "2"!
NO MORE GETTING PATTY MIXED UP WITH PEPPERMINT PATTY! WE CAN CALL THEM "8" AND "9"!
OH, DEAR...
MY DAD HAD THAT SAME CRAZY LOOK IN HIS EYES TOO...

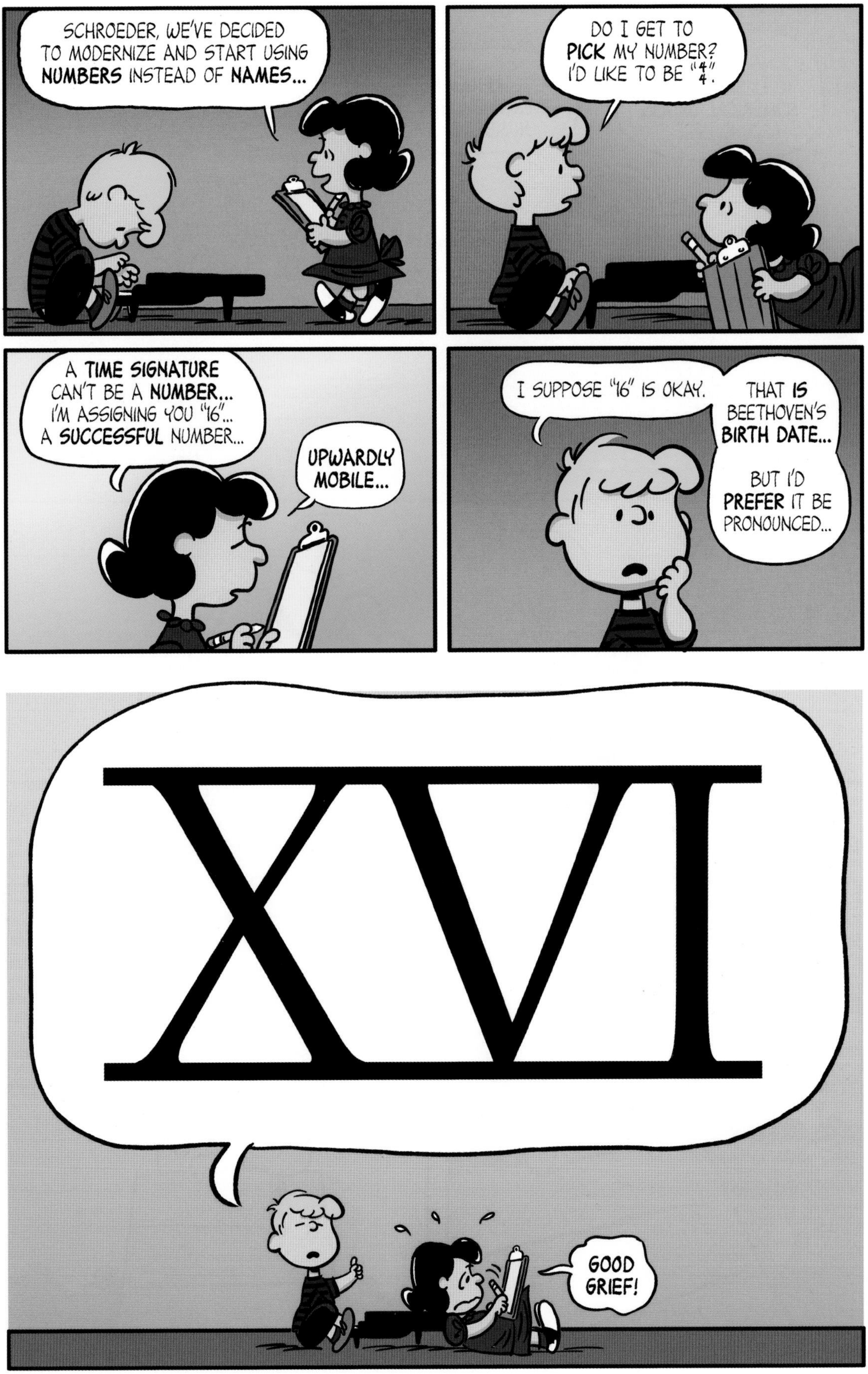
SCHROEDER, WE'VE DECIDED TO MODERNIZE AND START USING **NUMBERS** INSTEAD OF **NAMES...**
DO I GET TO **PICK** MY NUMBER? I'D LIKE TO BE "4/4".
A **TIME SIGNATURE** CAN'T BE A **NUMBER...** I'M ASSIGNING YOU "16"... A **SUCCESSFUL** NUMBER...
UPWARDLY MOBILE...
I SUPPOSE "16" IS OKAY.
THAT **IS** BEETHOVEN'S **BIRTH DATE...**
BUT I'D **PREFER** IT BE PRONOUNCED...
XVI
GOOD GRIEF!

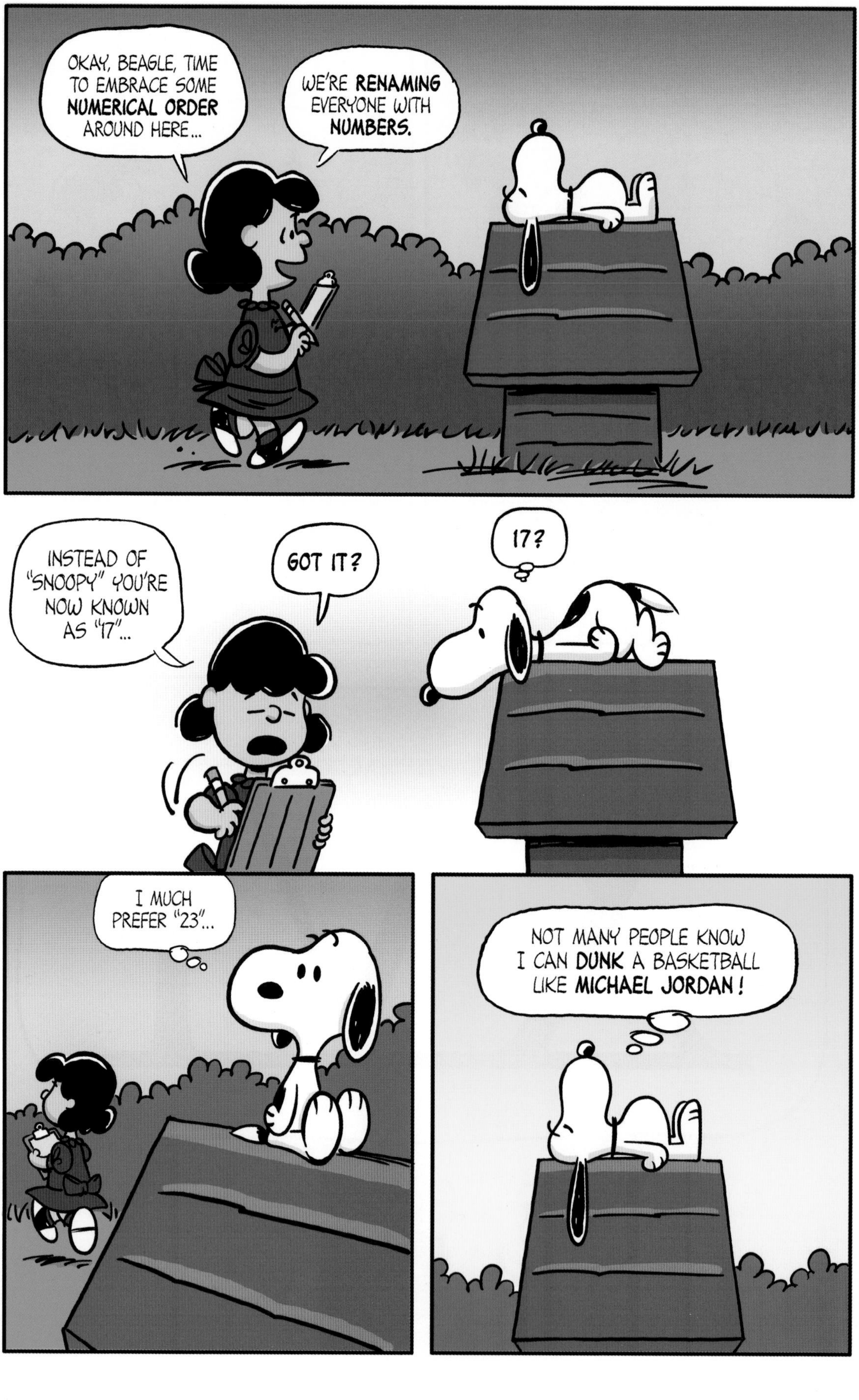

OKAY, BEAGLE, TIME TO EMBRACE SOME **NUMERICAL ORDER** AROUND HERE...
WE'RE **RENAMING** EVERYONE WITH **NUMBERS.**
INSTEAD OF "SNOOPY" YOU'RE NOW KNOWN AS "17"...
GOT IT?
17?
I MUCH PREFER "23"...
NOT MANY PEOPLE KNOW I CAN **DUNK** A BASKETBALL LIKE **MICHAEL JORDAN**!

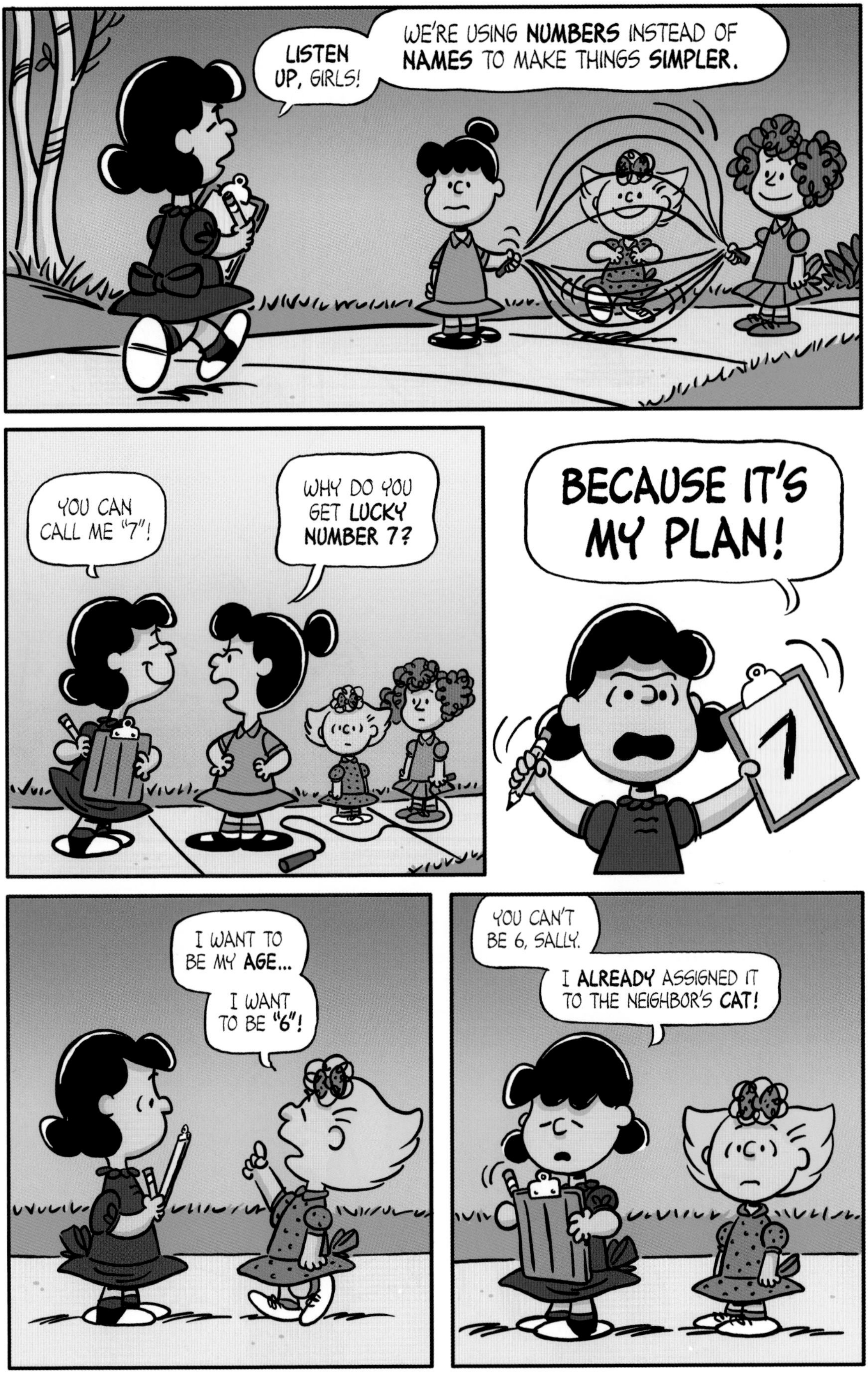
LISTEN UP, GIRLS!
WE'RE USING NUMBERS INSTEAD OF NAMES TO MAKE THINGS SIMPLER.
YOU CAN CALL ME "7"!
WHY DO YOU GET LUCKY NUMBER 7?
BECAUSE IT'S MY PLAN!
7
I WANT TO BE MY AGE...
I WANT TO BE "6"!
YOU CAN'T BE 6, SALLY.
I ALREADY ASSIGNED IT TO THE NEIGHBOR'S CAT!

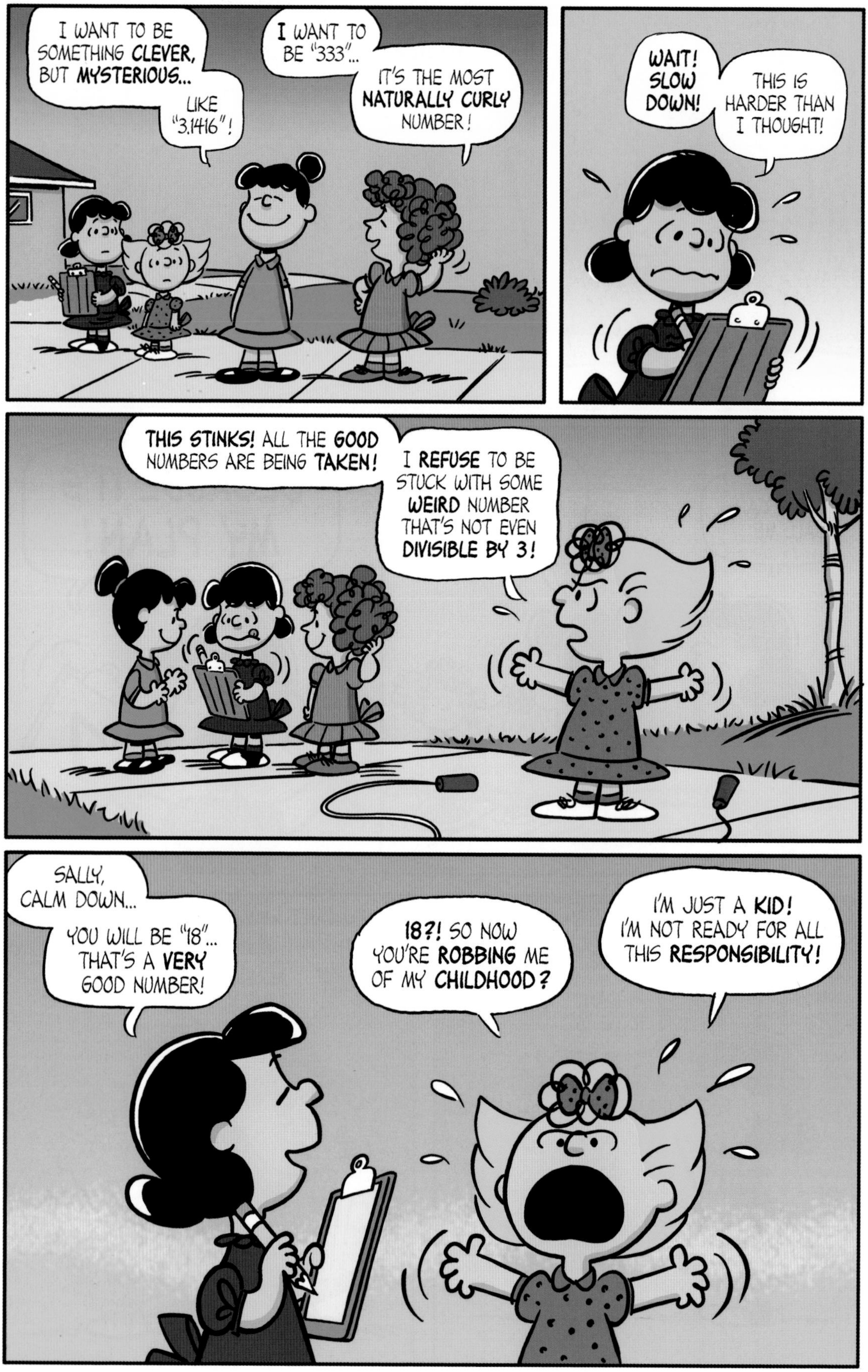

I WANT TO BE SOMETHING CLEVER, BUT MYSTERIOUS...
LIKE "3.1416"!
I WANT TO BE "333"...
IT'S THE MOST NATURALLY CURLY NUMBER!
WAIT! SLOW DOWN!
THIS IS HARDER THAN I THOUGHT!
THIS STINKS! ALL THE GOOD NUMBERS ARE BEING TAKEN!
I REFUSE TO BE STUCK WITH SOME WEIRD NUMBER THAT'S NOT EVEN DIVISIBLE BY 3!
SALLY, CALM DOWN...
YOU WILL BE "18"... THAT'S A VERY GOOD NUMBER!
18?! SO NOW YOU'RE ROBBING ME OF MY CHILDHOOD?
I'M JUST A KID! I'M NOT READY FOR ALL THIS RESPONSIBILITY!

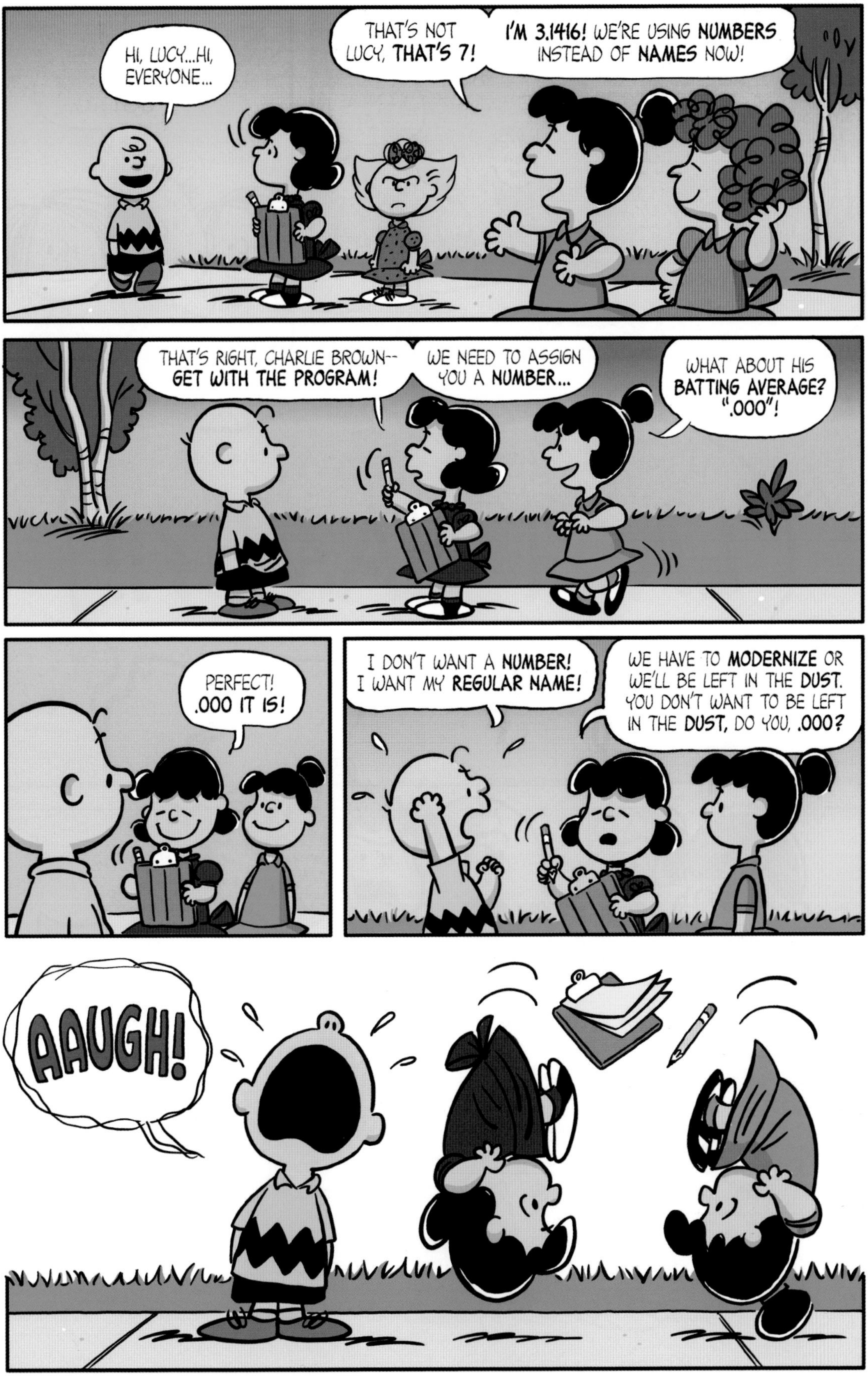
HI, LUCY...HI, EVERYONE...
THAT'S NOT LUCY, THAT'S 7!
I'M 3.1416! WE'RE USING NUMBERS INSTEAD OF NAMES NOW!
THAT'S RIGHT, CHARLIE BROWN-- GET WITH THE PROGRAM!
WE NEED TO ASSIGN YOU A NUMBER...
WHAT ABOUT HIS BATTING AVERAGE? ".000"!
PERFECT! .000 IT IS!
I DON'T WANT A NUMBER! I WANT MY REGULAR NAME!
WE HAVE TO MODERNIZE OR WE'LL BE LEFT IN THE DUST. YOU DON'T WANT TO BE LEFT IN THE DUST, DO YOU, .000?
AAUGH!

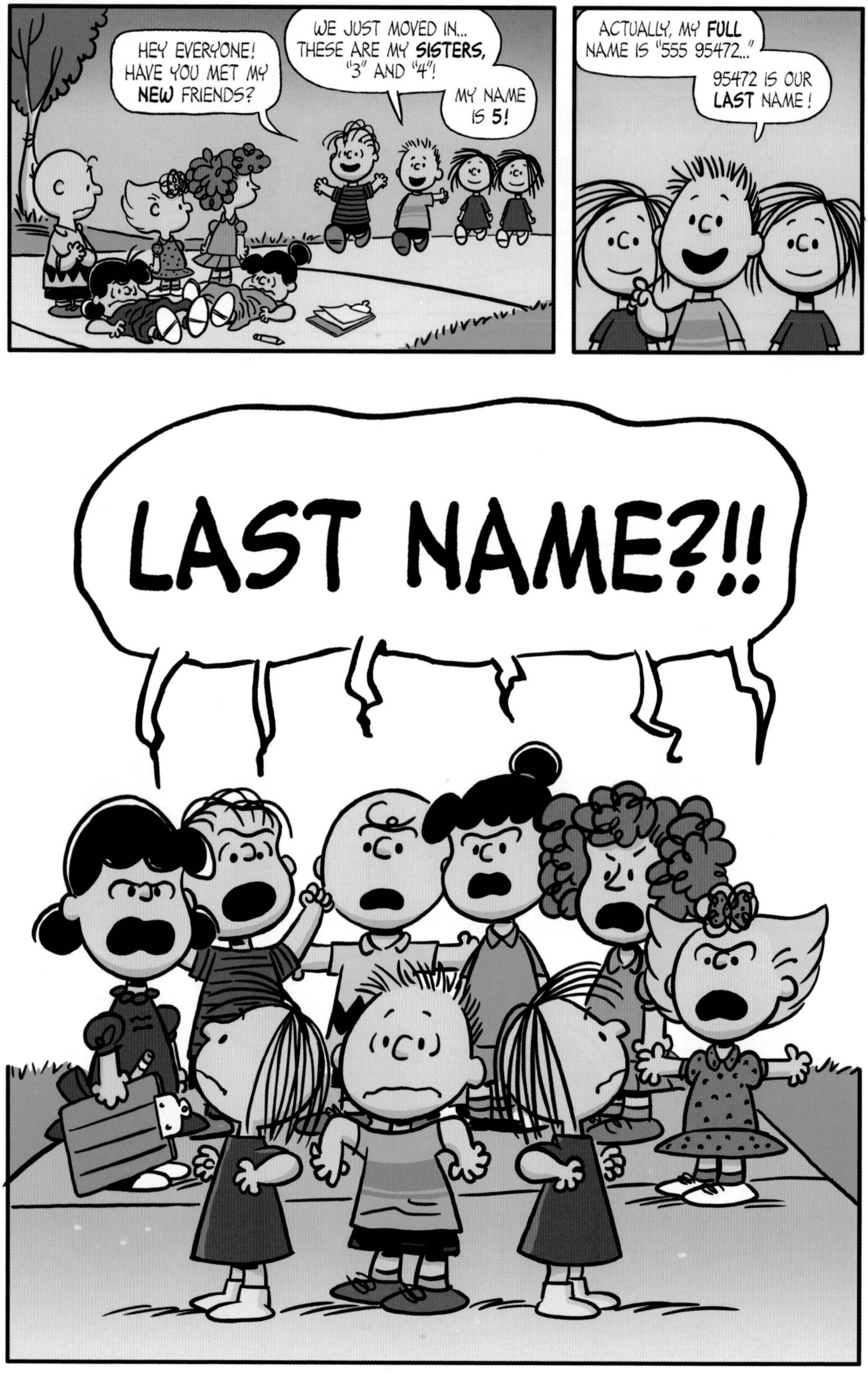
HEY EVERYONE! HAVE YOU MET MY NEW FRIENDS?
WE JUST MOVED IN... THESE ARE MY SISTERS, "3" AND "4"!
MY NAME IS 5!
ACTUALLY, MY FULL NAME IS "555 95472..."
95472 IS OUR LAST NAME!
LAST NAME?!!

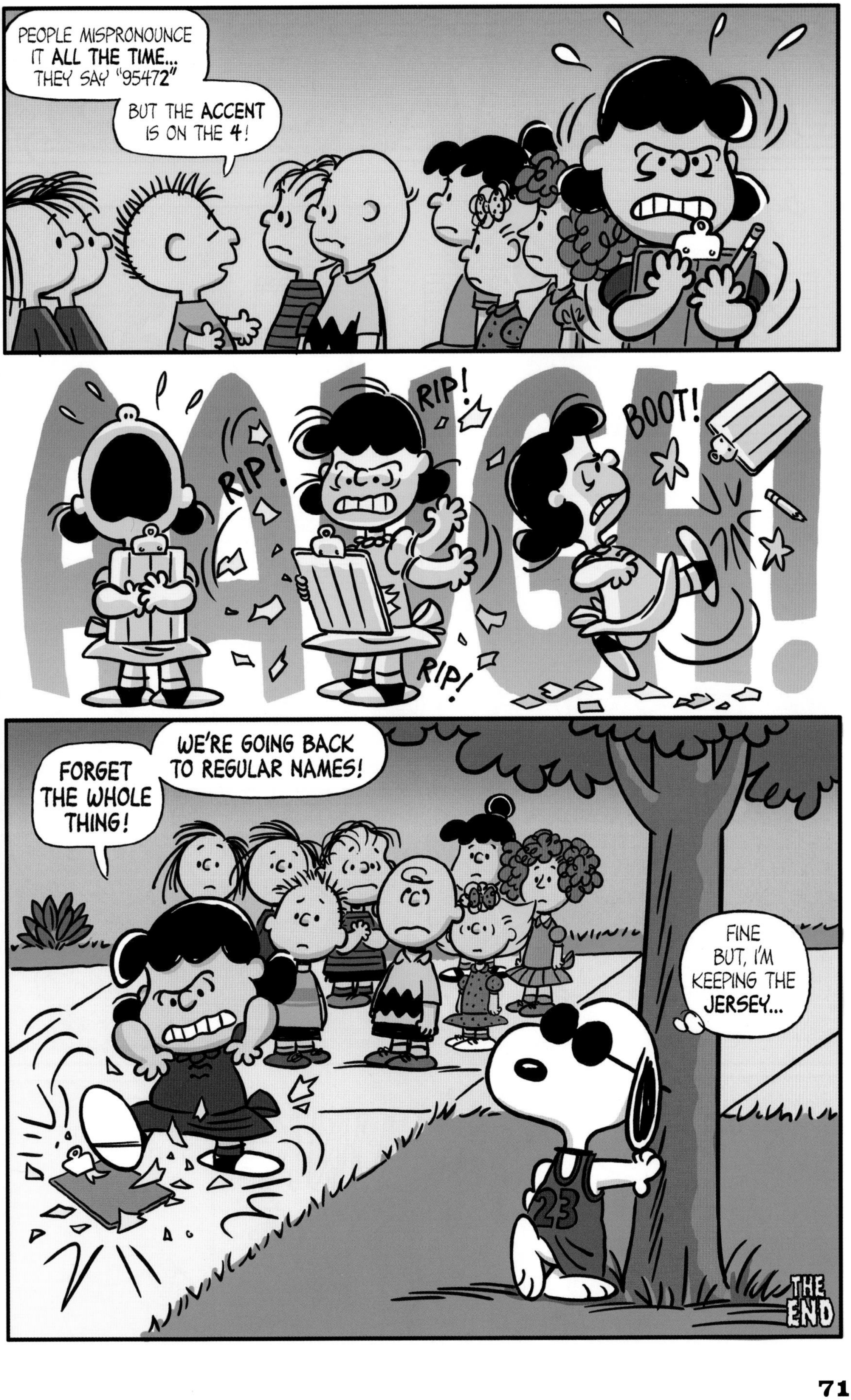

PEOPLE MISPRONOUNCE IT ALL THE TIME... THEY SAY "95472"
BUT THE ACCENT IS ON THE 4!
AAUGH!
RIP!
RIP!
BOOT!
RIP!
FORGET THE WHOLE THING!
WE'RE GOING BACK TO REGULAR NAMES!
FINE BUT, I'M KEEPING THE JERSEY...
23
THE END

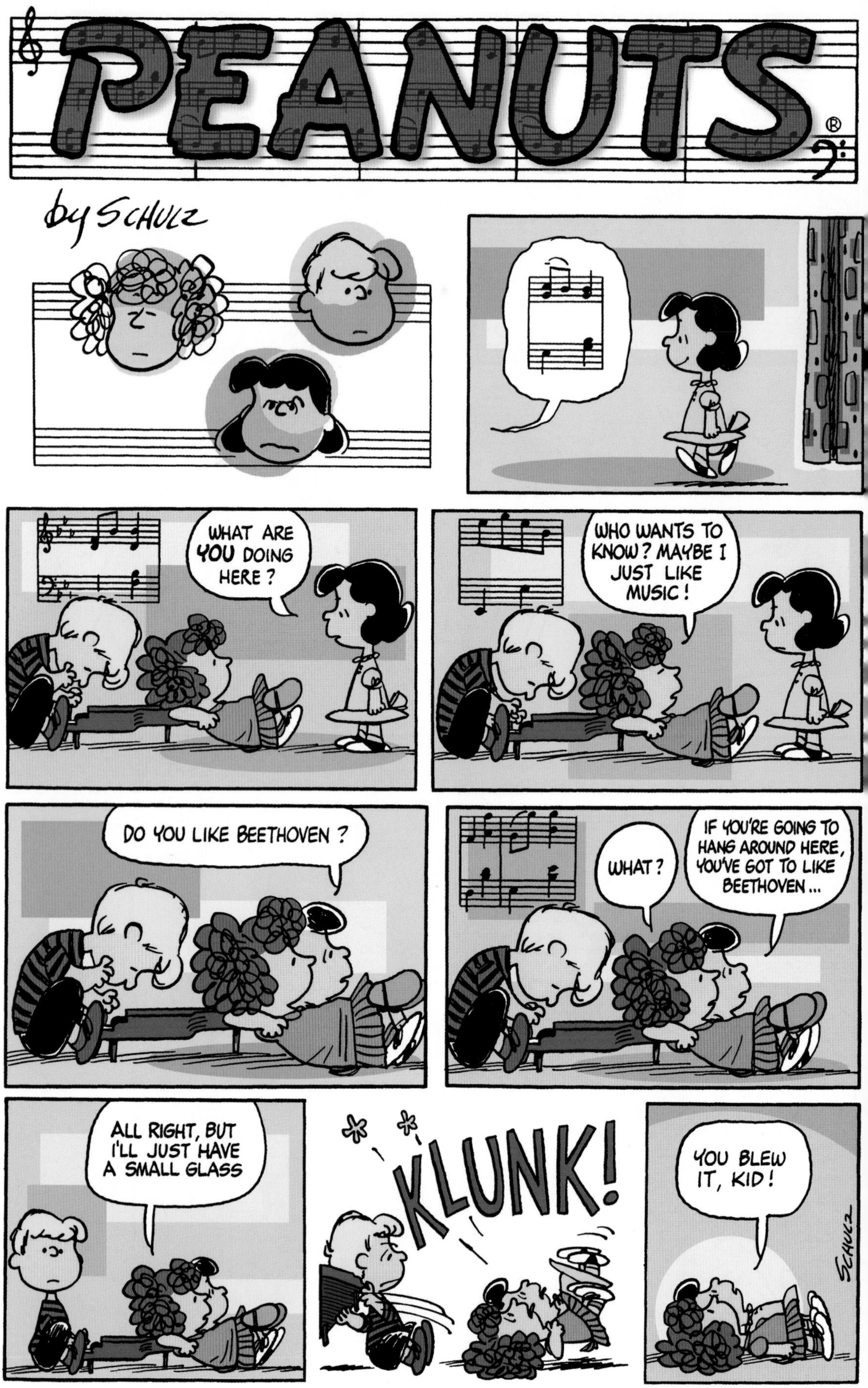
PEANUTS®
by SCHULZ
WHAT ARE YOU DOING HERE?
WHO WANTS TO KNOW? MAYBE I JUST LIKE MUSIC!
DO YOU LIKE BEETHOVEN?
WHAT?
IF YOU'RE GOING TO HANG AROUND HERE, YOU'VE GOT TO LIKE BEETHOVEN...
ALL RIGHT, BUT I'LL JUST HAVE A SMALL GLASS
KLUNK!
YOU BLEW IT, KID!
SCHULZ

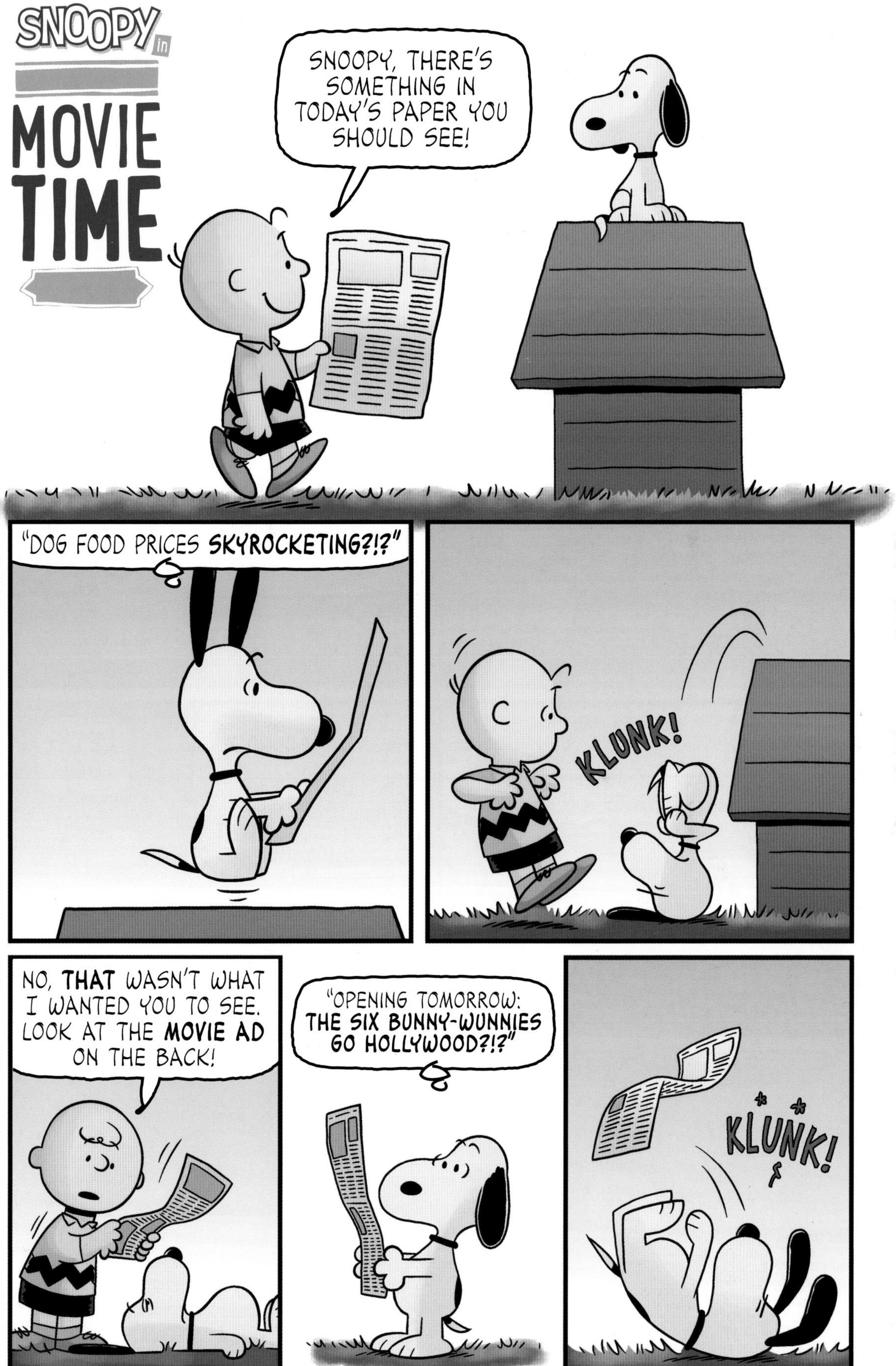
SNOOPY in
MOVIE TIME
SNOOPY, THERE'S SOMETHING IN TODAY'S PAPER YOU SHOULD SEE!
"DOG FOOD PRICES SKYROCKETING?!?"
KLUNK!
NO, THAT WASN'T WHAT I WANTED YOU TO SEE. LOOK AT THE MOVIE AD ON THE BACK!
"OPENING TOMORROW: THE SIX BUNNY-WUNNIES GO HOLLYWOOD?!?"
KLUNK!

THAT NIGHT:

WOODSTOCK, OLIVIER, BILL, CONRAD AND HARRIET, ALL HERE!

I KNOW TONIGHT'S BEAGLE SCOUT ACTIVITIES WERE SUPPOSED TO BE LEARNING **FIRST AID** AND **SURVIVAL PLANNING**, BUT SOMETHING MUCH MORE **IMPORTANT** HAS COME UP.

THERE'S A SIX BUNNY-WUNNIES MOVIE!

WHAT ARE THE **SIX BUNNY-WUNNIES?** ONLY THE STARS OF THE GREATEST WORKS OF **LITERATURE** OF ALL TIME!

AUTHOR **MISS HELEN SWEETSTORY** HAS CRAFTED SUCH LASTING MASTER-WORKS AS...

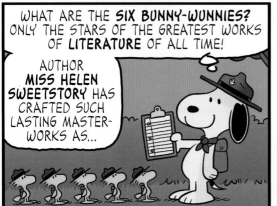

..."THE SIX BUNNY-WUNNIES AND THEIR PONY CART," "THE SIX BUNNY-WUNNIES MAKE COOKIES," "THE SIX BUNNY-WUNNIES TAKE A NAP," "THE SIX BUNNY-WUNNIES FREAK OUT," "THE SIX BUNNY-WUNNIES AND THEIR WATER BED," "THE SIX BUNNY-WUNNIES AND THEIR LAYOVER IN ANDERSON, INDIANA"...

..."THE SIX BUNNY-WUNNIES MEET THE SEVEN HAMSTER-WAMSTERS," "THE SIX BUNNY-WUNNIES FORM A PUNK BAND," AND "THE SIX BUNNY-WUNNIES FULFILL A CONTRACTUAL OBLIGATION!" **MASTERPIECES** ALL!

SUCH A CINEMATIC EVENT IS **BOUND** TO DRAW A CROWD. WE MUST WAIT IN LINE ALL NIGHT TO BE SURE TO GET INTO THE **FIRST** SHOWING.

LET'S GO!

HOW DO WE FIND A MOVIE THEATER? JUST FOLLOW **THE MOON!**

YOU SEE, THE MOON RISES DIRECTLY OVER HOLLYWOOD, AND IF WE FOLLOW IT, WE'RE SURE TO END UP AT A MOVIE THEATER!

Thump! Thump! Thump! Thump! Thump!

Thump!

FOUND IT! LET'S SET UP **CAMP!**

OPENING FRIDAY

SIX BUNNY-WUNNIES GO HOLLYWOOD

MARTIANS FROM SPACE

Z

Z Z Z Z Z

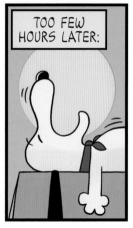

TOO FEW HOURS LATER:

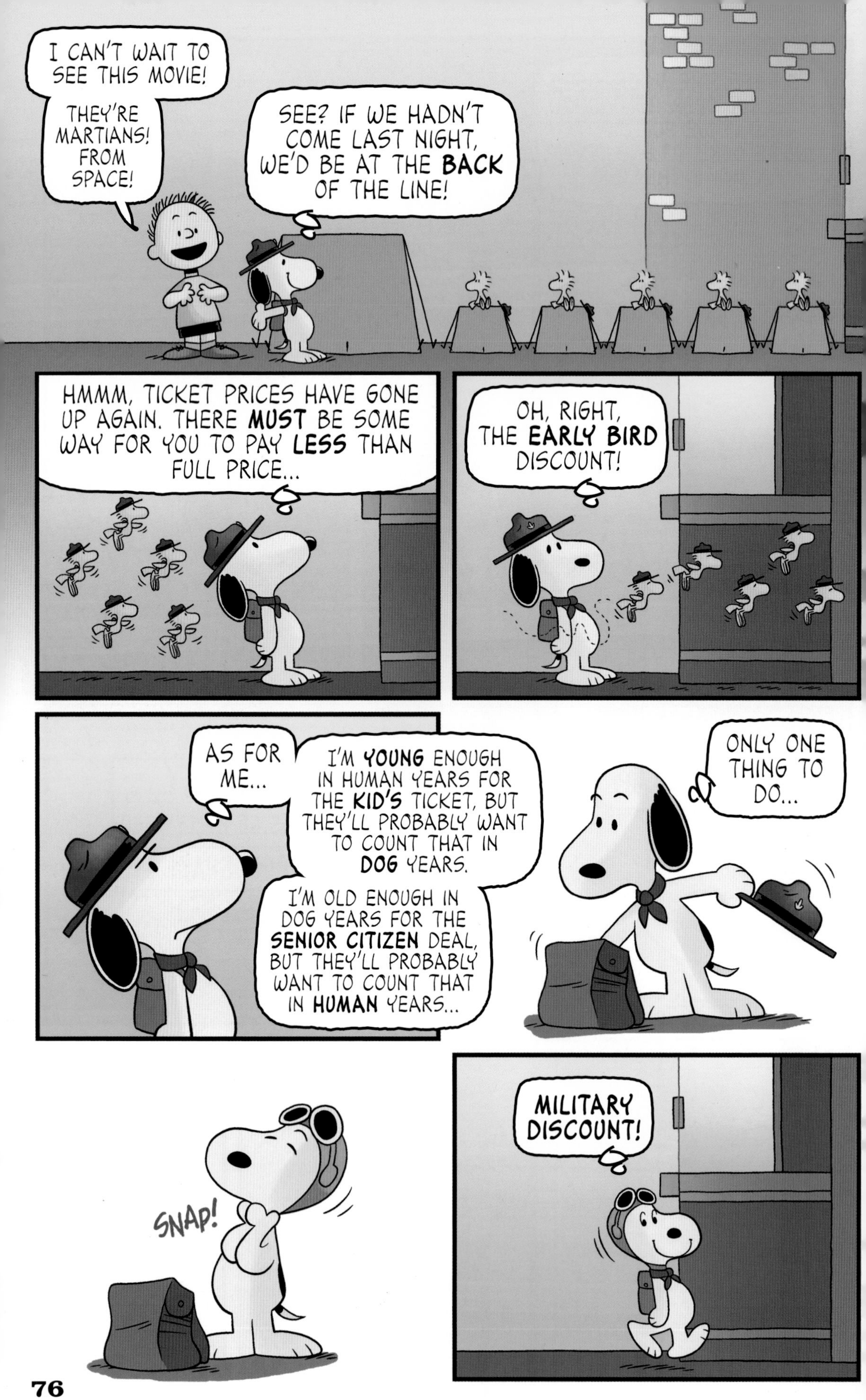

I CAN'T WAIT TO SEE THIS MOVIE!
THEY'RE MARTIANS! FROM SPACE!
SEE? IF WE HADN'T COME LAST NIGHT, WE'D BE AT THE **BACK** OF THE LINE!
HMMM, TICKET PRICES HAVE GONE UP AGAIN. THERE **MUST** BE SOME WAY FOR YOU TO PAY **LESS** THAN FULL PRICE...
OH, RIGHT, THE **EARLY BIRD** DISCOUNT!
AS FOR ME...
I'M **YOUNG** ENOUGH IN HUMAN YEARS FOR THE **KID'S** TICKET, BUT THEY'LL PROBABLY WANT TO COUNT THAT IN **DOG** YEARS.
I'M OLD ENOUGH IN DOG YEARS FOR THE **SENIOR CITIZEN** DEAL, BUT THEY'LL PROBABLY WANT TO COUNT THAT IN **HUMAN** YEARS...
ONLY ONE THING TO DO...
SNAP!
MILITARY DISCOUNT!

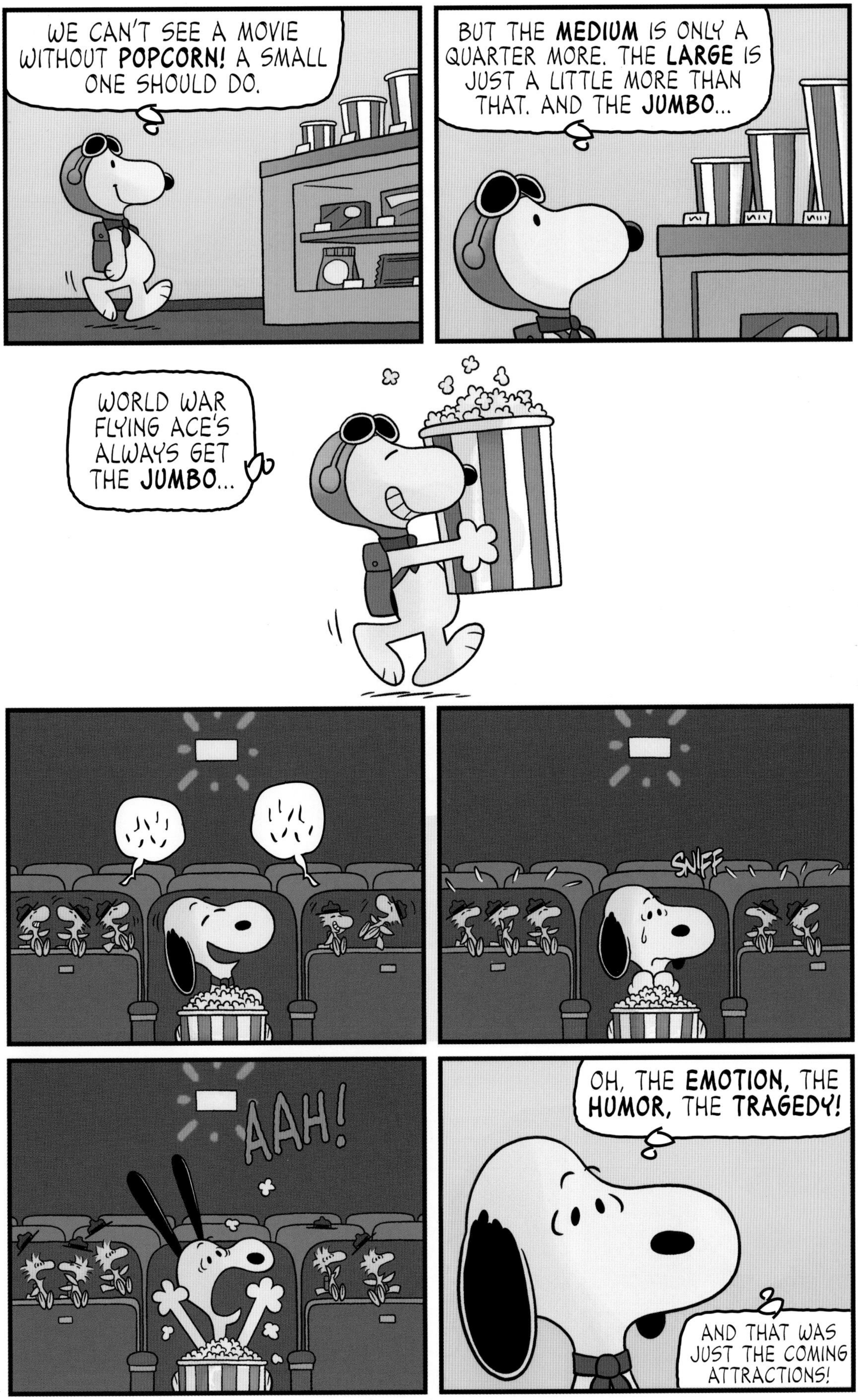
WE CAN'T SEE A MOVIE WITHOUT **POPCORN!** A SMALL ONE SHOULD DO.
BUT THE **MEDIUM** IS ONLY A QUARTER MORE. THE **LARGE** IS JUST A LITTLE MORE THAN THAT. AND THE **JUMBO**...
WORLD WAR FLYING ACE'S ALWAYS GET THE **JUMBO**...
SNIFF
AAH!
OH, THE **EMOTION**, THE **HUMOR**, THE **TRAGEDY!**
AND THAT WAS JUST THE COMING ATTRACTIONS!

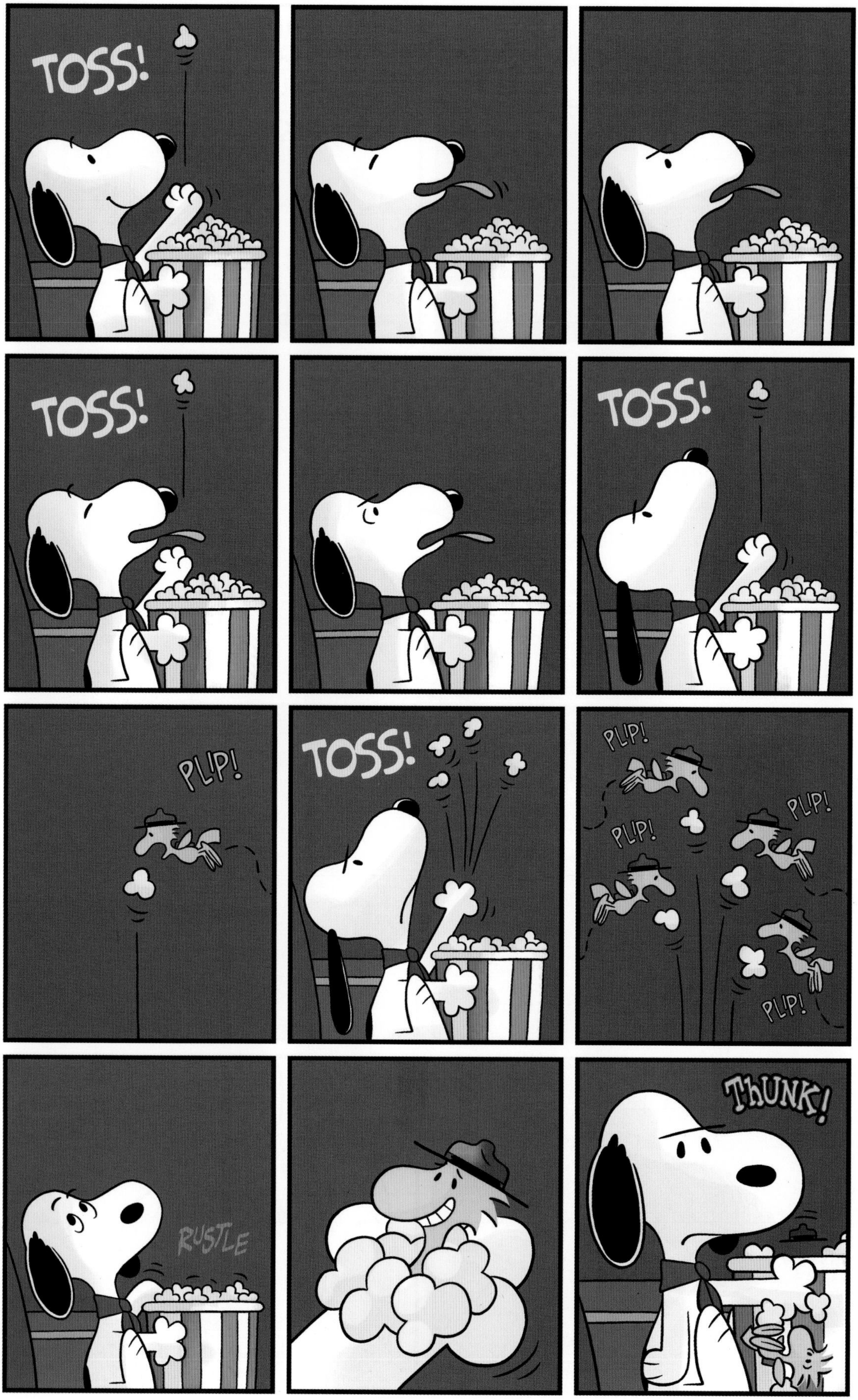
TOSS!
TOSS!
TOSS!
PLIP!
TOSS!
PLIP!
PLIP!
PLIP!
PLIP!
RUSTLE
THUNK!

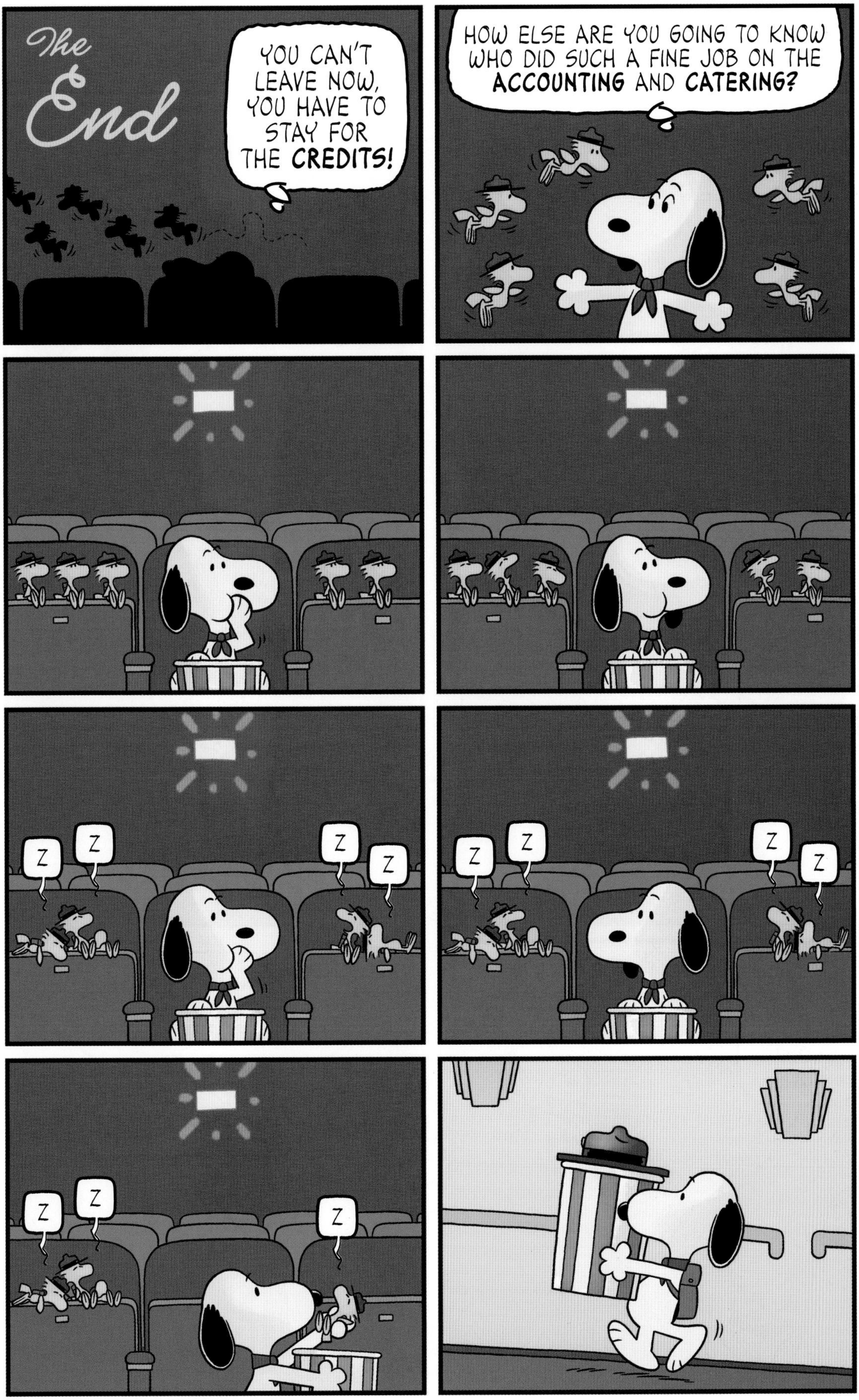
The End
YOU CAN'T LEAVE NOW, YOU HAVE TO STAY FOR THE **CREDITS!**
HOW ELSE ARE YOU GOING TO KNOW WHO DID SUCH A FINE JOB ON THE **ACCOUNTING** AND **CATERING?**
Z
Z
Z
Z
Z
Z
Z
Z
Z
Z
Z

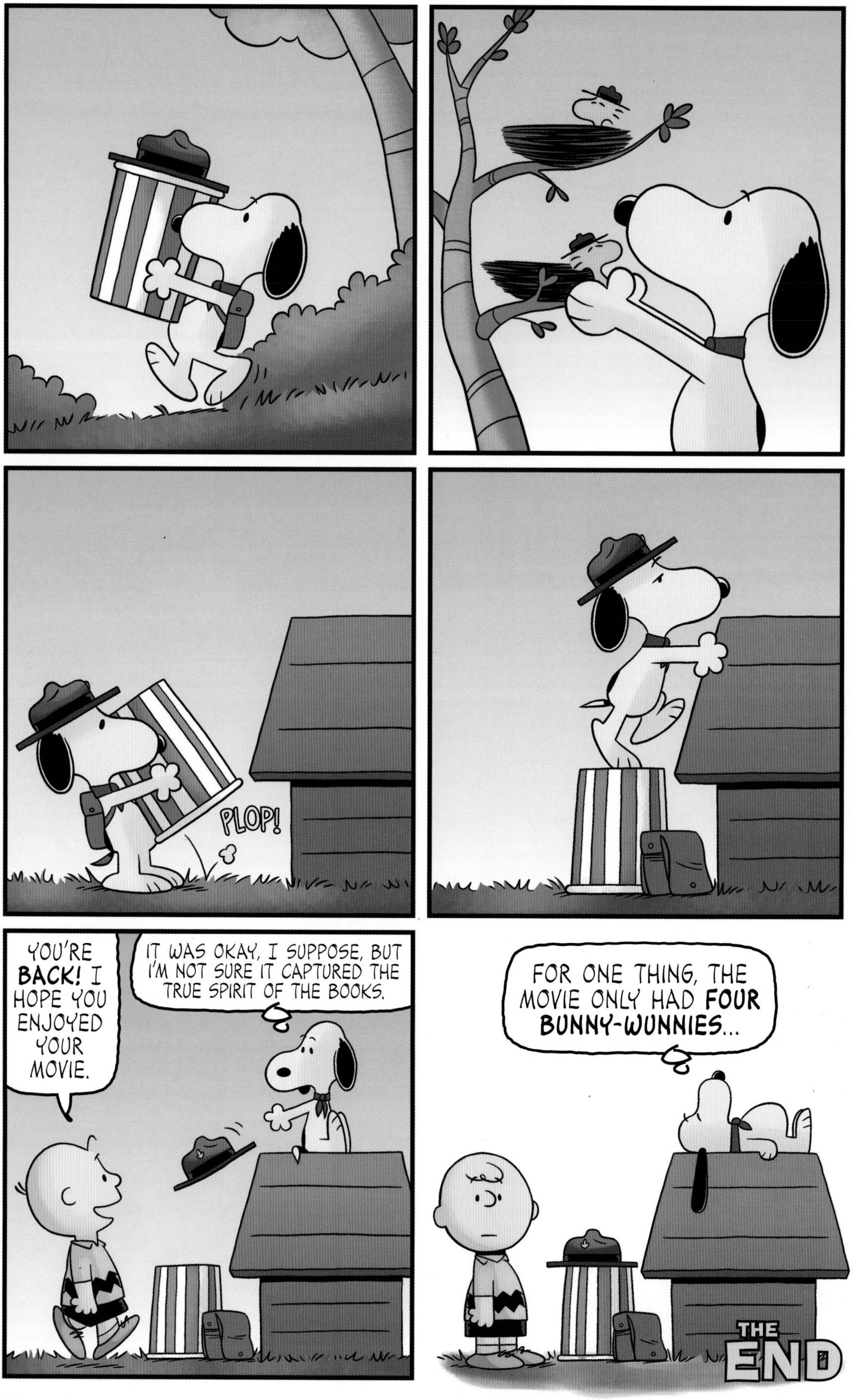
PLOP!
YOU'RE BACK! I HOPE YOU ENJOYED YOUR MOVIE.
IT WAS OKAY, I SUPPOSE, BUT I'M NOT SURE IT CAPTURED THE TRUE SPIRIT OF THE BOOKS.
FOR ONE THING, THE MOVIE ONLY HAD FOUR BUNNY-WUNNIES...
THE END

From the Drawing Board

Charlie Brown
by Schulz
LATELY EVERYTHING SEEMS TO BOTHER ME...
HOW DO YOU MEAN?
WHAT DO YOU THINK SECURITY IS, CHUCK?
SECURITY?
SECURITY IS SLEEPING IN THE BACK SEAT OF THE CAR...
WHEN YOU'RE A LITTLE KID, AND YOU'VE BEEN SOMEWHERE WITH YOUR MOM AND DAD, AND IT'S NIGHT, AND YOU'RE RIDING HOME IN THE CAR, YOU CAN SLEEP IN THE BACK SEAT..
YOU DON'T HAVE TO WORRY ABOUT ANYTHING... YOUR MOM AND DAD ARE IN THE FRONT SEAT, AND THEY DO ALL THE WORRYING...THEY TAKE CARE OF EVERYTHING...
THAT'S REAL NEAT!
BUT IT DOESN'T LAST! SUDDENLY, YOU'RE GROWN UP, AND IT CAN NEVER BE THAT WAY AGAIN!
8-6
SUDDENLY, IT'S OVER, AND YOU'LL NEVER GET TO SLEEP IN THE BACK SEAT AGAIN! NEVER!
NEVER?
ABSOLUTELY NEVER!
HOLD MY HAND, CHUCK!!
SCHULZ

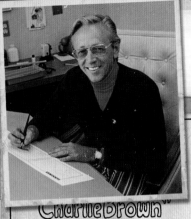

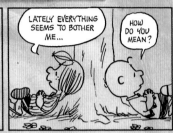

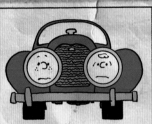

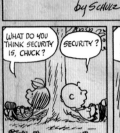

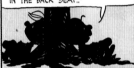

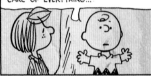

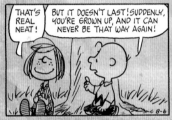

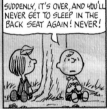

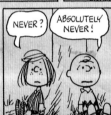

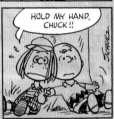

"Another cartoon I recall is one about security, where Charlie Brown says that when you are a little kid you can lie in the back seat of your parent's car in the evening when you've been someplace and you can sleep and you don't have to worry about anything, your parents are in the front seat, they're driving home, and you have no worries, but when you grow up you have to sit in the front seat, you can never lie in the back seat again.

And Peppermint Patty was terror-stricken at the thought of this and she says, "Hold my hand, Chuck."

And I think this is true, this is one of the things that bothers adults too.

They've grown up, now they're on their own, they can't back up, there's no turning back, they're committed and we're forced to be mature.

We don't want to be mature, we keep wanting to slip back where somebody else will take care of these things for us and we can't."

–Charles M. Schulz

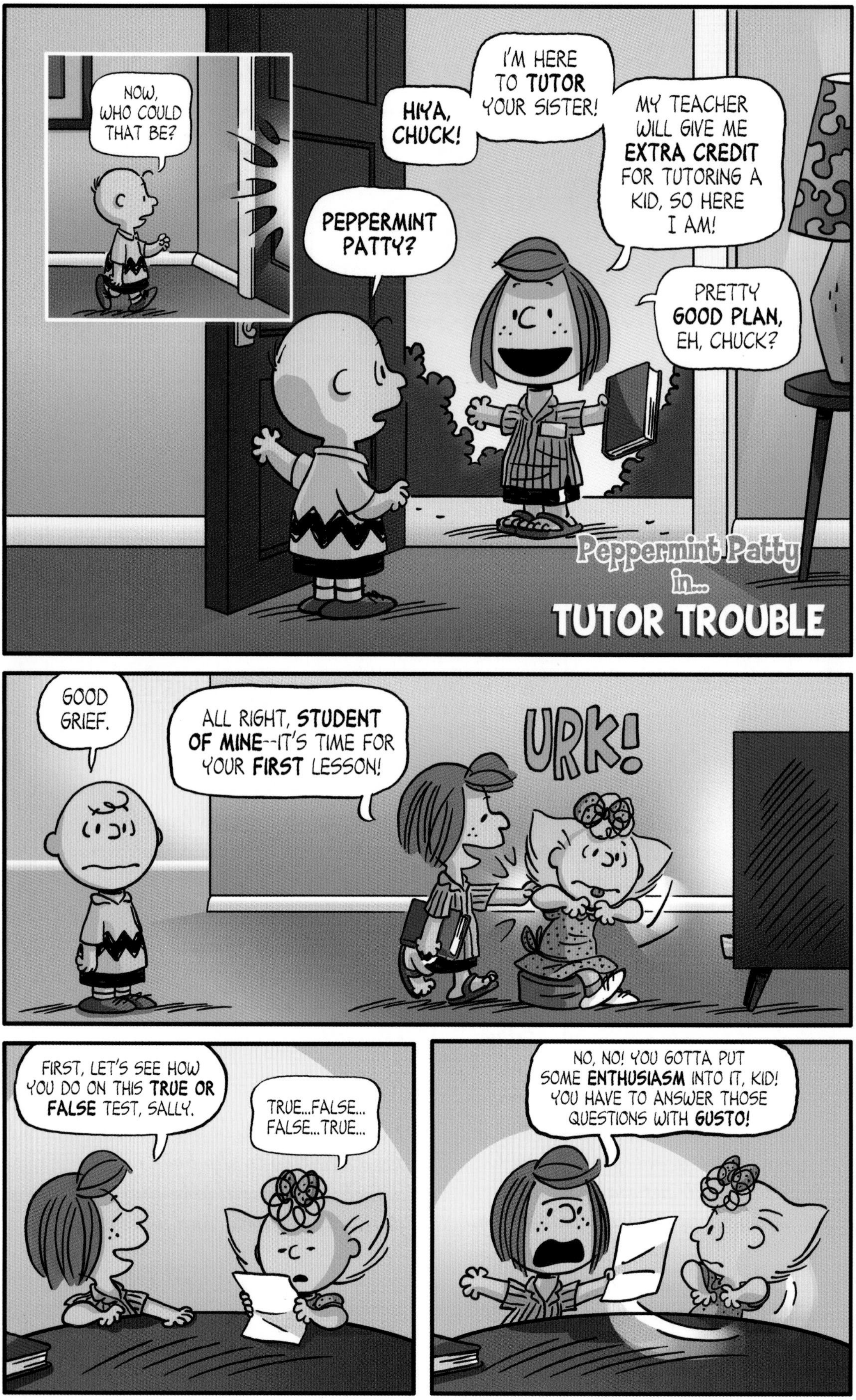
NOW, WHO COULD THAT BE?
HIYA, CHUCK!
I'M HERE TO TUTOR YOUR SISTER!
MY TEACHER WILL GIVE ME EXTRA CREDIT FOR TUTORING A KID, SO HERE I AM!
PEPPERMINT PATTY?
PRETTY GOOD PLAN, EH, CHUCK?
Peppermint Patty in...
TUTOR TROUBLE
GOOD GRIEF.
ALL RIGHT, STUDENT OF MINE--IT'S TIME FOR YOUR FIRST LESSON!
URK!
FIRST, LET'S SEE HOW YOU DO ON THIS TRUE OR FALSE TEST, SALLY.
TRUE...FALSE... FALSE...TRUE...
NO, NO! YOU GOTTA PUT SOME ENTHUSIASM INTO IT, KID! YOU HAVE TO ANSWER THOSE QUESTIONS WITH GUSTO!

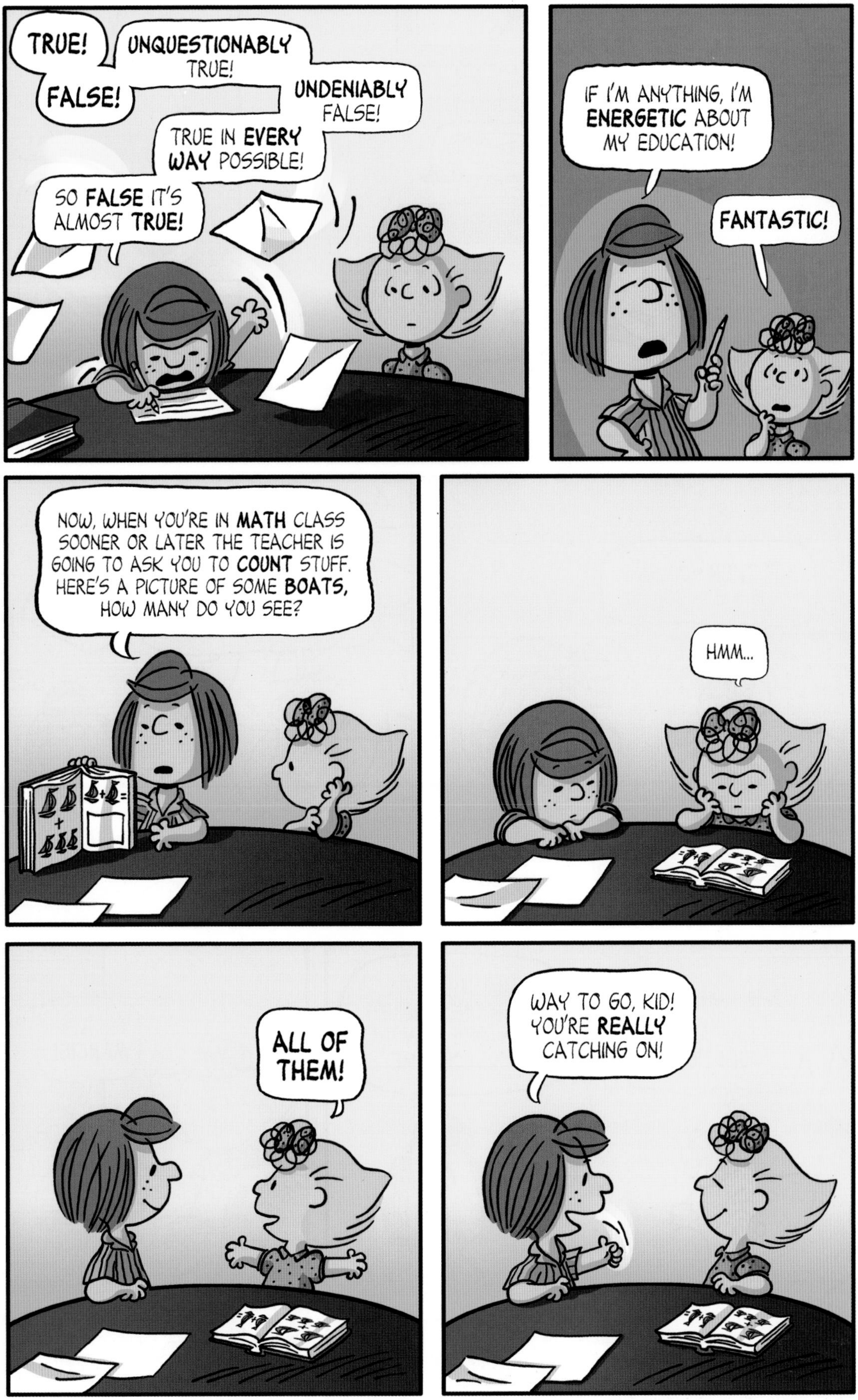
TRUE!
UNQUESTIONABLY TRUE!
FALSE!
UNDENIABLY FALSE!
TRUE IN EVERY WAY POSSIBLE!
SO FALSE IT'S ALMOST TRUE!
IF I'M ANYTHING, I'M ENERGETIC ABOUT MY EDUCATION!
FANTASTIC!
NOW, WHEN YOU'RE IN MATH CLASS SOONER OR LATER THE TEACHER IS GOING TO ASK YOU TO COUNT STUFF. HERE'S A PICTURE OF SOME BOATS, HOW MANY DO YOU SEE?
HMM...
ALL OF THEM!
WAY TO GO, KID! YOU'RE REALLY CATCHING ON!

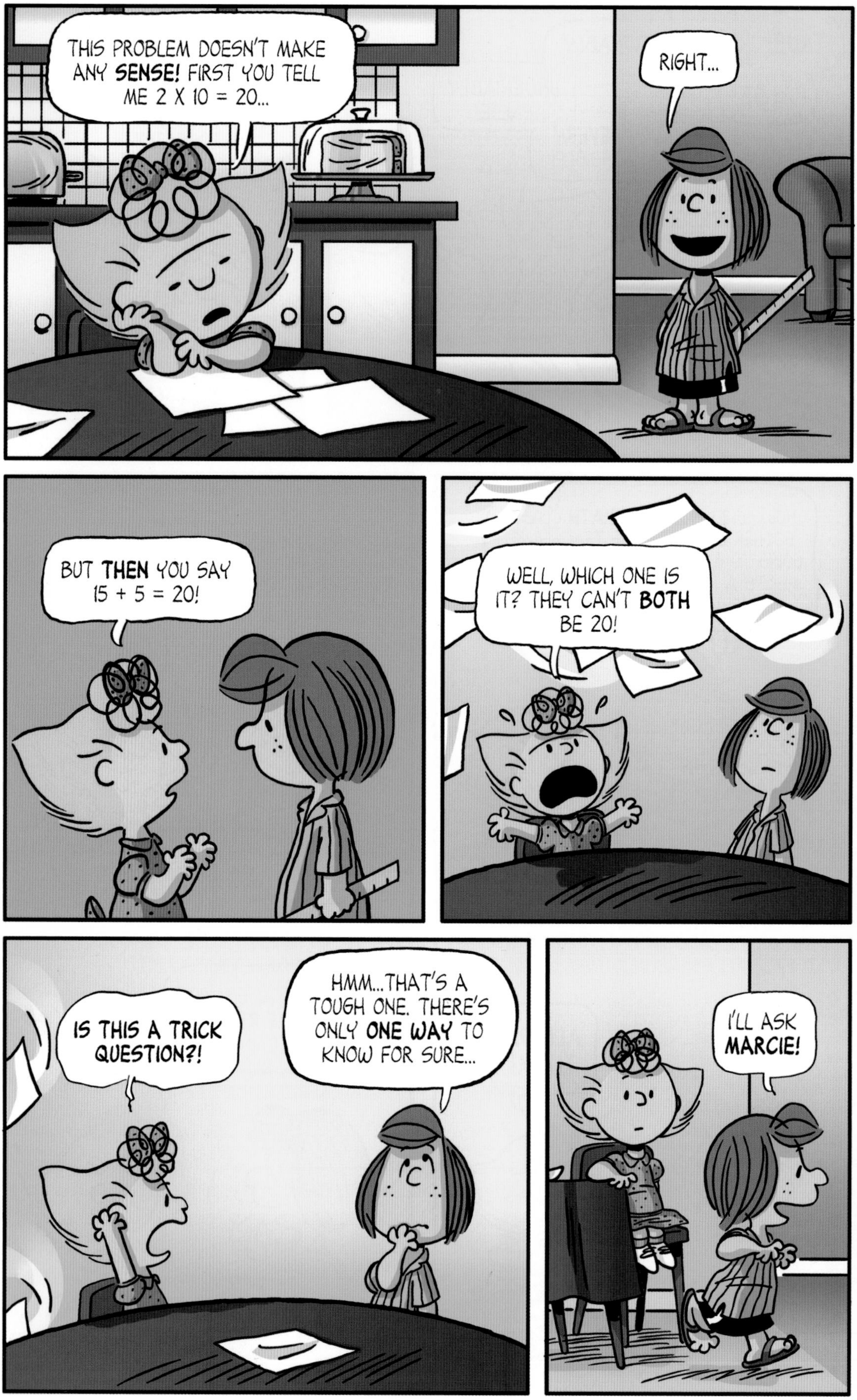
THIS PROBLEM DOESN'T MAKE ANY **SENSE!** FIRST YOU TELL ME 2 X 10 = 20...
RIGHT...
BUT **THEN** YOU SAY 15 + 5 = 20!
WELL, WHICH ONE IS IT? THEY CAN'T **BOTH** BE 20!
IS THIS A TRICK QUESTION?!
HMM...THAT'S A TOUGH ONE. THERE'S ONLY **ONE WAY** TO KNOW FOR SURE...
I'LL ASK **MARCIE!**

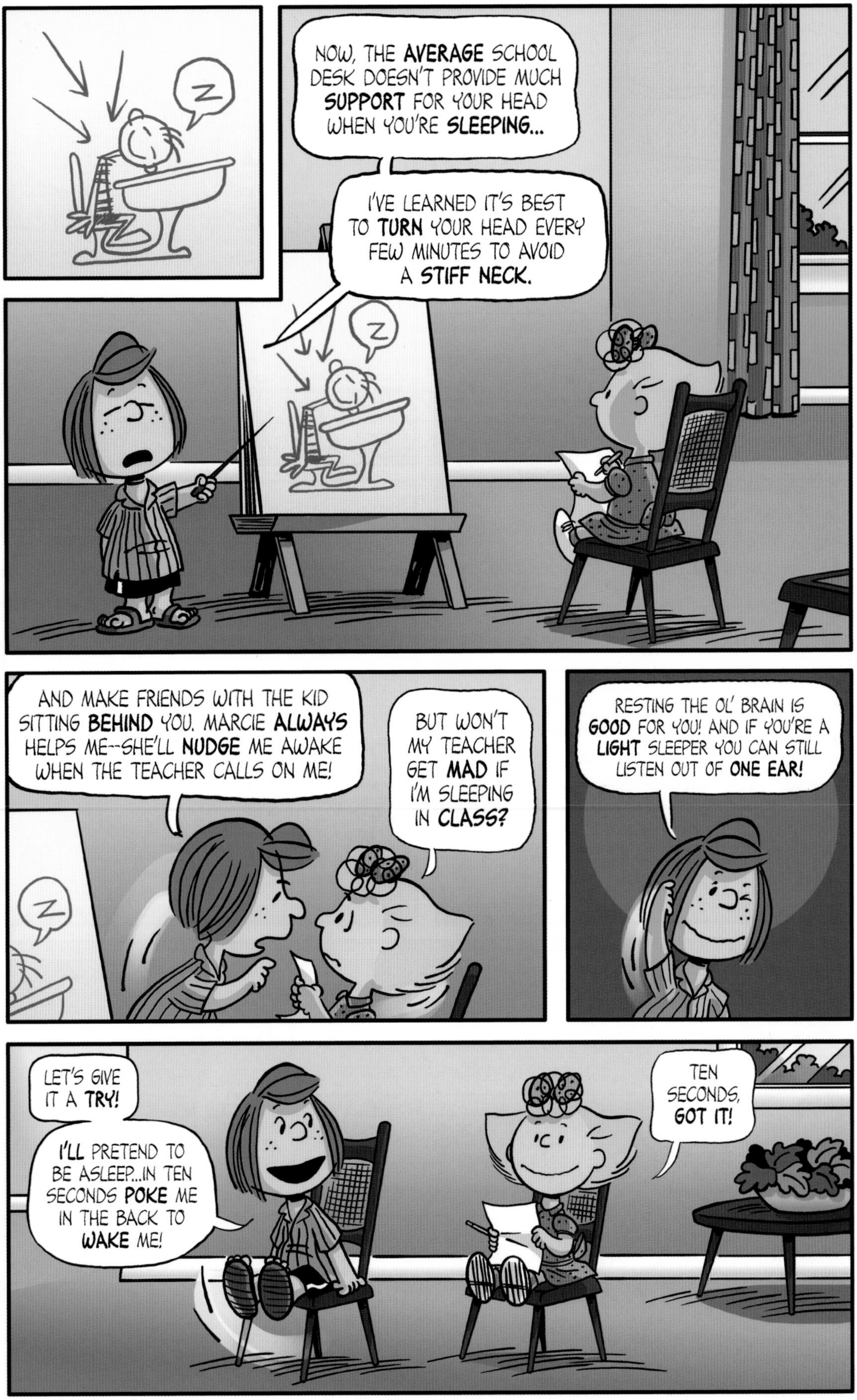
Z
NOW, THE AVERAGE SCHOOL DESK DOESN'T PROVIDE MUCH SUPPORT FOR YOUR HEAD WHEN YOU'RE SLEEPING...
I'VE LEARNED IT'S BEST TO TURN YOUR HEAD EVERY FEW MINUTES TO AVOID A STIFF NECK.
Z
AND MAKE FRIENDS WITH THE KID SITTING BEHIND YOU. MARCIE ALWAYS HELPS ME--SHE'LL NUDGE ME AWAKE WHEN THE TEACHER CALLS ON ME!
BUT WON'T MY TEACHER GET MAD IF I'M SLEEPING IN CLASS?
Z
RESTING THE OL' BRAIN IS GOOD FOR YOU! AND IF YOU'RE A LIGHT SLEEPER YOU CAN STILL LISTEN OUT OF ONE EAR!
LET'S GIVE IT A TRY!
I'LL PRETEND TO BE ASLEEP...IN TEN SECONDS POKE ME IN THE BACK TO WAKE ME!
TEN SECONDS, GOT IT!

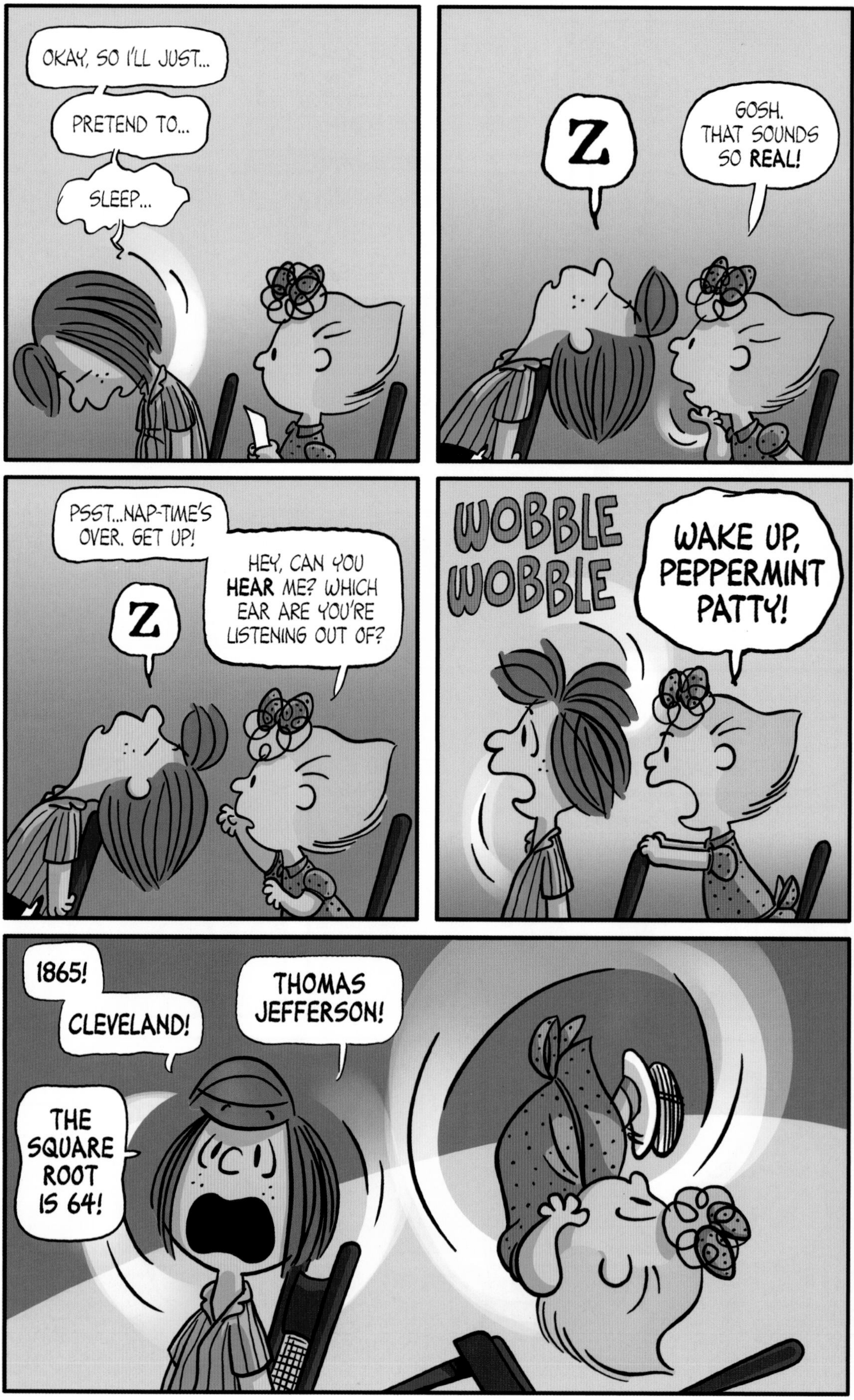
OKAY, SO I'LL JUST...
PRETEND TO...
SLEEP...
Z
GOSH. THAT SOUNDS SO REAL!
PSST...NAP-TIME'S OVER. GET UP!
Z
HEY, CAN YOU HEAR ME? WHICH EAR ARE YOU'RE LISTENING OUT OF?
WOBBLE WOBBLE
WAKE UP, PEPPERMINT PATTY!
1865!
CLEVELAND!
THOMAS JEFFERSON!
THE SQUARE ROOT IS 64!

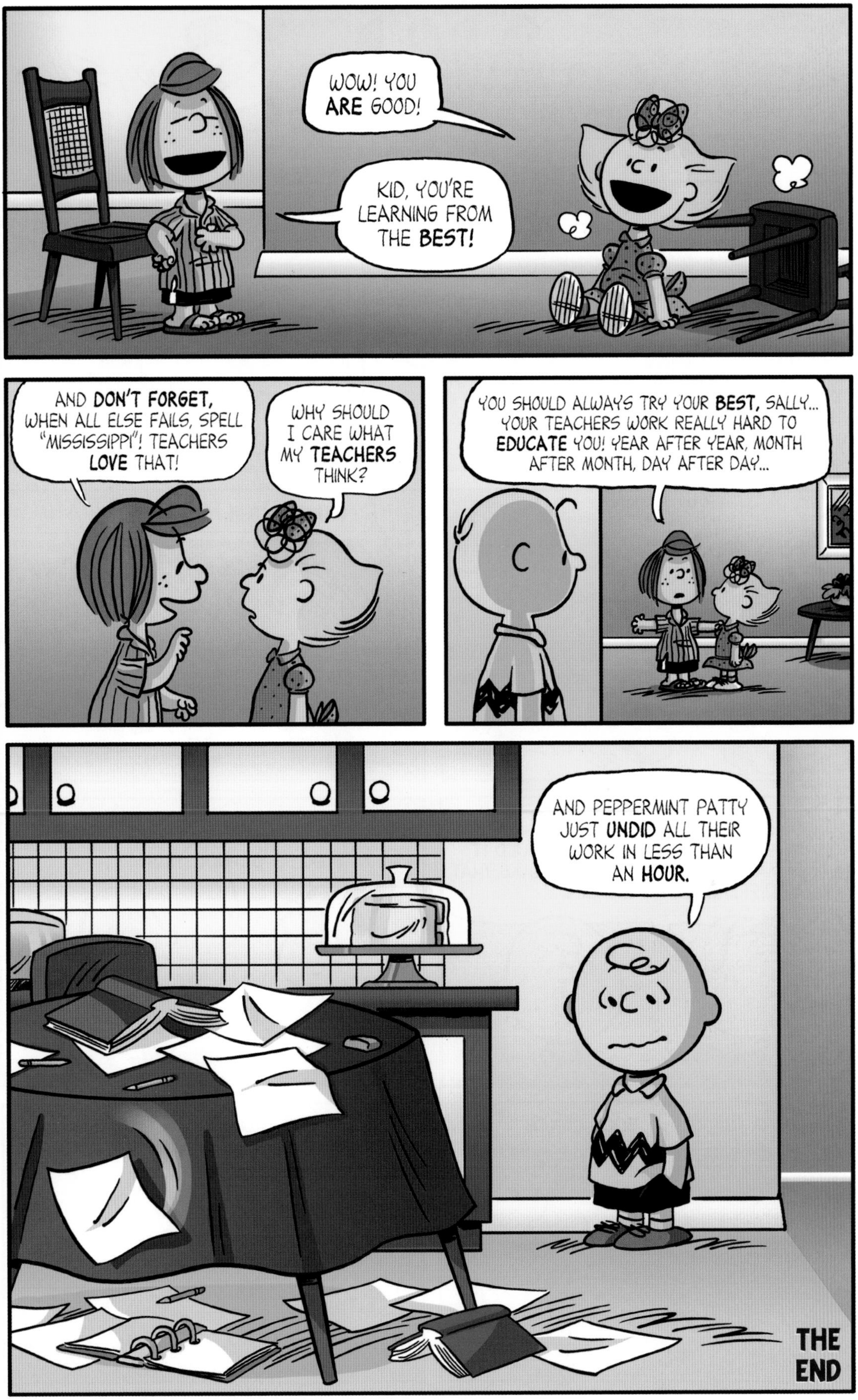
WOW! YOU **ARE** GOOD!
KID, YOU'RE LEARNING FROM THE **BEST!**
AND **DON'T FORGET,** WHEN ALL ELSE FAILS, SPELL "MISSISSIPPI"! TEACHERS **LOVE** THAT!
WHY SHOULD I CARE WHAT MY **TEACHERS** THINK?
YOU SHOULD ALWAYS TRY YOUR **BEST,** SALLY... YOUR TEACHERS WORK REALLY HARD TO **EDUCATE** YOU! YEAR AFTER YEAR, MONTH AFTER MONTH, DAY AFTER DAY...
AND PEPPERMINT PATTY JUST **UNDID** ALL THEIR WORK IN LESS THAN AN **HOUR.**
THE END

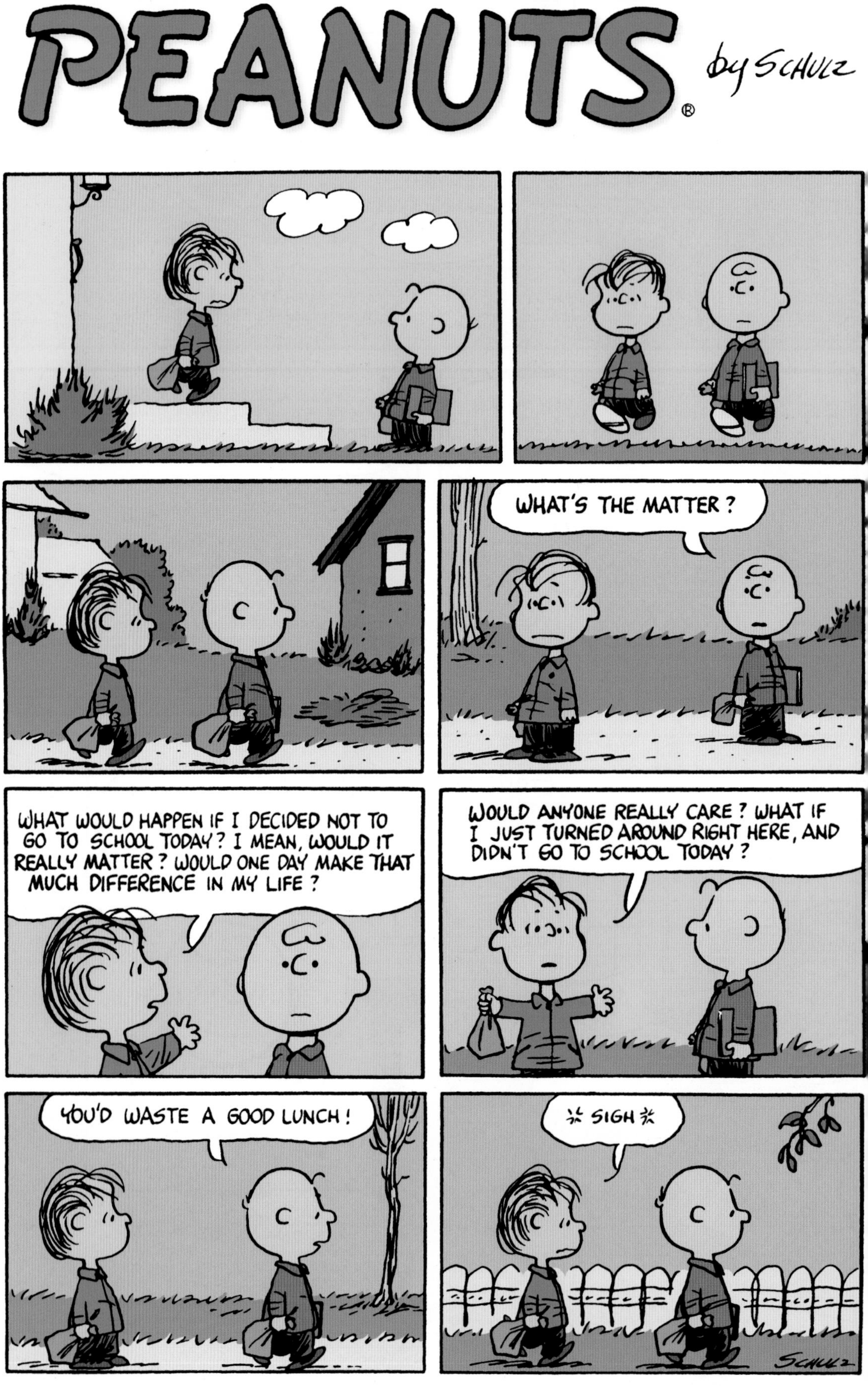
PEANUTS
by SCHULZ
WHAT'S THE MATTER?
WHAT WOULD HAPPEN IF I DECIDED NOT TO GO TO SCHOOL TODAY? I MEAN, WOULD IT REALLY MATTER? WOULD ONE DAY MAKE THAT MUCH DIFFERENCE IN MY LIFE?
WOULD ANYONE REALLY CARE? WHAT IF I JUST TURNED AROUND RIGHT HERE, AND DIDN'T GO TO SCHOOL TODAY?
YOU'D WASTE A GOOD LUNCH!
SIGH
SCHULZ

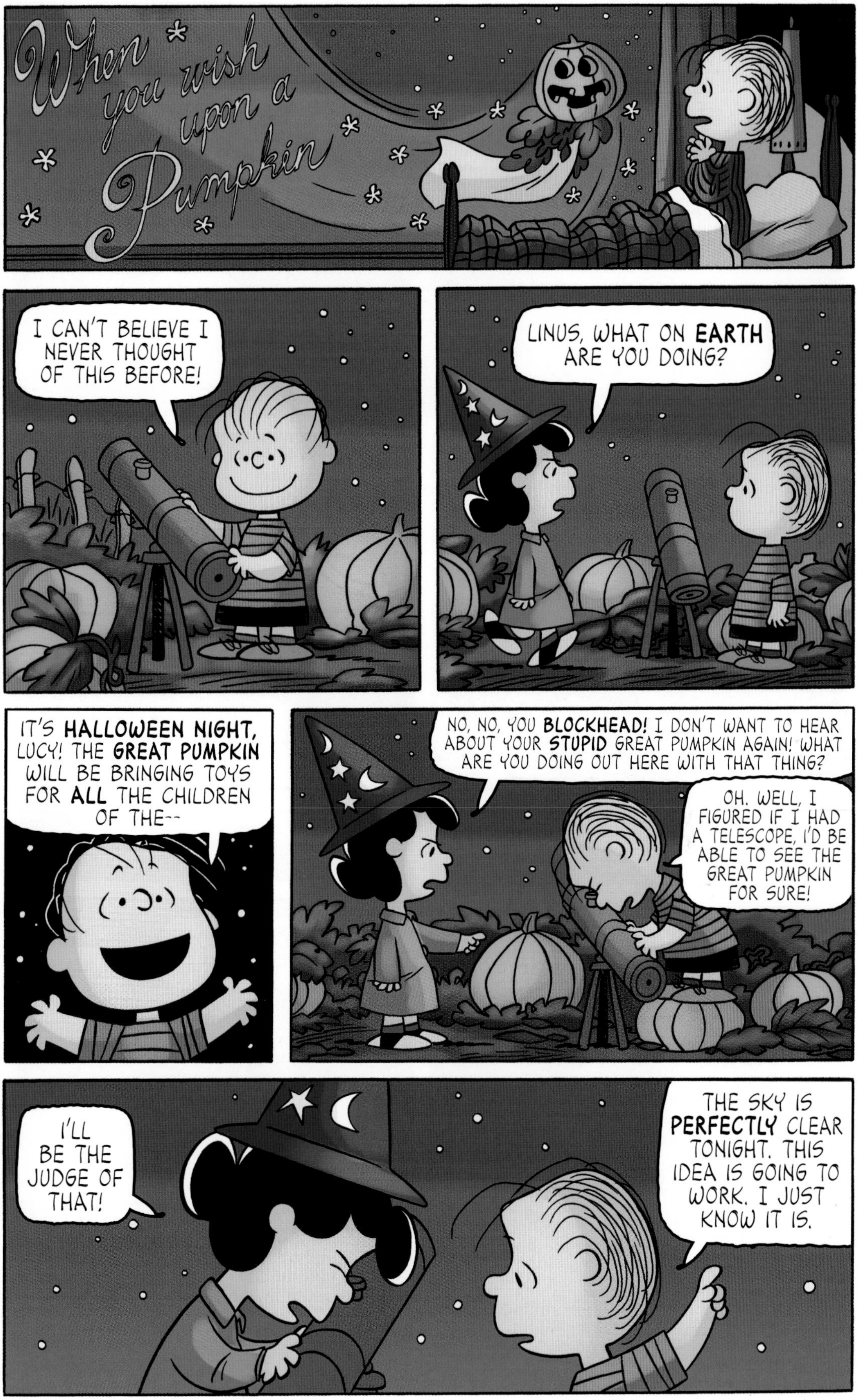
When you wish upon a Pumpkin
I CAN'T BELIEVE I NEVER THOUGHT OF THIS BEFORE!
LINUS, WHAT ON **EARTH** ARE YOU DOING?
IT'S **HALLOWEEN NIGHT,** LUCY! THE **GREAT PUMPKIN** WILL BE BRINGING TOYS FOR **ALL** THE CHILDREN OF THE--
NO, NO, YOU **BLOCKHEAD!** I DON'T WANT TO HEAR ABOUT YOUR **STUPID** GREAT PUMPKIN AGAIN! WHAT ARE YOU DOING OUT HERE WITH THAT THING?
OH. WELL, I FIGURED IF I HAD A TELESCOPE, I'D BE ABLE TO SEE THE GREAT PUMPKIN FOR SURE!
I'LL BE THE JUDGE OF THAT!
THE SKY IS **PERFECTLY** CLEAR TONIGHT. THIS IDEA IS GOING TO WORK. I JUST KNOW IT IS.

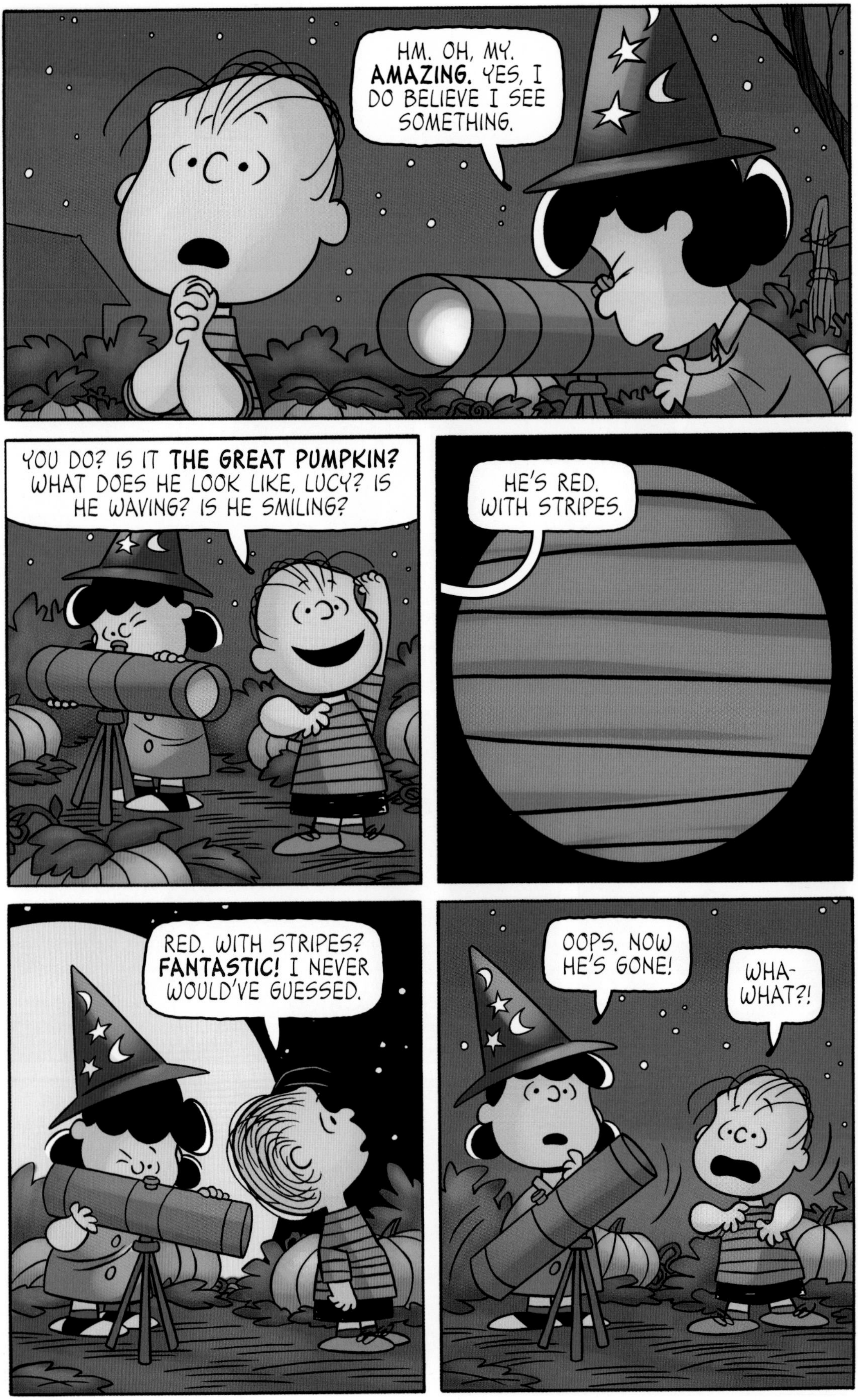
HM. OH, MY. **AMAZING.** YES, I DO BELIEVE I SEE SOMETHING.
YOU DO? IS IT **THE GREAT PUMPKIN?** WHAT DOES HE LOOK LIKE, LUCY? IS HE WAVING? IS HE SMILING?
HE'S RED. WITH STRIPES.
RED. WITH STRIPES? **FANTASTIC!** I NEVER WOULD'VE GUESSED.
OOPS. NOW HE'S GONE!
WHA-WHAT?!

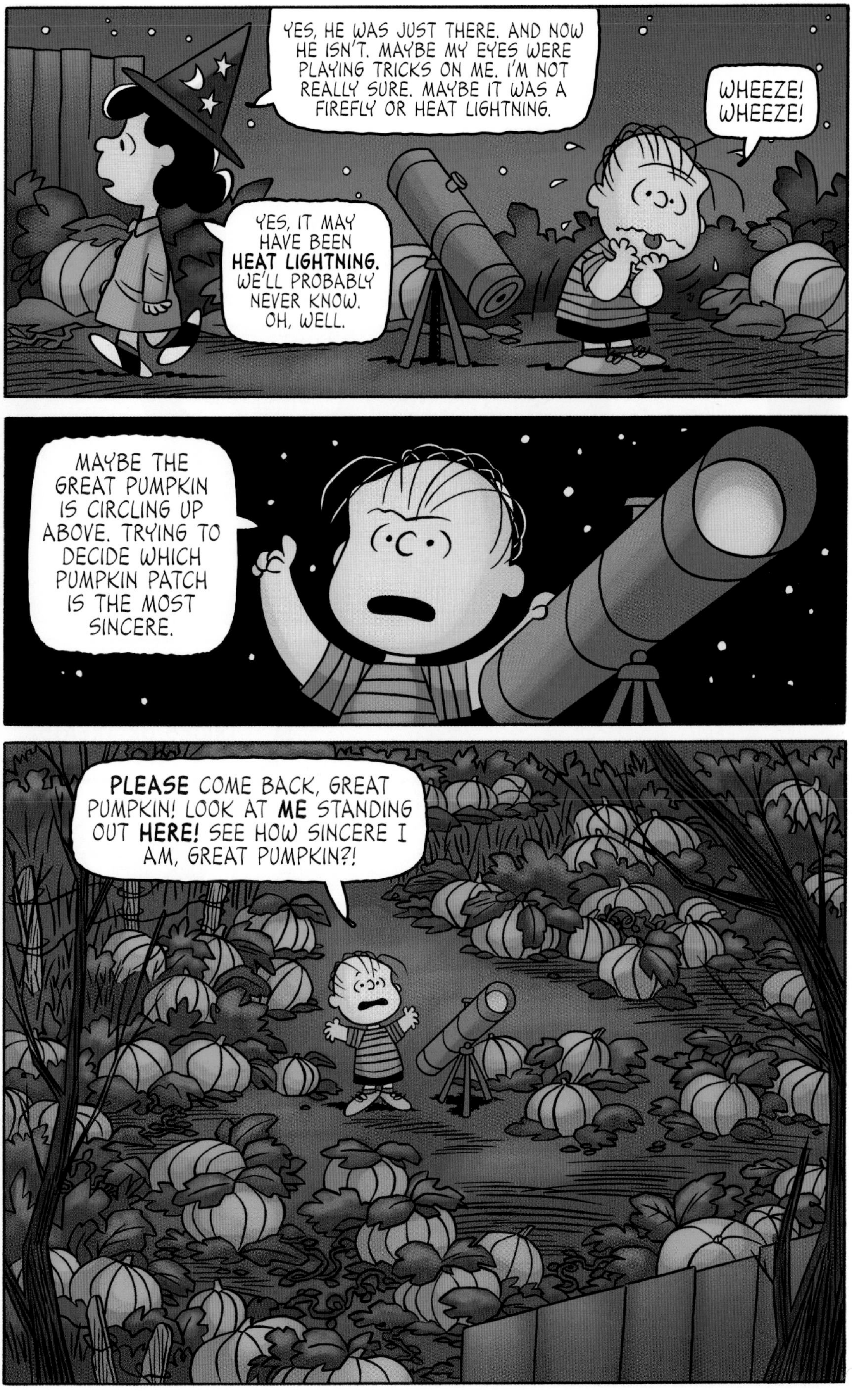
YES, HE WAS JUST THERE. AND NOW HE ISN'T. MAYBE MY EYES WERE PLAYING TRICKS ON ME. I'M NOT REALLY SURE. MAYBE IT WAS A FIREFLY OR HEAT LIGHTNING.
WHEEZE! WHEEZE!
YES, IT MAY HAVE BEEN **HEAT LIGHTNING.** WE'LL PROBABLY NEVER KNOW. OH, WELL.
MAYBE THE GREAT PUMPKIN IS CIRCLING UP ABOVE. TRYING TO DECIDE WHICH PUMPKIN PATCH IS THE MOST SINCERE.
PLEASE COME BACK, GREAT PUMPKIN! LOOK AT **ME** STANDING OUT **HERE!** SEE HOW SINCERE I AM, GREAT PUMPKIN?!

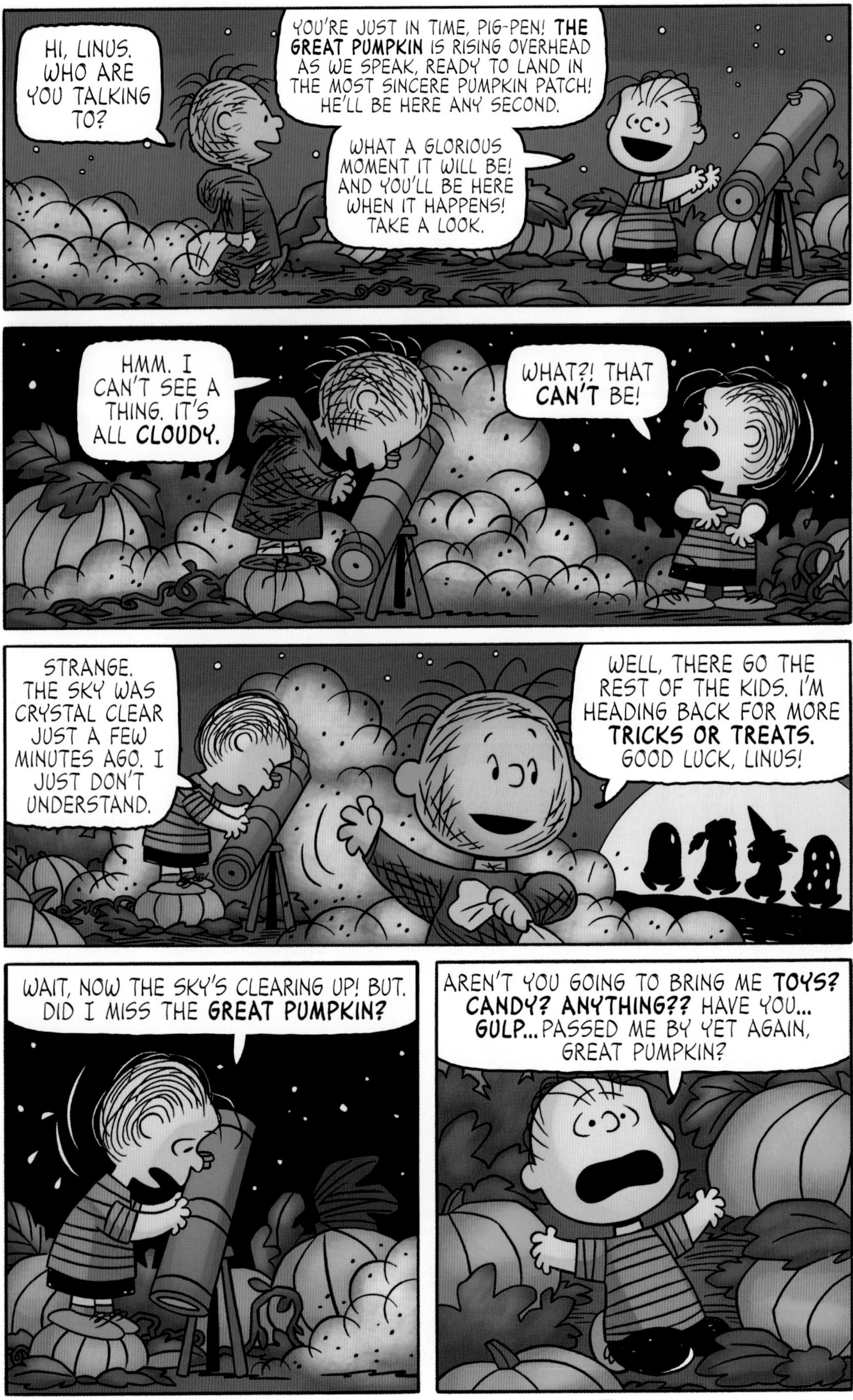
HI, LINUS. WHO ARE YOU TALKING TO?
YOU'RE JUST IN TIME, PIG-PEN! **THE GREAT PUMPKIN** IS RISING OVERHEAD AS WE SPEAK, READY TO LAND IN THE MOST SINCERE PUMPKIN PATCH! HE'LL BE HERE ANY SECOND.
WHAT A GLORIOUS MOMENT IT WILL BE! AND YOU'LL BE HERE WHEN IT HAPPENS! TAKE A LOOK.
HMM. I CAN'T SEE A THING. IT'S ALL **CLOUDY.**
WHAT?! THAT **CAN'T** BE!
STRANGE. THE SKY WAS CRYSTAL CLEAR JUST A FEW MINUTES AGO. I JUST DON'T UNDERSTAND.
WELL, THERE GO THE REST OF THE KIDS. I'M HEADING BACK FOR MORE **TRICKS OR TREATS.** GOOD LUCK, LINUS!
WAIT, NOW THE SKY'S CLEARING UP! BUT. DID I MISS THE **GREAT PUMPKIN?**
AREN'T YOU GOING TO BRING ME **TOYS? CANDY? ANYTHING??** HAVE YOU... **GULP...**PASSED ME BY YET AGAIN, GREAT PUMPKIN?

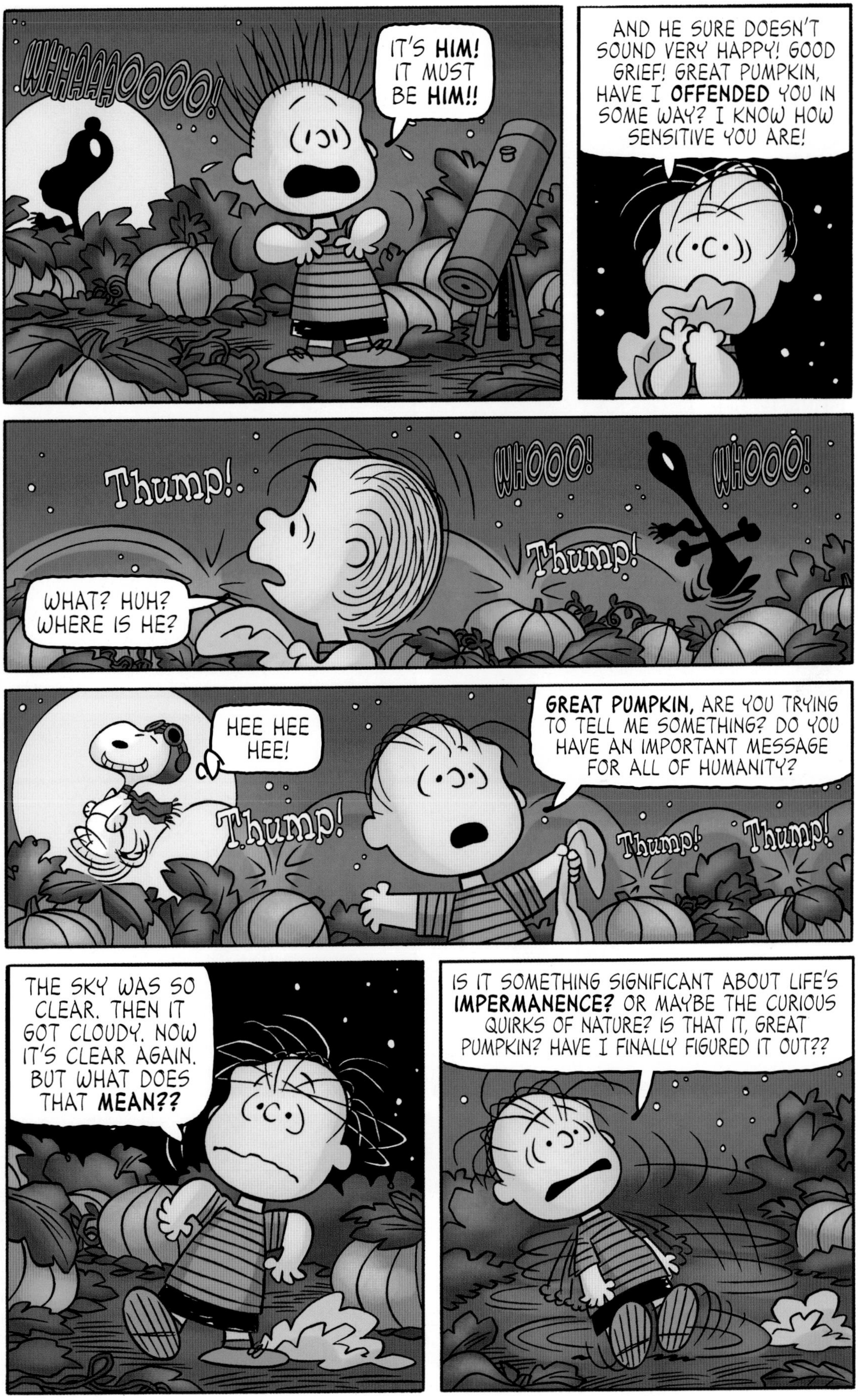
WHHAAAOOOO!
IT'S HIM! IT MUST BE HIM!!
AND HE SURE DOESN'T SOUND VERY HAPPY! GOOD GRIEF! GREAT PUMPKIN, HAVE I OFFENDED YOU IN SOME WAY? I KNOW HOW SENSITIVE YOU ARE!
Thump!
WHOOO!
WHOOO!
Thump!
WHAT? HUH? WHERE IS HE?
HEE HEE HEE!
GREAT PUMPKIN, ARE YOU TRYING TO TELL ME SOMETHING? DO YOU HAVE AN IMPORTANT MESSAGE FOR ALL OF HUMANITY?
Thump!
Thump!
Thump!
THE SKY WAS SO CLEAR. THEN IT GOT CLOUDY. NOW IT'S CLEAR AGAIN. BUT WHAT DOES THAT MEAN??
IS IT SOMETHING SIGNIFICANT ABOUT LIFE'S IMPERMANENCE? OR MAYBE THE CURIOUS QUIRKS OF NATURE? IS THAT IT, GREAT PUMPKIN? HAVE I FINALLY FIGURED IT OUT??

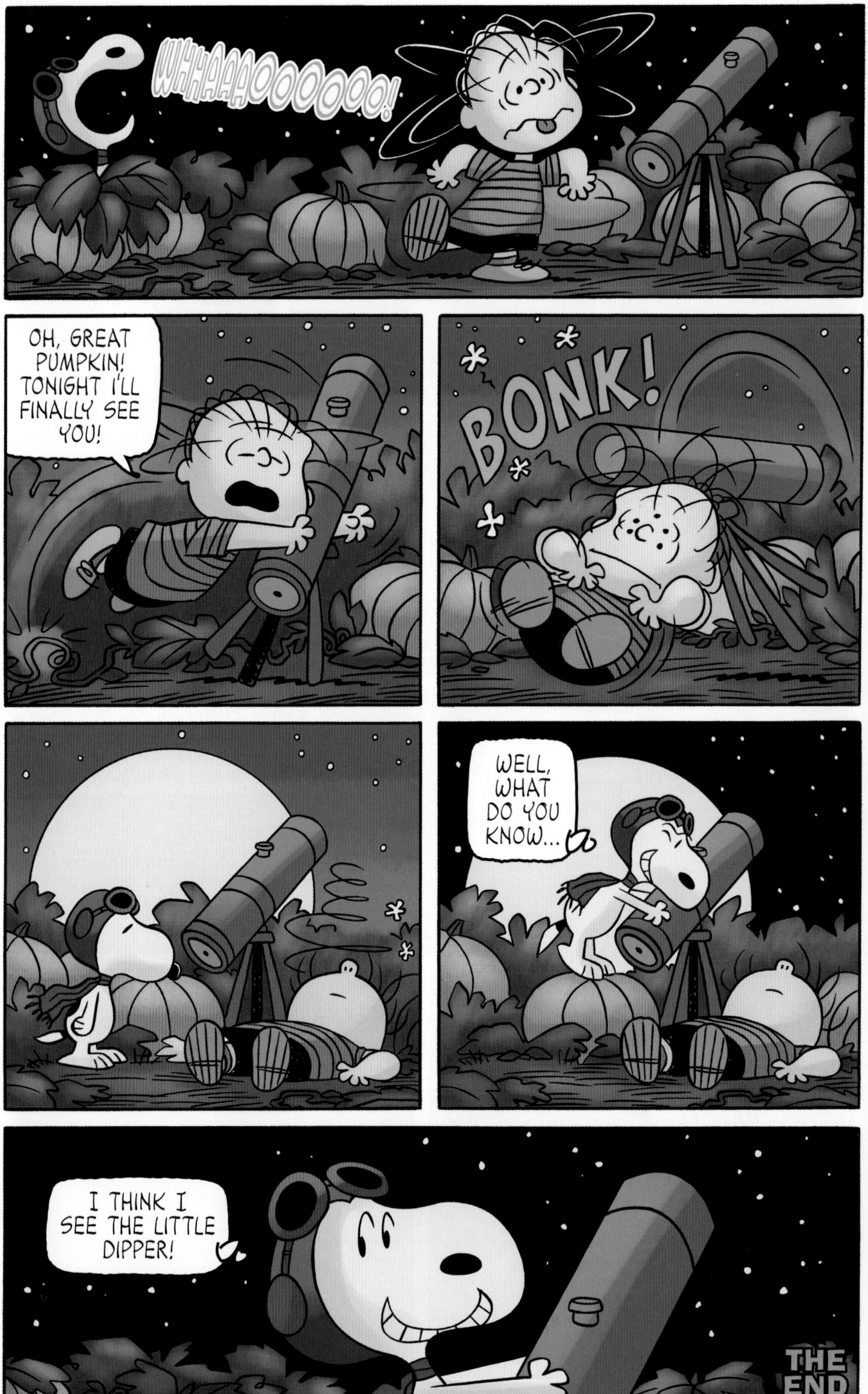
WHHAAAOOOOOOO!
OH, GREAT PUMPKIN! TONIGHT I'LL FINALLY SEE YOU!
BONK!
WELL, WHAT DO YOU KNOW...
I THINK I SEE THE LITTLE DIPPER!
THE END

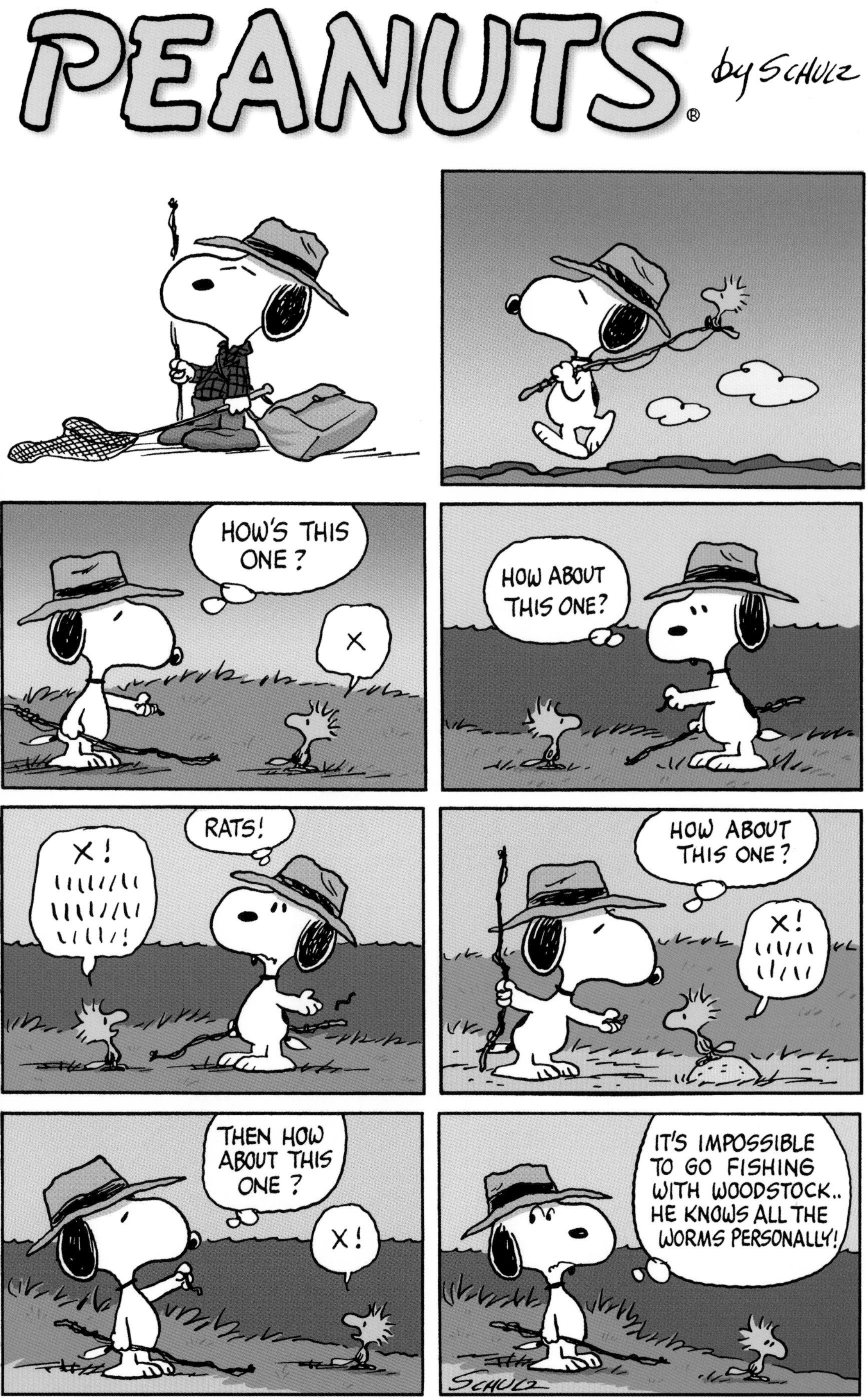
PEANUTS
by SCHULZ
HOW'S THIS ONE ?
X
HOW ABOUT THIS ONE?
RATS!
X !
HOW ABOUT THIS ONE ?
X !
THEN HOW ABOUT THIS ONE ?
X !
IT'S IMPOSSIBLE TO GO FISHING WITH WOODSTOCK.. HE KNOWS ALL THE WORMS PERSONALLY!
SCHULZ

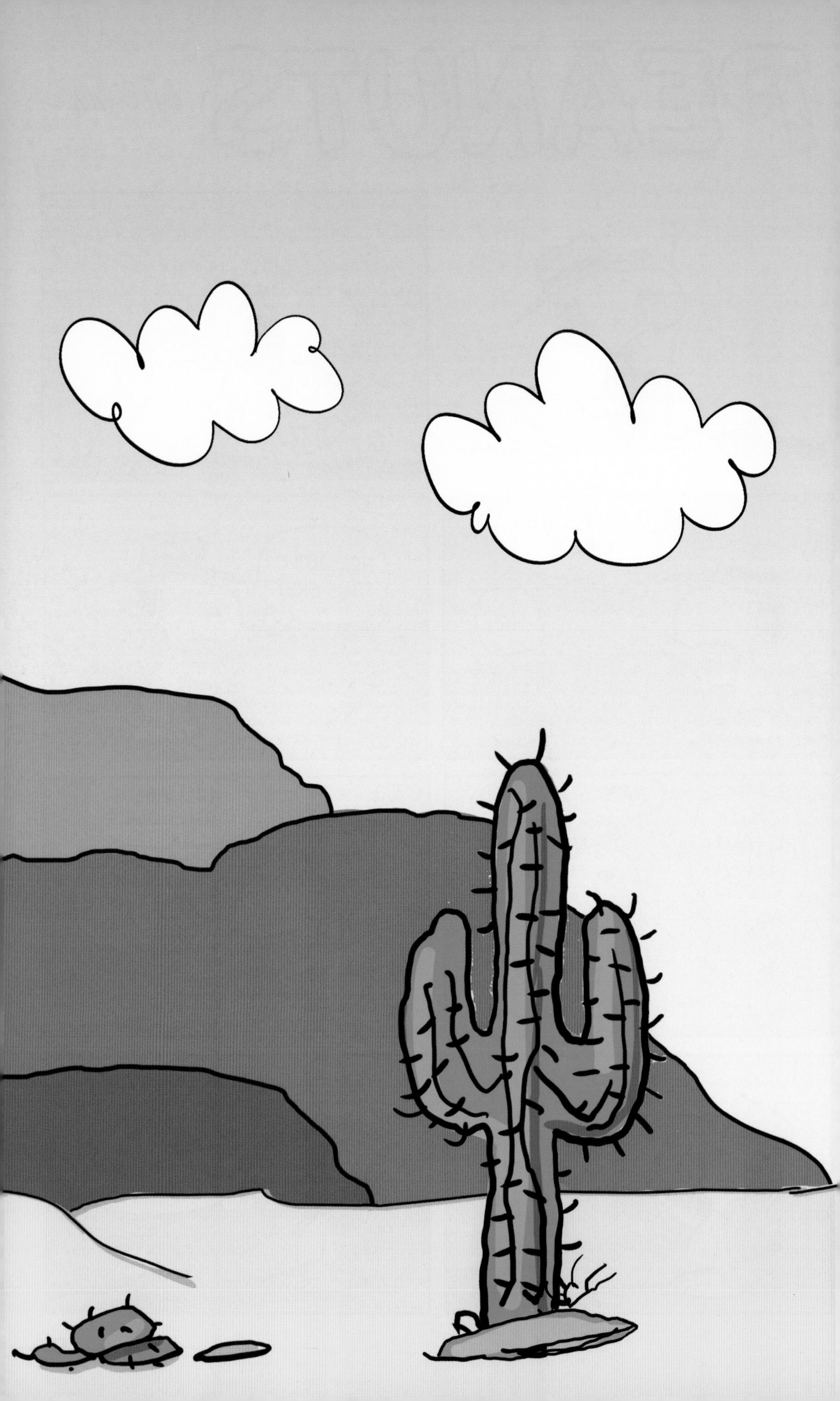

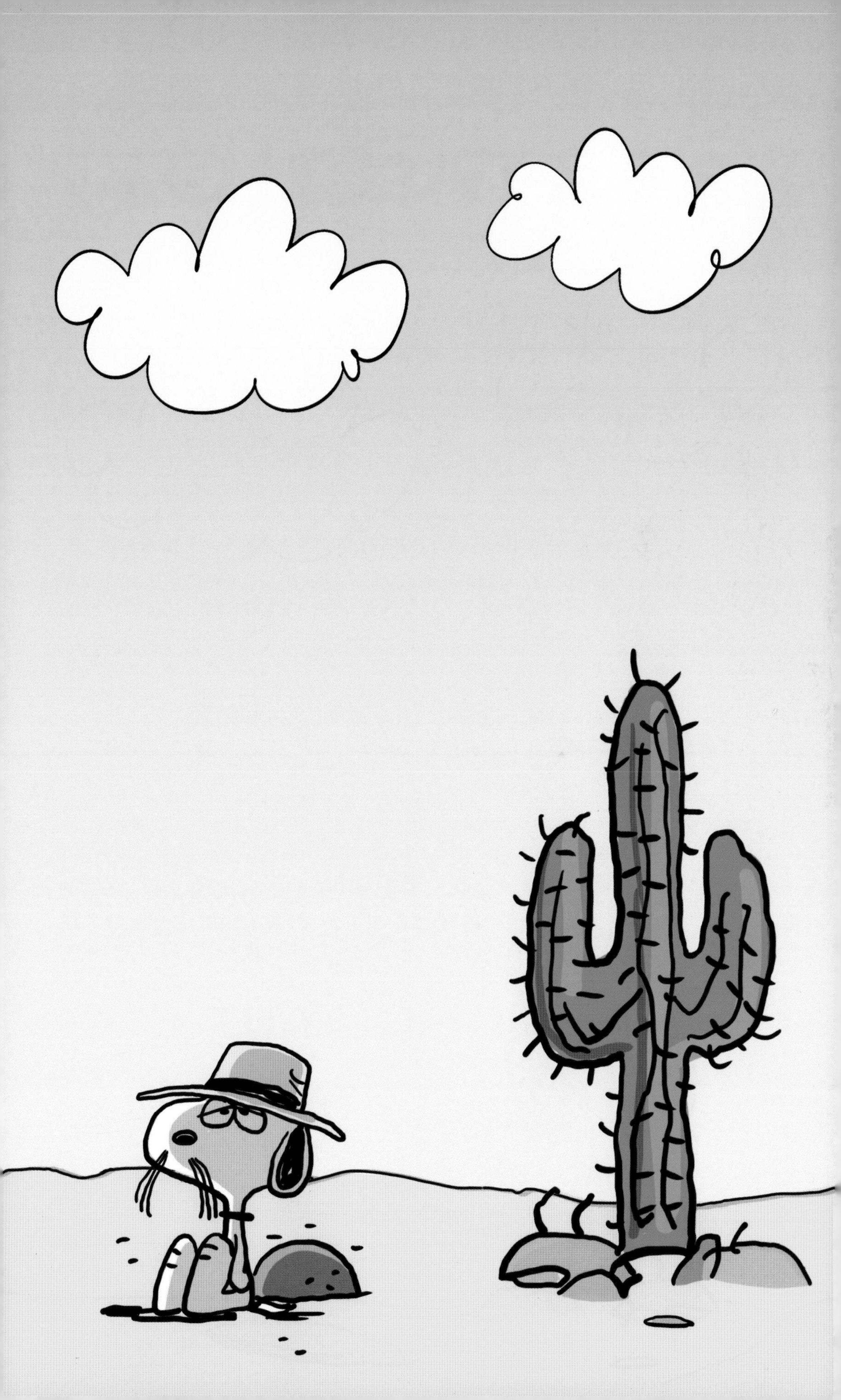

Cover Gallery

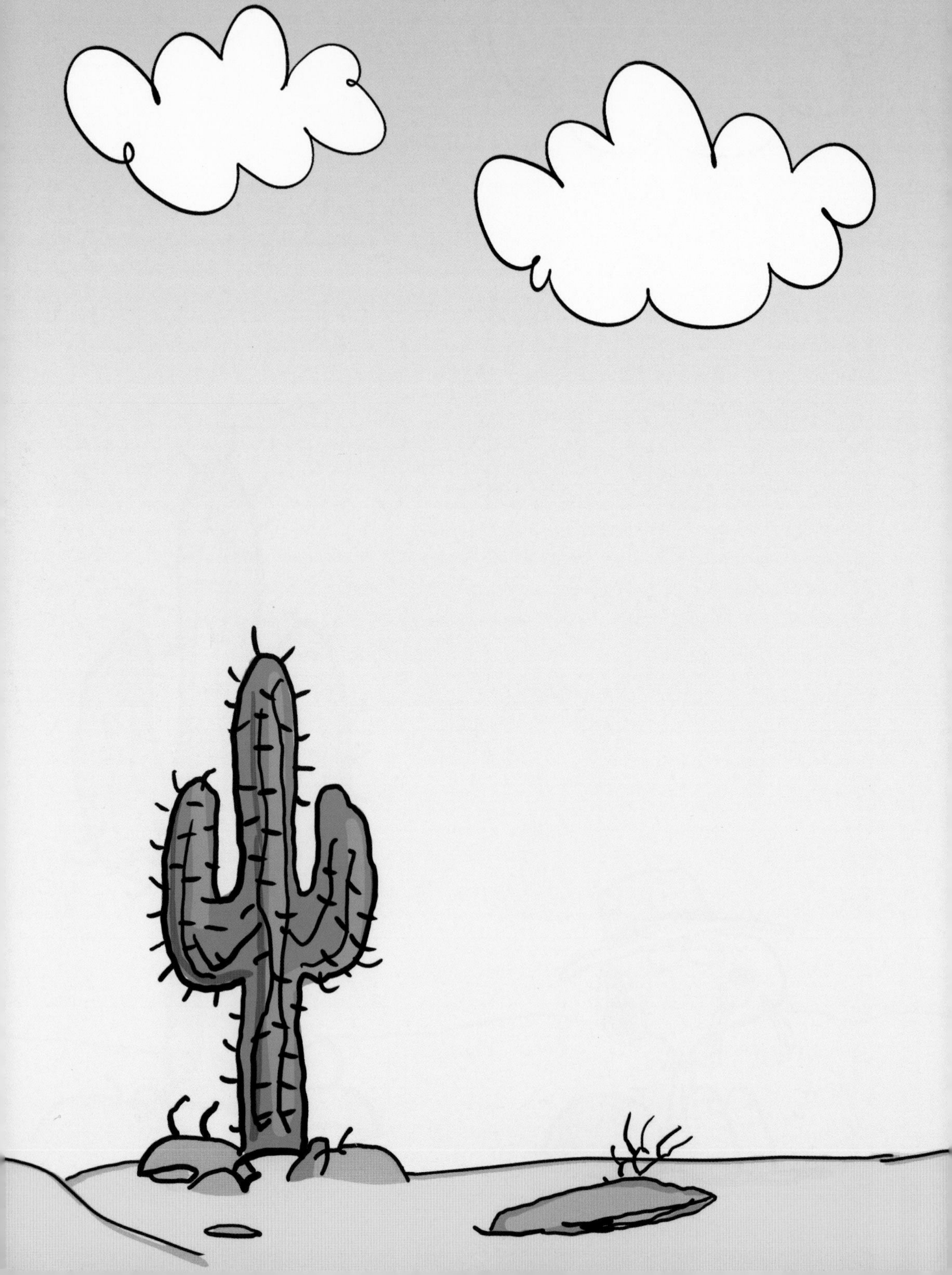

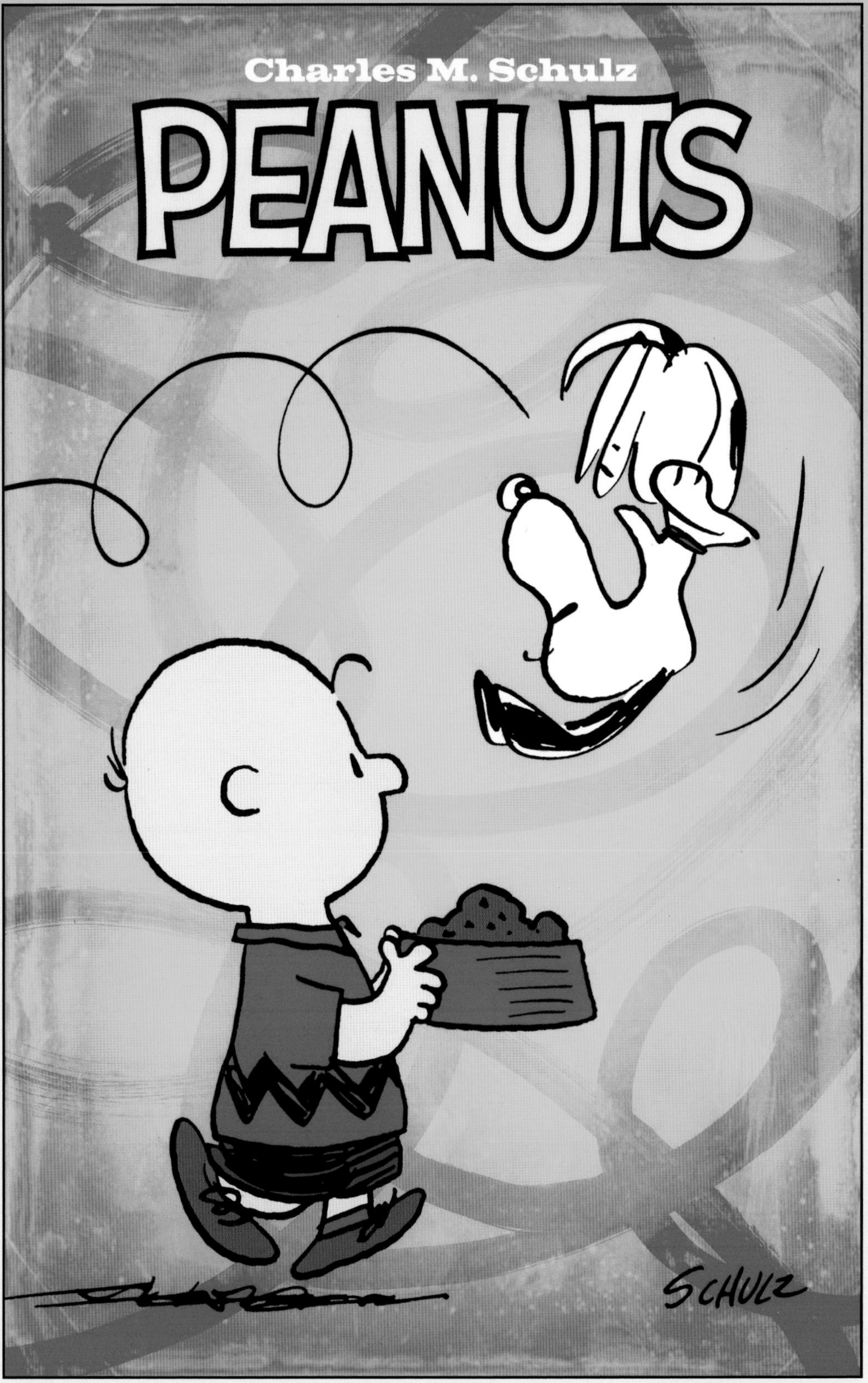
Charles M. Schulz
PEANUTS
SCHULZ

By Charles M. Schulz
Design by Iain R. Morris

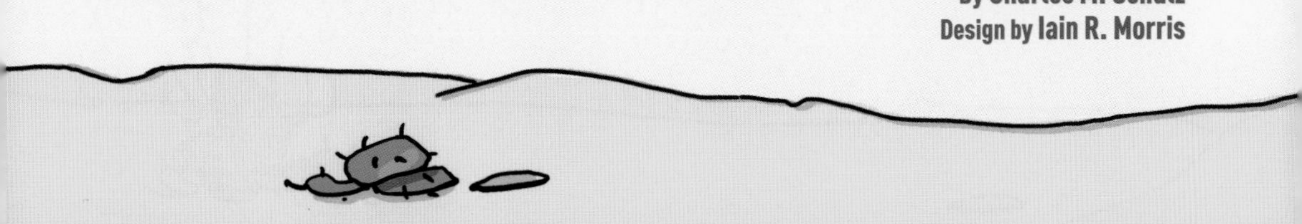

Peanuts #9 SDCC Exclusive

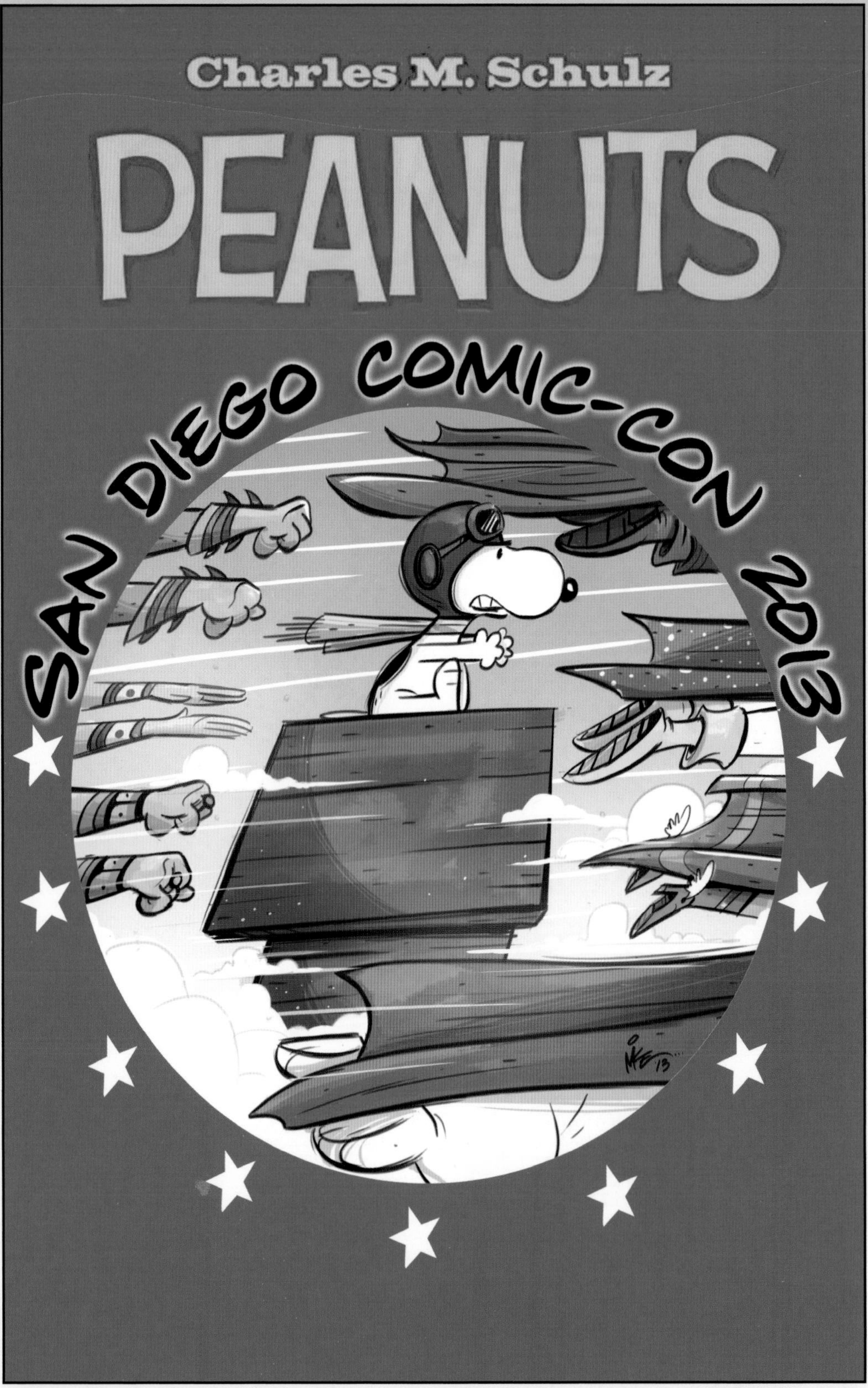
Charles M. Schulz
PEANUTS
SAN DIEGO COMIC-CON 2013

By Mike Kunkel

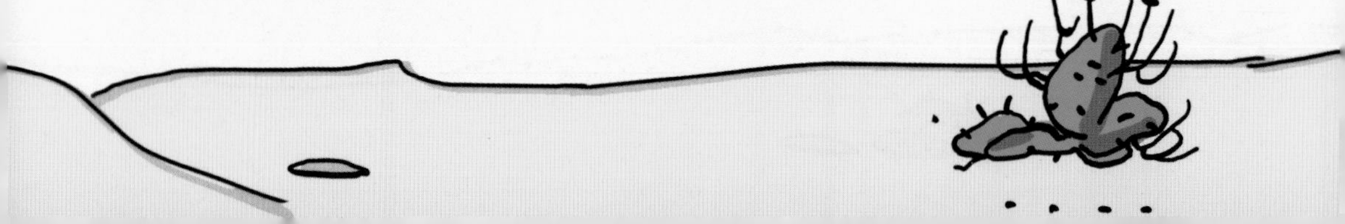

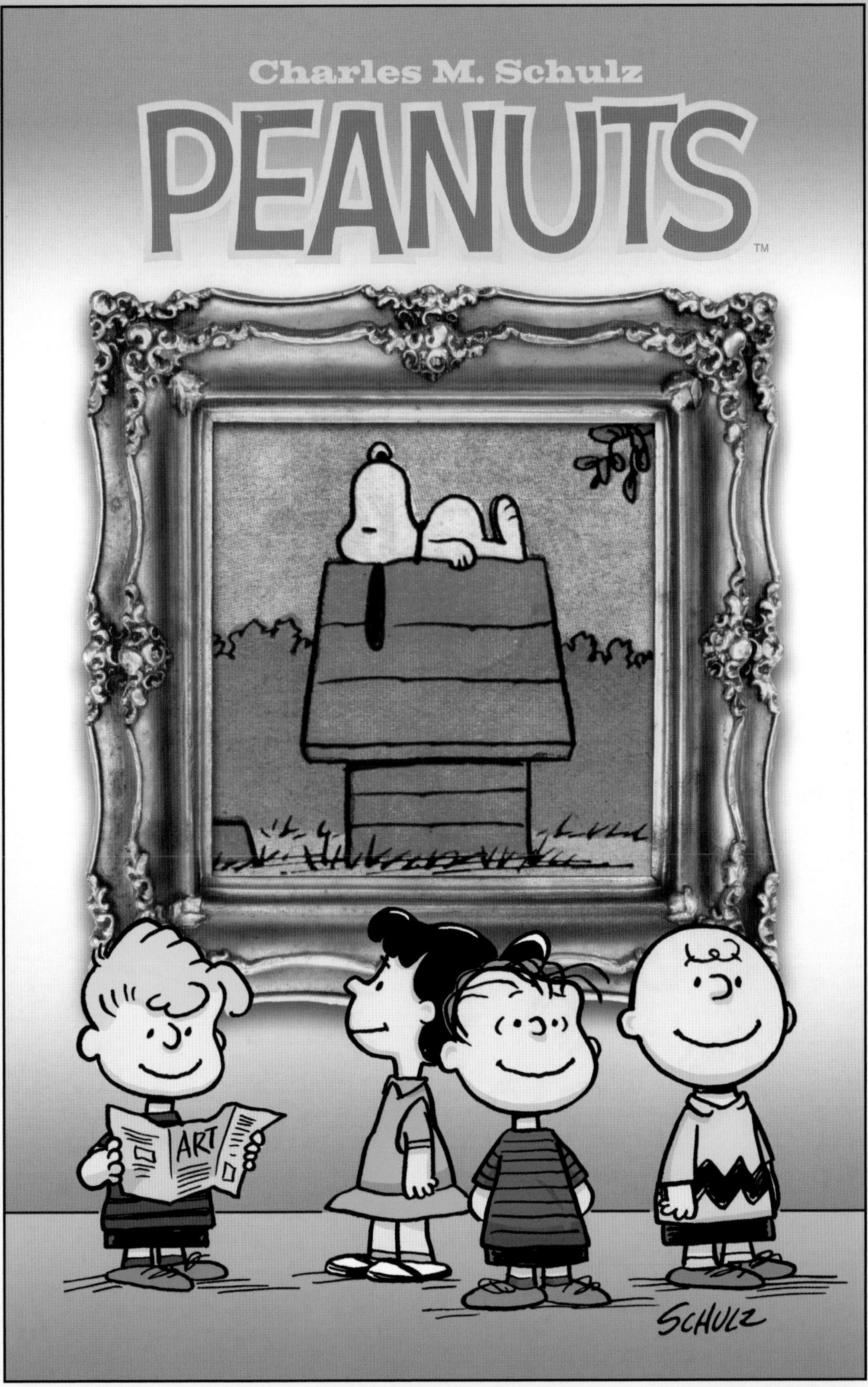
Charles M. Schulz
PEANUTS
TM
ART
SCHULZ

Pencils by Vicki Scott
Inks by Paige Braddock
Colors by Art Roche
Design by Iain R. Morris

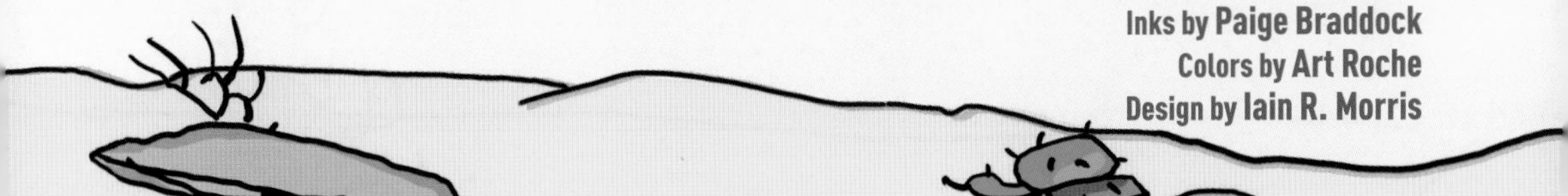

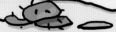

Peanuts #11

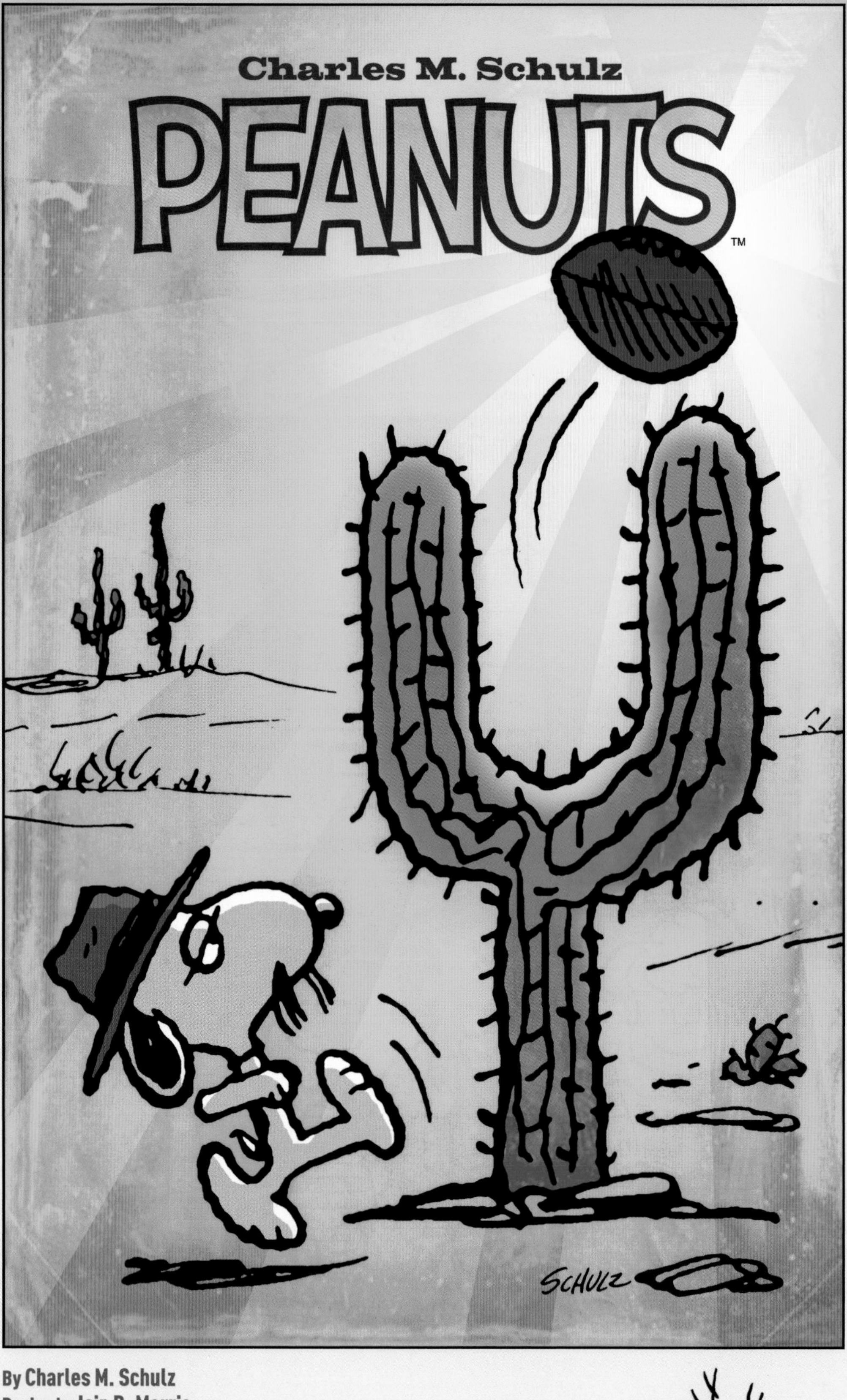

Charles M. Schulz
PEANUTS
TM
SCHULZ

By Charles M. Schulz
Design by Iain R. Morris

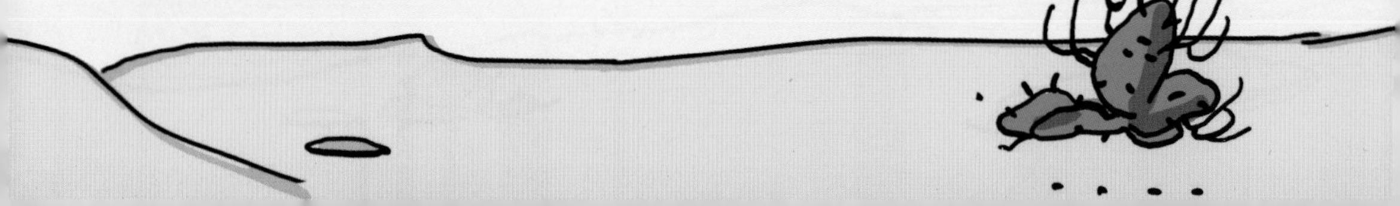

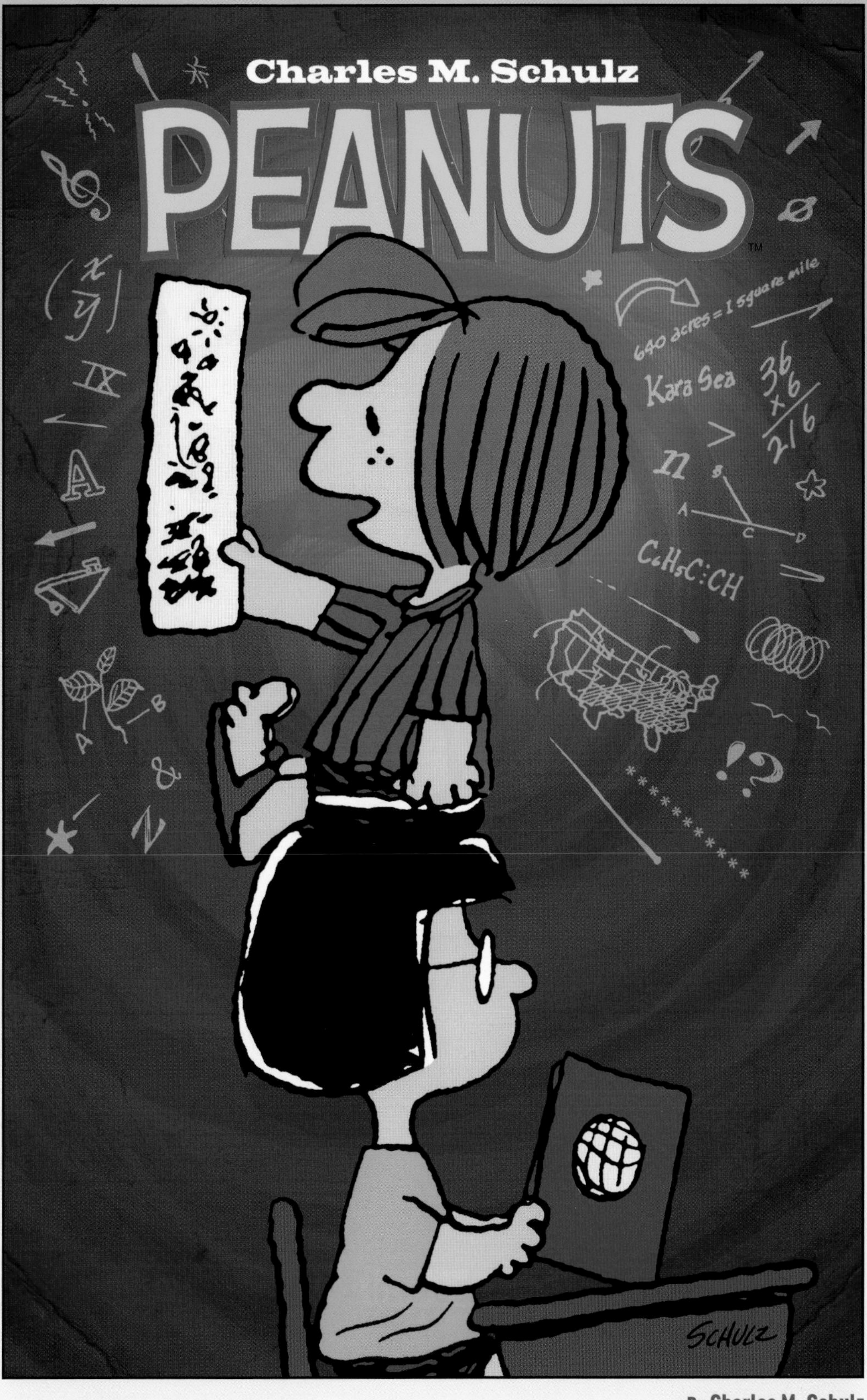

Charles M. Schulz
PEANUTS
™
640 acres = 1 square mile
Kara Sea
36
x6
216
C6H5C:CH
SCHULZ

By Charles M. Schulz
Design by Iain R. Morris

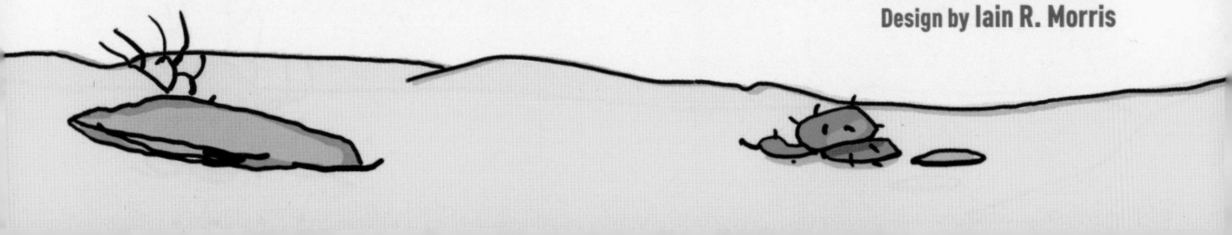

Peanuts #9 Beagle Scout
First Appearance

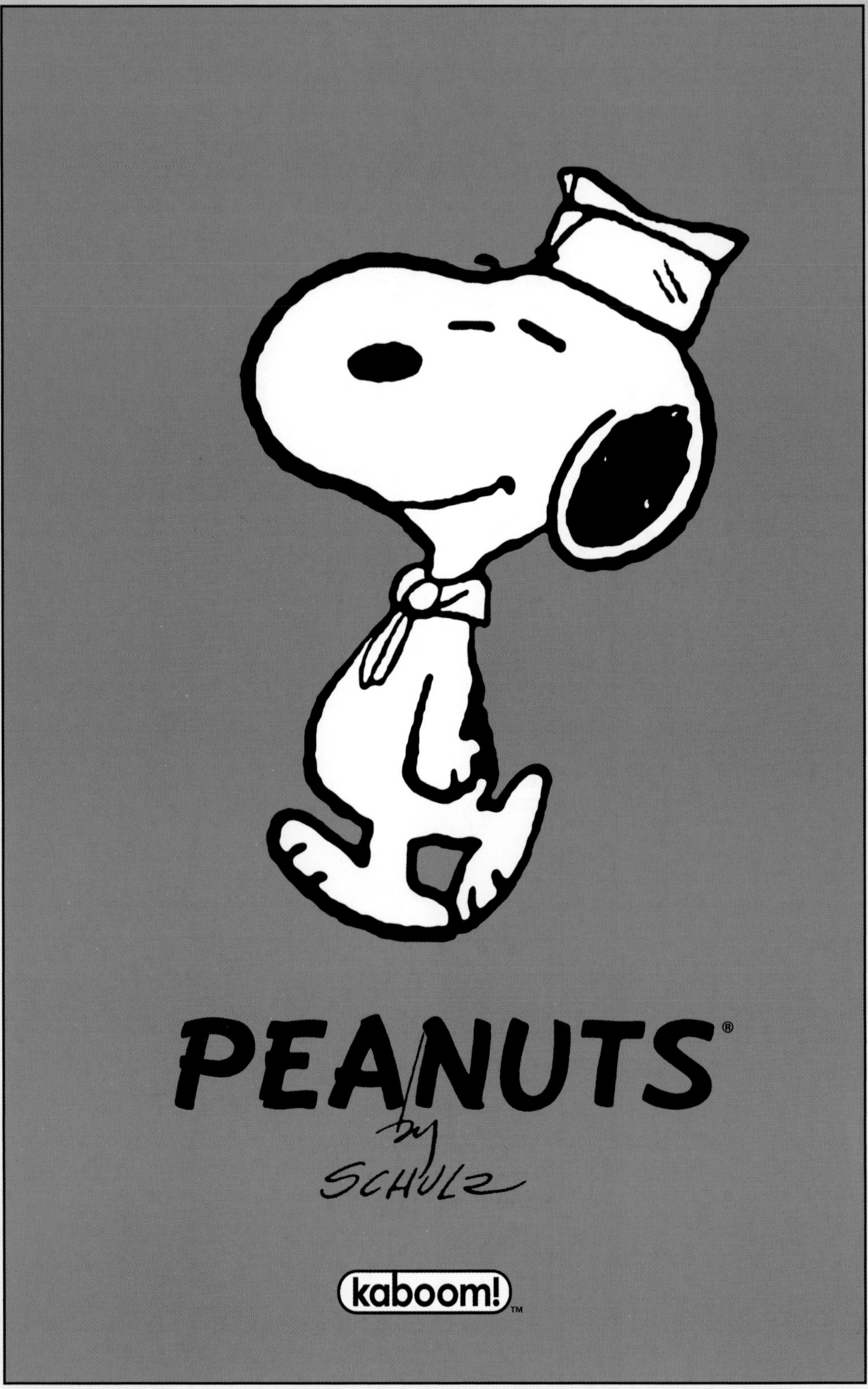
PEANUTS®
by SCHULZ
kaboom!™

By Charles M. Schulz
Design by Emily Chang

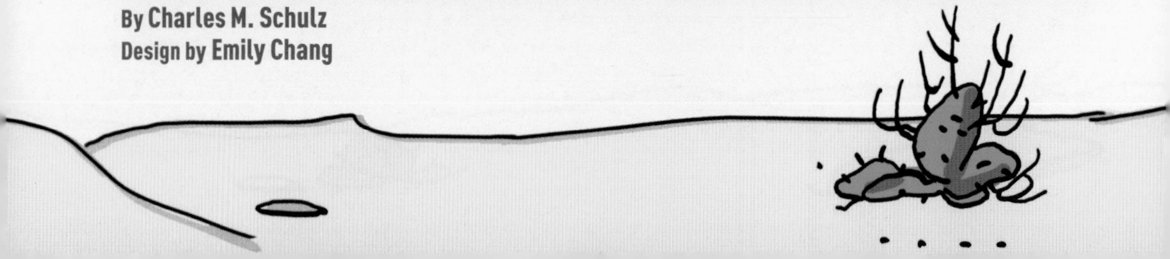

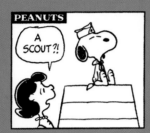

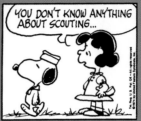

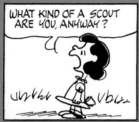

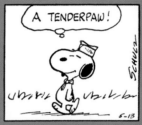

PEANUTS

by SCHULZ

PEANUTS
A SCOUT?!
YOU DON'T KNOW ANYTHING ABOUT SCOUTING...
WHAT KIND OF A SCOUT ARE YOU, ANYWAY?
A TENDERPAW!
SCHULZ
5-13

BEAGLE SCOUT

FIRST APPEARANCE

MAY 13, 1974

kaboom!™

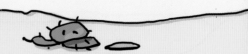

SELECT SERIES IV

ISSUE NINE

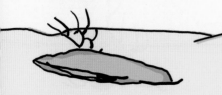

Peanuts #10 Violet
First Appearance

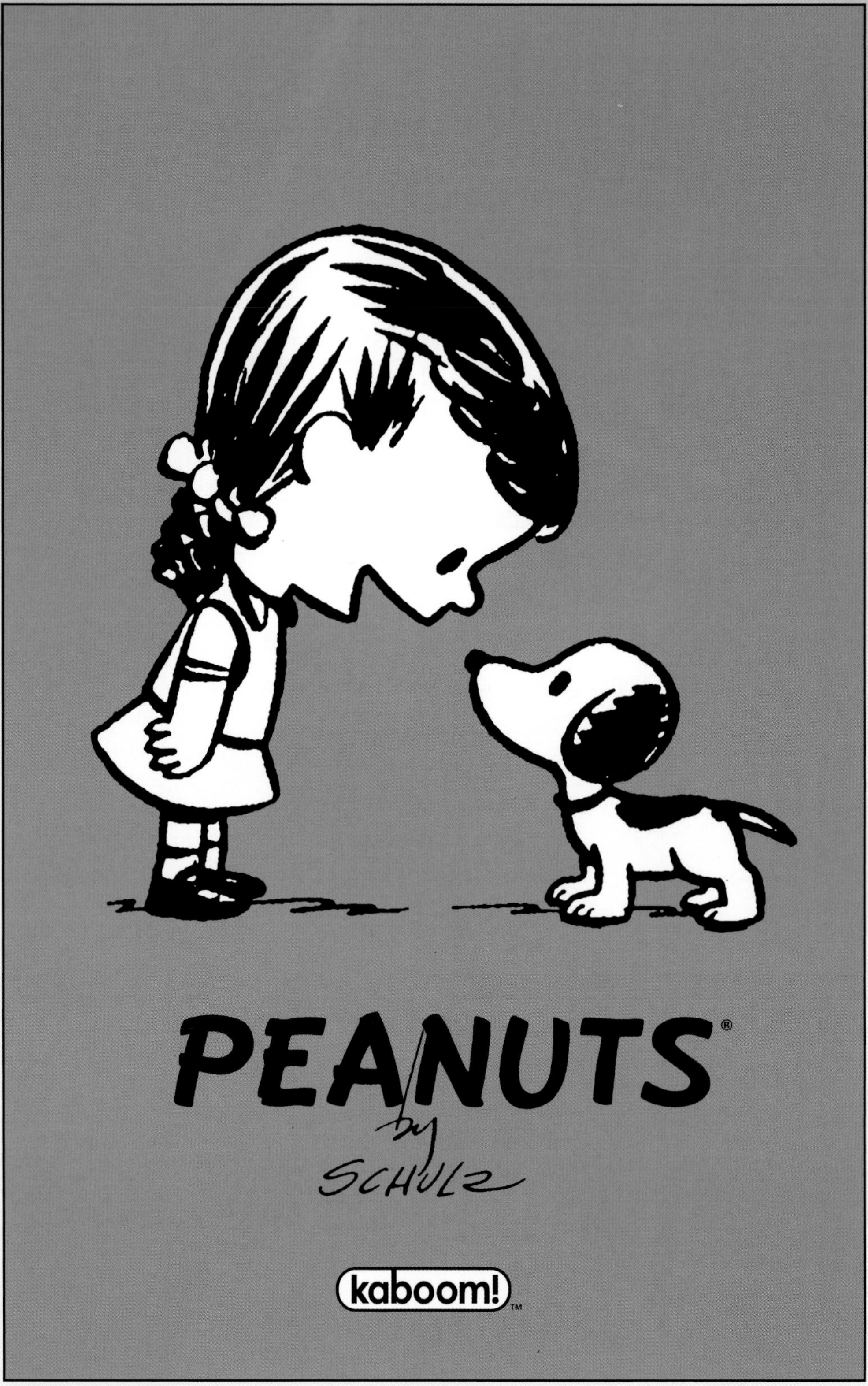
PEANUTS®
by
SCHULZ
kaboom!™

By Charles M. Schulz
Design by Emily Chang

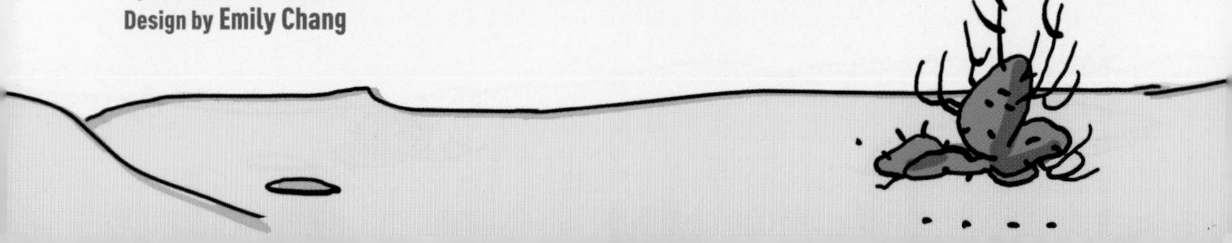

PEANUTS
by
SCHULZ

"PEANUTS"
WELL, HELLO, THERE!
?
YOU DON'T KNOW ME, DO YOU? MY NAME IS "VIOLET"
AHEM
YOU'RE REAL CUTE...
AHEM!!
WELL, WHY DIDN'T YOU INTRODUCE ME?!
2-7
SCHULZ

VIOLET
FIRST APPEARANCE
FEBRUARY 7, 1951

kaboom!™

SELECT SERIES IV
ISSUE TEN

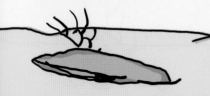

Peanuts #11 Spike
First Appearance

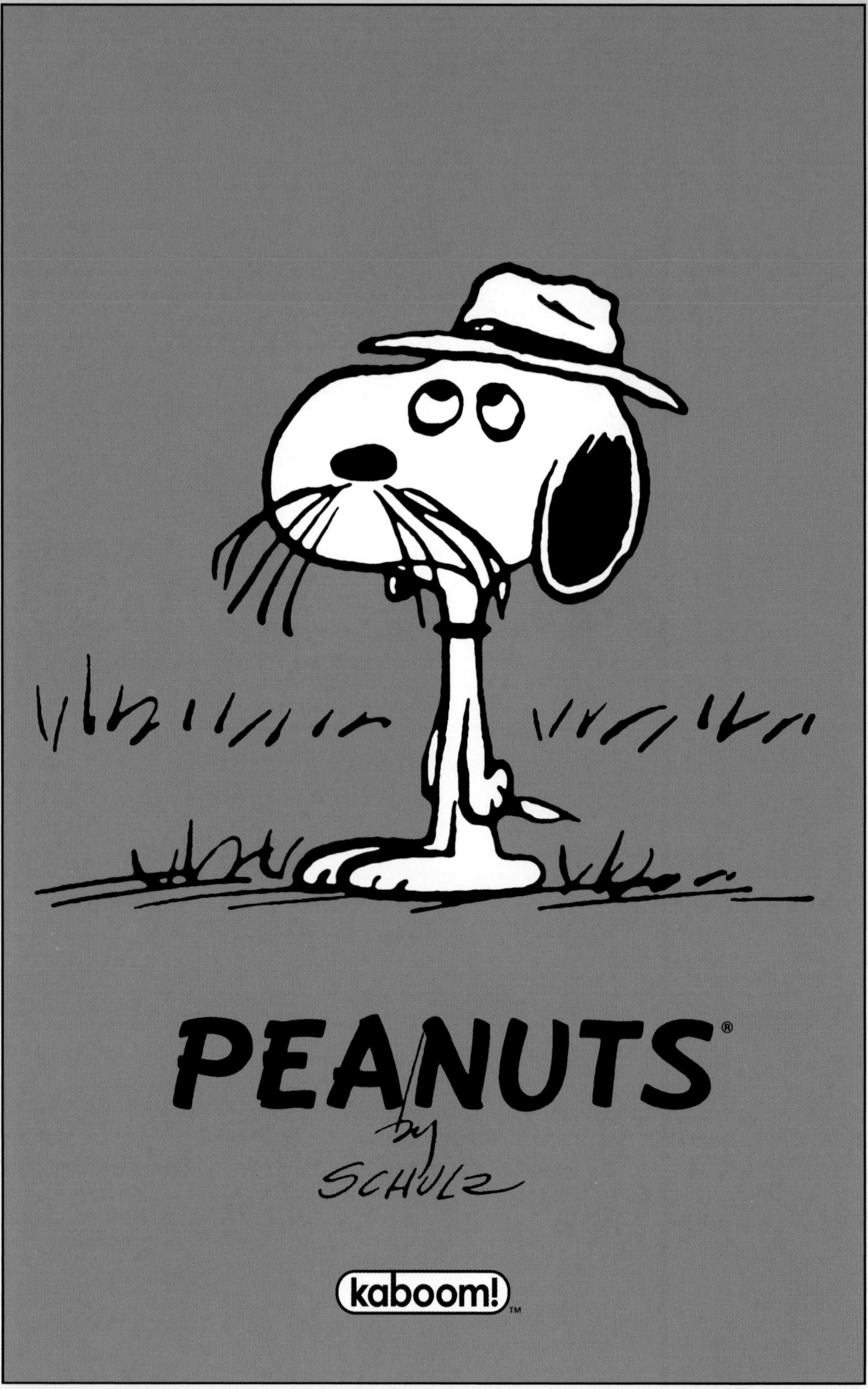
PEANUTS®
by
SCHULZ
kaboom!™

By Charles M. Schulz
Design by Emily Chang

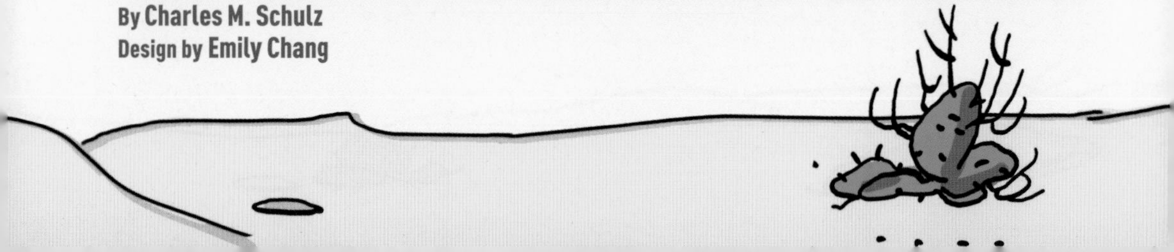

PEANUTS

by SCHULZ

MY BROTHER HAS ARISEN!
EGGS BENEDICT FOR MY BROTHER, SPIKE!
8-13
I THINK YOU'D BETTER MAKE THAT TEN POUNDS OF BUFFALO STEAK...
SCHULZ

SPIKE

FIRST APPEARANCE

AUGUST 13, 1975

kaboom!™

SELECT SERIES IV

ISSUE ELEVEN

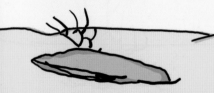

Peanuts #12 Joe Cool
First Appearance

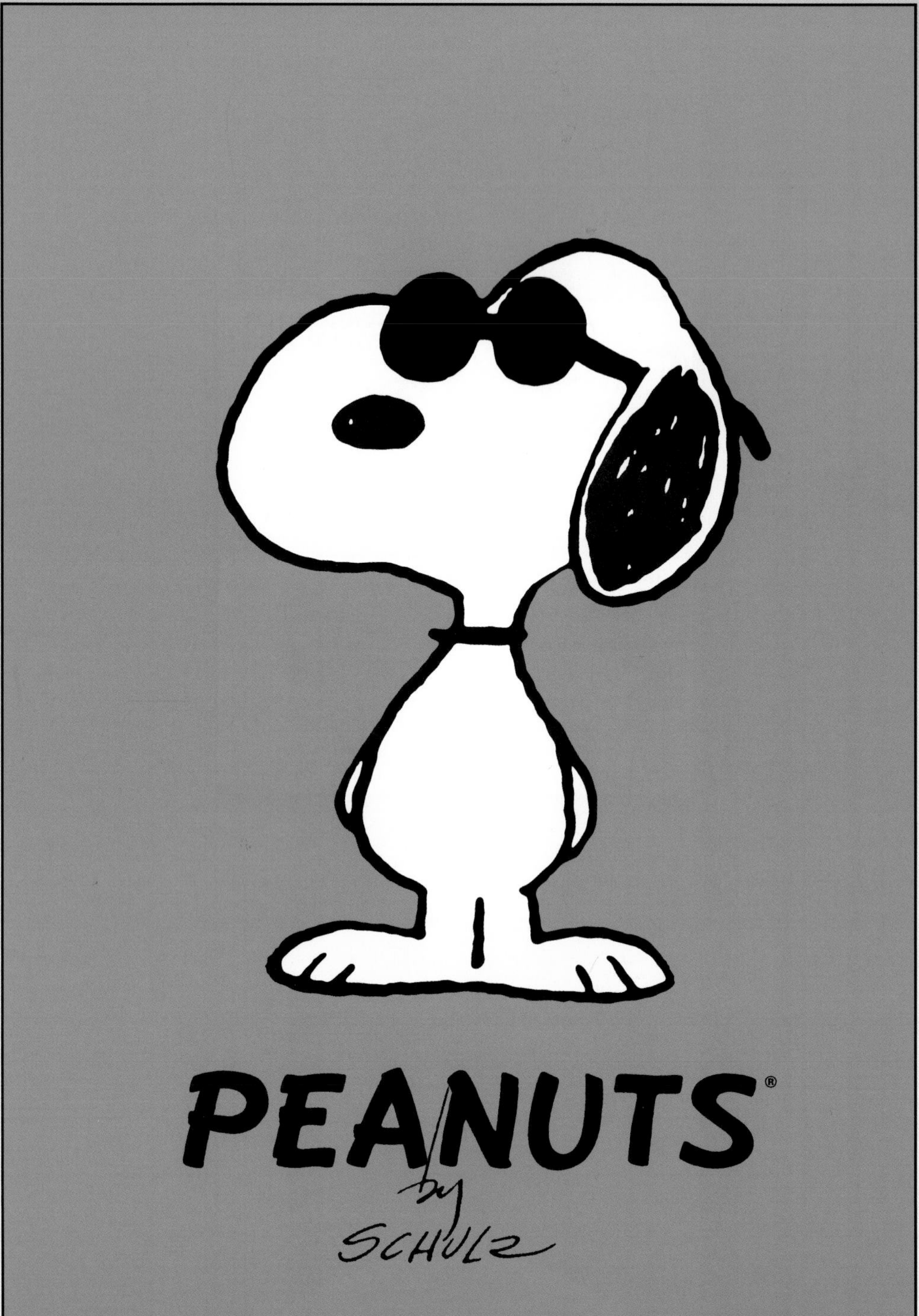
PEANUTS®
by
SCHULZ
kaboom!™

By Charles M. Schulz
Design by Emily Chang

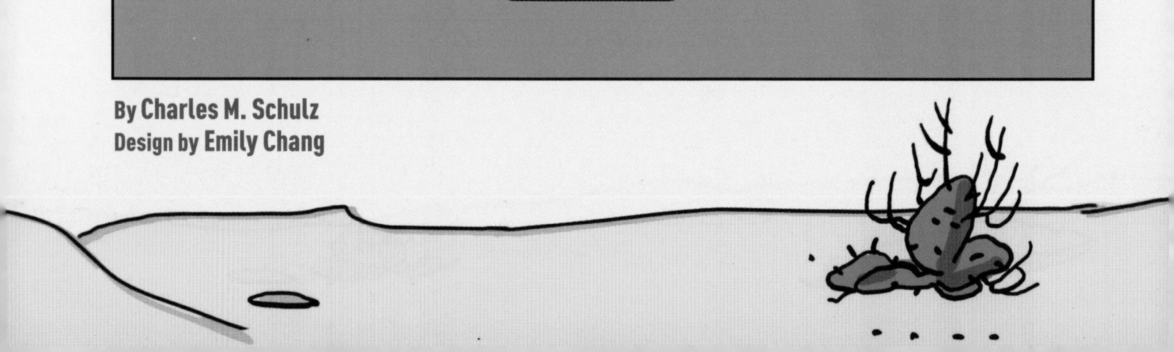

PEANUTS
by SCHULZ

PEANUTS
THE WOLVERINE IS A REMARKABLE ANIMAL
WHEN HE IS LOOKING FOR SOMETHING IN THE DISTANCE, HE WILL ACTUALLY SHADE HIS EYES WITH HIS PAW...
6-13
HE'S THE ONLY ANIMAL BESIDES MAN WHO HAS THIS ABILITY...
WHO NEEDS IT ?
SCHULZ

JOE COOL

FIRST APPEARANCE

JUNE 13, 1975

kaboom!™

SELECT SERIES IV

ISSUE TWELVE

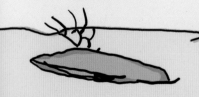

Charles M. Schulz once described himself as "born to draw comic strips." Born in Minneapolis, at just two days old, an uncle nicknamed him "Sparky" after the horse Spark Plug from the "Barney Google" comic strip, and throughout his youth, he and his father shared a Sunday morning ritual reading the funnies. After serving in the Army during World War II, Schulz's first big break came in 1947 when he sold a cartoon feature called "Li'l Folks" to the *St. Paul Pioneer Press*. In 1950, Schulz met with United Feature Syndicate, and on October 2 of that year, PEANUTS, named by the syndicate, debuted in seven newspapers. Charles Schulz died in Santa Rosa, California, in February 2000—just hours before his last original strip was to appear in Sunday papers.